JONATHAN & JESSE
KELLERMAN
A MEASURE
OF DARKNESS

HEADLINE

First published in the United States in 2018 by Ballantine Books,
an imprint of Random House, a Penguin Random House Company

First published in Great Britain in 2018 by
HEADLINE PUBLISHING GROUP

First published in paperback in Great Britain in 2019 by
HEADLINE PUBLISHING GROUP

1

Cataloguing in Publication Data is available from the British Library

(B-format) ISBN 9781 4722 3845 0
(A-format) ISBN 9781 4722 6225 7

Typeset in 9.9/15.31 pt Sabon LT Std by Jouve (UK), Milton Keynes

Printed and bound in Great Britain by Clays Ltd, Elcograf S.p.A.

HEADLINE PUBLISHING GROUP
An Hachette UK Company
Carmelite House
50 Victoria Embankment
London
EC4Y 0DZ

www.headline.co.uk
www.hachette.co.uk

Jesse Kellerman won the Princess Grace Award for best young American playwright and is the author of *Sunstroke*, *Trouble*, *The Genius* (for which he won the 2010 Grand Prix des Lectrices de Elle), *The Executor*, and *Potboiler* (for which he was nominated for the Edgar Award for Best Novel). He lives in California.

Praise for Jonathan and Jesse Kellerman:

'They have a way of scaring you, of chasing sleep away, these psychological thrillers that send your heart thumping. Imagine, then, what you're in for when two masters of the genre decide to collaborate' *Huffington Post*

'This is a witty, propulsive, and frequently chilling read; as ambitious as it is entertaining' *Kirkus Reviews*

'Sophisticated, cleverly plotted and satisfying' *Sunday Telegraph*

'With exceptional verve and flair, the Kellermans have created a heart-stopper of a story' *Daily Mail*

To Faye

—Jonathan Kellerman

To Gavri

—Jesse Kellerman

ONE

The House on Almond Street

CHAPTER 1

Friday, December 21

They were going to have a nice evening together. Hattie had been planning for a week, since Isaiah called to tell her he was home from school. He wanted to know was it okay for him to come by and pay her a visit.

Okay? How could it not be? Hattie couldn't remember when she'd last seen her grandson. That distressed her, both the not-seeing and the not-remembering. A year? Maybe longer. Too long, at any rate.

It got lonely. She didn't get many visitors. People had their own lives. Her children had gone and gotten children for themselves. They'd found places in the world. That alone was proof of a life well lived.

It got lonely, though.

Curtis—Isaiah's father, her youngest—made the drive down once a month or so. You'd think it was a thousand miles instead of forty. Hattie sometimes made up reasons to call him. The kitchen outlets did go bad a lot. Standing at the breaker box, he would remind her again in that weary patient way of his that the whole sub-panel needed replacing.

Her baby boy, graying. It must have happened at some point that she stopped scolding him and it started coming back the other way. There must have been a day.

She couldn't remember that, either.

The neighborhood's changing he said.

She fixed coffee and let him make his case. They were fleeing the city, pouring over the bridge. Computer people. Couldn't be stopped. They wanted to be near the train. Ten minutes to downtown San Francisco. They paid cash. Did she know what she could get for this old place?

He took after his own father. Unsentimental.

It's too much house for one person he said.

And where was she supposed to live, according to this plan?

With us.

Hattie snorted. *I guess you didn't ask Tina how she feels about that.*

Mom, please. She'd love to have you.

He was missing the point. Change was nothing new to her. All her life she'd lived in Oakland, half those years on Almond Street, and never could she remember the scenery standing still. Now he expected her to pick up and run? What from? White folks wielding new countertops?

She'd weathered worse.

Not to say she wasn't tempted. Most of her friends had left, passed on, or else lost their leases. Curtis wasn't the only one trying to show her the light. Real estate agents kept calling her up, knocking on her door, sliding their slick postcards into her mailbox.

Please call me to discuss an exciting opportunity.

Once she went to put out the trash, and a young fellow in a jacket and tie appeared at her side. Hattie thought he must have been sitting in his car, waiting for her. Like an eel, darting out from the rocks to snap. He offered to bring the can down to the curb for her.

No, thank you, she could manage on her own.

He left her with a card (SEAN GODWIN, LICENSED REALTOR) and a sheet of paper listing recent neighborhood sales. On Almond Street alone there were three, including the big wreck across the street. A ruined beauty, with a cratered roof, blank window frames, walls spray-painted in wrathful scrawls. Hattie's eyes nearly fell out of her head when she saw the price. She counted the string of zeros and expected bulldozers any day.

The buyer was a white lady, with other ideas. Plank by plank, dab by dab, the skeleton knit itself back together, grew flesh, skin, acquired a healthful glow. Hattie monitored the process through her curtains. A crew of Spanish men did the heavy work. Often, though, she saw the lady herself out there, her and her husband, or boyfriend more likely, smoking and laughing as they rolled paint, drove out a horde of raccoons. Or the lady alone, wearing overalls to hang wire for a chicken coop. Planting bamboo that rose to shut out the world.

Everything changes, nothing remains. Hattie knew that. She accepted it. Truth be told it excited her a little—the unexpected. Her husband, God rest him, called her a dreamer. She used to hide her mystery novels under the kitchen sink so he wouldn't lecture her.

For this reason, perhaps, she harbored a particular closeness to Isaiah: he was a dreamer, too.

I might come by and see you, Grandma. Is that okay?

Was it *okay*.

Hattie baked a coconut cake.

ISAIAH CLOCKED HER disappointment as soon as she opened the door. She'd begun moving in for a kiss, freezing as her eye picked out the metal bead snugged in the crease beneath his lower lip, as though it might sting her.

He was going to have to take the initiative. He brought her into his arms and held her against him, smelling her scalp, the floral bite of her hairspray. She felt like straw.

"Good to see you, Grandma."

"You too, honey."

She didn't say a word about the stud. He did catch her staring over dinner, or maybe that was him being paranoid. On the train down, he'd thought about taking it out, but he wasn't supposed to do that for a month or the hole could close up. He was aware of gumming up consonants—*F, V, P, B*—the backing clicking against his teeth. Certain foods presented a challenge. Hattie had prepared enough for ten. Chicken, beans, yams. He didn't dare refuse. He chewed with purpose, seated beneath the portrait of Grandpa William in his starched Navy uniform.

"How are your parents?" she said.

"Fine." His mother had seen the piercing and sighed. *Isaiah. Really.* "They say hi."

"Tell me about school. What classes are you taking?"

Structure of the Family, Imagining Ethnography, Comp 2, American Cultural Methodologies. He'd settled on sociology as a major.

"Next semester I have a class on interviewing," he said. "I'm gonna call you up."

"Me?" She waved him away. "What for?"

But he could tell she was pleased. "You've seen some things," he said.

"I'm old, you mean."

"Grandma."

"It's all right," she said. "I *am* old."

She carried his empty plate into the kitchen, returning with a high cake smothered in coconut flakes and thick buttercream frosting. She fetched clean plates and a knife and bent to cut him a huge slice. He was trying to figure out how to decline when from out in the street came a deafening belch of static.

"Shit," he said, twisting in his seat.

Hattie clucked her tongue at him.

He spread his palms on the vinyl tablecloth. His heart was going. "What was that?"

She shook her head.

He pushed back his chair, went over to the bay window, parted the curtains. The side gate of the mansion across the street was propped, and a portly, bearded white man was unloading a van, dollying a keg up a path toward the backyard.

"Someone lives there?" he said.

"A lady bought it," Hattie said.

"What lady?"

"She calls herself an artist."

Isaiah studied the house, its windows warm, multicolored lights outlining the eaves. As long as he could remember, the place had served as a lair for junkies and squatters. Growing up—before his parents dragged him and his sister out to the suburbs—he had been forbidden from going anywhere near it.

A second blast of static made him jump.

"She's probably having one of her parties," Hattie said. She tapped the plate with the back of the knife. "Eat up, honey."

In the time it took him to consume his dessert there were four more eruptions of noise, a man's amplified voice: *Testing, one two, one two.*

House music boomed.

Isaiah set down his fork. "Don't they have any respect?"

"It's not that bad," Hattie said.

"Are you kidding? It's like a bomb going off."

"Since when did you ever hear a bomb?"

"You can't sleep with that," he said.

"It'll be over by midnight."

He goggled at her. "Midnight?"

She shrugged.

The music cut out a few minutes later, as he was setting his backpack down on the guest room bed. The silence was as startling as the noise, causing him to tense all over, and then to flood with hot relief.

He dug out his phone. Tuan had texted him an address. Isaiah replied he'd be there in thirty and went back downstairs, calling, "Yo Grandma."

He found her hunched over the sink, skinny arms inside floppy yellow dish gloves.

"Yes, honey?"

"Hey," he said. Faltering, because she looked so frail. "Why don't I do that for you?"

"Guests don't do the dishes." She gestured toward the living room, flinging soapy droplets. "Make yourself comfortable. *Jeopardy!*'s on. I'll come join you when I'm done."

"Yeah, okay. Just," he said, scratching at his neck, "I kind of told some friends I might meet up with them."

In the brief interval that followed he watched an unspoken hope of hers crumble.

"But I can stay," he said.

"Don't be silly. You go have fun. Which friends?"

"Jalen."

"That's Gladys Coombs's boy."

He nodded. He didn't mention Tuan, she wouldn't approve.

"It's nice you two keep in touch," Hattie said.

"Yeah, for sure."

She stripped off the dish gloves and went over to the kitchen table. Taking her pocketbook from her purse, she extracted a ten-dollar bill. "Here."

"That's okay, I'm fine."

"Go on. Make an old lady happy."

He accepted the money. "Thanks, Grandma."

"You're welcome. Get the key off the hook before you go."

She presented her cheek.

He pursed his lips out far to kiss her, so that she wouldn't feel metal.

HATTIE LISTENED TO the front door close. She'd intended to finish the washing up but felt overcome by fatigue. It could wait till tomorrow.

Upstairs, sitting on the edge of the bathtub, she let the running water cascade through her fingers, its glassy whisper soon crushed by the wallop of a bass drum.

ISAIAH PEERED INTO the back of the open van. Inside lay several more kegs.

"Something I can help you with."

The white guy with the beard stood on the sidewalk, his torso angled away, the dolly squared between them like a shield. Sharp eyes, tight mouth.

Isaiah smiled reflexively, stepped back from the van, feeling in quick succession shame and anger. The guy assumed he was there to steal.

And look at him. Look at how he'd deferred. When he was the one in the right. What did he have to smile about? Ashamed of what? All he was doing was standing there. *They* were the ones making a racket. But the man had spoken and Isaiah had hopped to like one of those trained rats in his psych textbook.

Confront your internalized racism. A TA had written that in the margins of his midterm.

He pointed. "That's my grandmother's house."

"All right."

"You need to show some respect. People live here."

The guy put his hands up. "Not my department, man."

"Whose department is it?"

The guy indicated the backyard.

Isaiah started across the front lawn. A lawn to cross—that was new. He followed a long flowerbed toward the gate, pausing as he came to a sign staked by a willow tree.

BLACK
LIVES
MATTER

The music started up, like a blow to the head.

Isaiah pushed through the gate.

IT WAS A dizzying spectacle that greeted him, and he hesitated. The view from the street gave no hint of the property's true depth. It was huge, a huge mess, clogged with an incredible collection of junk: garden gnomes, plastic flamingos, Mexican skulls, statuary, wicker. Clusters of trees and stray bits of fencing disrupted perspective. As Isaiah stood there, trying to pinpoint the source of the noise, a goat darted by, causing him to start.

He settled himself down, followed a dirt path studded with clamshells; past a roller-coaster car helmed by mannequins; around the gigantic chicken coop, its residents running in frantic circles.

In the center of the yard was a fire pit piled with logs. Nearby was a DJ table, speakers, twin projection screens. A papier-mâché goblin turned in the breeze on a stake.

Cross-legged on the ground, unraveling a tangle of extension cords, was another white guy.

Isaiah waited in vain to be noticed. "Excuse me," he yelled.

The guy looked up. He, too, was bearded, wearing brown plastic glasses and a green flannel shirt. He stood, wiping his hands on his jeans, sauntered over to the DJ table, and touched an iPad. The music choked out. "We're not open till nine," he said.

"I'm from across the street."

"From . . . ?"

"Eleven-twelve. Your neighbor."

"Oh yeah. Nice. What can I do for you?"

"Are you aware of how loud that is?"

"I'm getting the levels set," the man said. "Sorry. I can turn it down a little."

"You need to turn it down a lot," Isaiah said.

"Yeah, bro. No worries."

"How late do you plan on going?"

"I mean . . . There's a problem, just let me know."

"That's what I'm doing," Isaiah said. "I'm letting you know."

The man gave a small, condescending smile. "Roger that. Listen, you want a beer? We got tons."

"I'm good."

"Cool." The man went back to his wires. "Have a good night."

On his way out, Isaiah nosed around a bit. There was no shortage of things to look at, and curiosity had gotten the better of him. The night was cloudy and cold, a few stars struggling to stay relevant. He ended up following a curling chain-link fence to where it converged with the back end of the house, creating a sort of triangular alley that contained yet more junk.

Bicycles. Milk crates. A plywood shed, shoulder height, with double doors. Two city trash cans, green and burgundy, pushed flush to the siding. A third can, gray for recyclables, sat several feet off, as though shunned by its companions. At the far point of the triangle, a gate led to 11th.

He started forward, intending to exit that way, rather than hike through the yard.

Ahead, a stirring in the dark.

Isaiah halted.

With mute shock he watched the disturbance assume the shape of a man. A lump springing up between the two cans, seeming to grow straight out of the ground, a giant malignant weed vomited up by the earth.

He was close. Fifteen feet, at most. Swaddle of greasy overcoat, sloppy scarf, head smashed flat at the temples, like it had been jammed in a vise.

A smell reached Isaiah. Acrid and fermented: piss and body odor.

The man didn't seem to notice Isaiah. He rolled the gray can into line with the others, against the house. Then he turned, tentacles of hair swinging, and stepped over to the shed. He opened the doors and ducked down behind them.

You could hear him messing around in there.

Definitely time to find the exit.

Isaiah stepped back and his heel touched something, something insubstantial, too late to avoid putting his weight down.

Aluminum crinkled.

The man shot up to his full and terrible height.

A gasp of moonlight broke through and for the first time Isaiah could see the man's face. White, with a beard.

Everyone here was white, with a beard.

The man shut the shed doors and stared at Isaiah.

He was holding a knife.

With a rattling gait he advanced, pushing before him a towering wave of stench. The music had stopped, so that Isaiah could hear the limbs swinging beneath many stiff layers of clothing, could hear the mouth chewing in wet anticipation. Ten feet between them and the face sharpened, every trench and pit, the moles jutting like obscene thumbs, the beard a tight mass of gray wires, gluey and twisted.

Isaiah wanted to run.

Why didn't he run?

Five feet.

The air was fetid, a rag in Isaiah's throat.

The man leaned forward.

Said, "Not you."

Like a burst steam pipe, he hissed.

Isaiah ran, smashing through obstacles, through branches that tore at his flesh.

When he found himself at the curb again, he had no idea how he'd gotten there.

He huddled by a parked car, sucking wind. His palms were bleeding. His shirt was wet. His crotch, too, hung heavy and moist, and he was briefly mortified, thinking he'd wet himself.

No. Just sweat.

He felt grateful, and that had him feeling stupid and weak.

Fumbling out his phone, the plastic blood-warm and soothing. Text from Tuan.

U coming

Isaiah blinked at the screen. He started to reply but his hands were shaking and he ended up typing a bunch of garbage. He erased it, tried again.

Yes

He dreaded facing his friends. One look at him and they would know his fear.

Yo, what the fuck? Laughing.

He had his breath back, and he could swallow again, but he was still crouched humiliatingly on the pavement like a child hiding from punishment.

He stood up tall, brushing leaves from his clothes and hair. His own reflection in the car window seemed to smirk at him.

Little bitch.

Shame tapped at the glass of his soul, and, again, without fail, close on its heels—

Rage.

Filling him up, straining his guts.

His phone chimed. Thumbs-up from Tuan.

Isaiah put the phone away.

The houses on the block, with their dark, drowned faces, observed him. He shook out his limbs, straightened his spine. Okay. He ran his tongue around the inside of his lower lip, feeling the backing. His grandmother was probably in bed already. He hoped she was. The van with the kegs was gone. He gave himself a final once-over. Okay, then.

Isaiah started toward the corner. As he turned onto 11th he felt the sudden and overwhelming conviction that tonight had a significance far beyond words. A bitter joy; it almost made him laugh, so strong and giddy was the sensation. He walked along, gorging on it. Tonight he felt ready for anything. Tonight, he could yet redeem himself, after all.

TWO

Aftermath

CHAPTER 2

Saturday, December 22

2:01 a.m.

I go to bed early and get up early, and even when I forget to set my alarm, I wake up around four thirty a.m.

Get dressed, grab a protein bar, in the car by quarter to. At that hour there's no traffic. Most days I'm at my desk with a couple minutes to spare.

That morning, I shot to the surface, mid-dream. The air felt bare and thick.

Amy was shaking me. "Clay. Wake up."

My phone was going off.

Moffett calling.

I climbed out of bed.

"What's wrong?" Amy asked.

"Nothing. Go back to sleep."

She flopped down and pulled the duvet over her head.

I found my uniform and boots in the dark and carried them to the kitchen. The phone had stopped ringing. I called Moffett back.

"Sorry to do this to you," he said.

I believed him. Before his promotion to night shift sergeant, Brad Moffett was my teammate for two and a half years. It wasn't in his nature to be melodramatic. "What's up?"

"Multiple shooting."

"How many?"

"At least three down, possibly more. Jurow's tied up in Albany. It's me and Nikki alone out here on a fuckin circus. I called your whole team. Lindsey's coming. I can't reach Zaragoza or Shoops."

He gave me an address: 11th and Almond, in the Lower Bottoms.

"That's close to you," he said.

"Close enough," I said.

2:24 a.m.

I had to park several blocks away. Traffic cops with light sticks were diverting non-emergency vehicles, and they'd cordoned off the length of 1100 Almond, plus a healthy chunk of 11th in either direction, a vast T that encompassed street, sidewalks, and structures. Best practice: easier to contract a crime scene than to expand it.

The downside was that it created three fronts to manage. Large crowds had gathered at each, shouting, sobbing, calling, texting, snapping pictures, shooting video, congregating improperly, disregarding commands. Oakland PD uniforms roved, attempting to corral witnesses, take statements, calm tempers, choreograph the chaos.

Picking my way toward the intersection, I noted a number of people wearing costumes. A young white woman in patent-leather go-go boots retched into the gutter while a friend tried to right the thermal blanket slipping off her shoulders. A young white man in a gorilla suit sat on the curb, gorilla head tucked flat in his armpit, actual head in his hands. There were EMTs, and two news vans. The neighborhood suffered its fair share of violent crime. It took a lot to bring residents out of their homes in the middle of the night. Yet there they were, on their porches in bathrobes and slippers, craning their necks.

The focal point of the activity was a giant gingerbread Victorian on the corner, its exterior smeared red and blue by flashers. Techs scoured the pavement and front yard.

In the middle of the intersection sat a single white flip-flop.

Thirty feet away, a body lay under a sheet.

I started to duck under the tape but was held up by a uniform.

"Coroner's," I said, in case he couldn't read.

"You gotta go around."

"Around where?"

"Staging area's at Twelfth."

"Come on," I said. "Are you serious?"

"Sorry, buddy. One way in, one way out."

I went around.

The far end of Almond Street sat in relative quiet, the eye of a hurricane, displaced. The roar of the crowd was a tidal murmur.

I signed in.

Emergency vehicles clogged the block. A hand-lettered sign gave the common radio frequency; there was an easel with an oversized paper pad. A uniform was using a marker to keep a running time line.

ShotSpotter had picked up gunfire at 2355. The first call to 911 had gone out at 0007, first call to the Coroner's at 0102. Nikki Kennedy had arrived at 0135; Moffett, twenty minutes later. He'd taken one look and started calling for backup.

I found the two of them leaning against a van, rubbing hands against the chill, watching the scene unfold. Forensics circled two more sheeted bodies lying in a puddle of lamplight.

Moffett said, "Hurry up and wait."

"Is there a story?" I asked.

Kennedy chinned at the Victorian. "They're having a party. Neighbors come over to ask, can you turn the music down. Exchange of words, it goes into the street, people start throwing punches. Someone pulls a gun."

"GSWs," Moffett said, pointing to the two nearest bodies. They had fallen within touching distance of each other; one of them lay half on the sidewalk, half off. "There's a third decedent, way down by the corner."

"Yeah, I saw," I said. "They made me go around."

"That one's a ped struck. Far as we can tell it was an accident. Shots go off, everyone's panicking, running, jumping in cars and speeding off without looking where they're going."

"She got dragged," Kennedy said.

"Fuck," I said.

"They have the driver. Some girl, totally freaked out."

"What about the shooter?"

Kennedy shook her head. "Got away."

Moffett said, "They took a couple more people to Highland. Don't know how bad the injuries are."

"So at least three," I said.

"As of right now, yeah."

"ID on any of them?"

He shook his head.

I looked at the Victorian. Triple-high, fancy paint scheme, elaborate shingling, gables, turrets, a widow's walk. There were other such examples throughout West Oakland, holdovers from a wealthier bygone era, but few in such good condition, and fewer still on that scale. The lot occupied half the western side of the block, squaring off against a run of slender row houses on the eastern side, some single-family, some subdivided.

Goliath versus the Seven Dwarfs.

"Big house," I said.

"Big party," Kennedy said.

"Uniforms are trying to track everyone down," Moffett said.

"I saw a few mixed in the crowd," I said.

I told them about the guy in the ape suit.

"Well," Moffett said, "that should help."

Hurry up and wait.

"Did you know," Kennedy said, reading from her phone, "that the Summerhof Mansion, located at eleven-oh-five Almond Street, was built in eighteen ninety-five for Franz Summerhof, owner of the Summerhof Ironworks in Oakland. The house, which is a classic example of the Queen Anne style, sits on over an acre and a half of land. It was home to Summerhof's family, including wife Gretchen and their nine children. After World War One it served as the headquarters of the German-American Friendship Society. At present it is under private ownership."

She looked at us. "Did you know?"

"I do now," I said.

WE WATCHED OTHER folks do their jobs. Tiptoeing among the yellow plastic evidence markers, sprouted like mushrooms after a heavy rain. Groaning as they bent to inspect a cigarette butt, a bottle, a shell casing. Striving, not always successfully, to avoid treading on one another's territory. It was like some confab of tribes negotiating an uneasy peace, each identifiable by its native tools and markings.

Evidence, with their gloves and bags.

Ballistics, with their residue kits and laser pointers and metal detectors.

Blood. Photography. Uniforms feathering the grass with pen-lights; uniforms going door-to-door.

Quite the turnout for Oakland.

I could make two detectives, sleepy-eyed white guys in slacks and parkas, standing on opposite sidewalks, talking to witnesses. Two: that's how I knew it was serious.

And us, here, in the on-deck circle, a tribe of three.

The meat people.

The bodies belonged to us. In theory we could shut everyone else down to stake our claim. But patience and diplomacy go a long way, especially when you deal with these same agencies over and over again. I recognized several of the people working, by face if not by name. As a unit, we try not to get possessive, unless it's called for.

"*Hey,*" Moffett barked.

Some uniforms were readying themselves to lift one of the GSWs in the street. "We need to clear this stuff out so we can move our vehicle."

"*No,*" Moffett said, starting forward, "you need to let these *people* be."

He proceeded to chew them out.

I turned to Kennedy. "Truth now: how is he as a boss?"

She tugged down her cap resolutely. "The best."

"You want to say that a little louder maybe, make sure he hears it?"

She laughed. "Let's wait till he comes back."

Behind us, a woman's voice: "Evening, people."

Lindsey Bagoyo jogged up, breathing steam. She bumped my fist. "I thought for sure I'd beat you here."

"I live five miles away."

"Yeah, but you drive like my grandma."

Moffett returned, shaking his head. "Idiots."

"Hey Nikki," I said, "what was that you were saying about your sergeant?"

"What, that he's the best?"

Ignoring us, Moffett turned to Lindsey. "Thanks for coming."

"No problem."

"Okay," he said. "Here's the deal. Priority number one is the decedent in the intersection. Get her concealed before people start tweeting."

While I admired his zeal, we all knew that ship had sailed.

"The detective said he needs another twenty minutes on the GSWs." He paused. "Anybody got a preference?"

Kennedy said, "I can—"

A scream buried her words.

CHAPTER 3

Up and down the block, heads raised, swinging around in confusion before they homed in on the source: a house on the east side of the street, where a woman had emerged onto the front lawn, tossing her arms and crying for help.

She collapsed as the uniforms reached her.

Radios crackled with a request for medical backup.

At this point, the one-way-in, one-way-out policy revealed its shortcomings. Nobody showed up for another fifteen minutes, by which time they'd laid the woman out on the grass. She was black, in her thirties, dressed in sleepwear unsuited to the cold. She keened, rolling sluggishly from side to side, like she was burning alive and unable to summon the will to save herself.

My baby. My baby.

While they covered her with jackets, worked to soothe her, the patrol sergeant entered the house with his firearm drawn.

A pair of EMTs came hurrying through the checkpoint and approached the woman on the lawn. She struggled up on her elbows, urging them toward the house instead.

Our team observed this dumbshow without comment.

Now the patrol sergeant came over the radio asking for assistance, eleven-twenty-four Almond, basement.

Can I get a detective, please.

The woman had curled up like a pietà in the arms of a uniform, moaning.

Kennedy said, "Fuck."

We all knew.

Our victim count had risen.

One of the detectives peeled off his witness, making *don't move* hands, and began shambling up the block.

Lindsey Bagoyo said, "On me."

She headed for the house.

Moffett rubbed his scalp. "I'm done sitting here like an asshole."

He addressed me. "Can you find out what's the deal with the ped struck? Start taking flicks. There's a pop-up in the Explorer."

STEPPING INTO THE intersection, I felt dozens of eyes on me.

Officer.

Back behind the line, please.

Hey. Officer. Hey.

A TV camera swung in my direction. A reporter began calling for comment.

I shunted these distractions to the margins of my awareness. Moving in a straight line toward the decedent, pausing every few feet to set down the pop-up, raise the Nikon, grab establishing shots.

Ma'am I asked you to step away.

Officer please—

On the sidewalk, on the street, a nauseating caption, scrawled in flesh, blood, and tire rubber. It began at the corner, where the driver had jumped the curb, bowing out toward the white flip-flop and running ten yards west along 11th to cease at the sheeted body.

Officer I need to hey don't touch me don't you touch me moth-erfucker.

A baby-faced uniform had been left to stand guard. He might've been a week out of the academy. He looked scared witless, body stiff and keyed to danger, attention yanked this way and that, flinching at each stray movement.

His hand bobbed near the butt of his gun.

This: this is how bad happens.

"Hey there"—I leaned in to read his tag—"Grelling. How's it going, buddy?"

"Yeah. Okay."

"Cold," I said.

He nodded.

"Listen, Grelling, you mind giving me a hand here?"

He said nothing, scanning past me, the mass of unknown faces.

Above us, a news helicopter carved arcs, ripping up the air.

"Grelling," I said.

He blinked. "Yeah." Dropped his gun hand. "Yeah, okay."

A pop-up is a three-paneled privacy barrier, forty-eight linear feet of aluminum tubing and two hundred sixteen square feet of white nylon, weighing about ten pounds; it folds up into a carrying bag for easy transport. Erecting one requires a single competent person and two minutes. With Grelling's assistance, I got it done in five.

Small price to pay. Nobody extra got shot.

I asked him who'd been over the scene. He shook his head as if it were a calculus problem.

I said, "The vehicle guys? They got their look?"

Hesitation. "I think so."

"Do me a solid, Grelling, go ask at the staging area. Check in with your sergeant while you're there. You don't have to come back with the answer, just hit me over comms. I'm Coroner's. Edison 3618. Otherwise I'm good here. You good?"

He nodded.

"I think they brought fresh coffee," I said. "Thanks for your help."

Officer Grelling departed on his new, fake mission. I'd already gotten the green light from the forensics team leader.

I stepped inside the pop-up, closed the panel behind, and knelt by the body.

Blood patched the sheet, less than one would expect given the violence of the trauma. In a perfect world, the first responders would not have covered the decedent; in a perfect world, there are no rubberneckers, and we arrive to find everything and everyone positioned precisely as they were at the instant of death.

Tonight was the world at its least perfect.

I folded the sheet back.

She was young. Twenty or a couple years past. Lying on her stomach, head wrenched to the left. The exposed half of her face was heavily made up, white pigments and silver glitter; the skin was unharmed and remarkably clean save a few flecks of road dirt and axle grease.

The side of her face ground into the asphalt—I was glad I couldn't see it.

She wore robes, flowing and white, now shredded. Strapped to her back was a mangled pair of angel's wings, white faux fur and feathers hot-glued to a hinged mechanical frame, a pull-chain dangling at the right hip. I guessed that the entire apparatus had gotten snarled in the vehicle's undercarriage, dragging her along.

Her feet were bare.

I took pictures, wondering where the second flip-flop was.

Without another set of hands to assist in turning her over, I decided to skip the full body exam. We'd have more time, space, and light at the morgue. I did do a cursory check to ensure I wasn't missing anything obvious and to look for identification. Despite the chill, she was well on her way toward full rigor; she had practically no fat on her to retard the process.

The robe had no pockets.

Under the robes, she had on white leggings.

Under the leggings, she had on compression shorts.

Under the shorts, she had a penis.

I couldn't find any ID.

No cash, either, or cards, or a phone, or keys.

In a bag, maybe. Left behind in the panic, or thrown clear of the body.

The pop-up shifted and Officer Grelling appeared. "Um."

I let the waistband snap back into place. "What's up."

"There's a woman out there screaming her head off she needs to talk to you."

"What about?"

"She says she knows the vic."

HE LED ME to the tape along the south side of 11th. A chunky, blond, spike-haired woman in a denim miniskirt stood rubbing the goose-pimpled flesh of her upper arms. Her mascara had run amok, watery black veins, like a map consisting wholly of dead ends.

She told me her name was Didi Flynn. She and Jasmine had come to the party together, sharing a Lyft.

I recognized her voice as the one that had been vying for my attention earlier.

Officer, please.

"Can you tell me Jasmine's last name?"

"Gomez."

"Thank you. I couldn't find any ID on her, a wallet or a phone. Was she carrying a bag?"

Didi blinked. "I have it."

From her own handbag she produced a plastic zip-top bag containing a battered flip phone, loose cash, cards held together with an alligator clip, and three keys on a key chain in the shape of a panda. "She asked me to carry it for her."

"Thanks. This is really helpful. I'm going to take it with me. We'll keep it safe."

Didi said, "What about Jasmine?"

"I'm with the Coroner's Bureau," I said. "I'm responsible for her body and her property, and for determining what took place. Eventually I'm going to transport her to our facility. Right now I'm examining the scene. So any information you can give me to help me understand what happened, I'd appreciate it."

She said, "I don't . . . There was a fight."

"Whatever you can remember is fine."

She rubbed at her raw nose. She was trembling. "Someone said they were fighting outside, we went to look. Everyone was—it was like a massive crowd of people, they were yelling and throwing shit. Jasmine wanted to get closer, so we could see, and so we're trying to get through. All of a sudden it goes *pop pop pop pop pop.* I didn't even realize what it was. It didn't sound like—I mean, I don't know anything about guns. But everyone started screaming, and running. I started running, too. I thought . . ."

She hiccuped miserably and began to cough on saliva.

I offered her a tissue. She shook her head. "I thought she was with me. I know she was. I saw her, she was right there, next to me. I tried to hold on to her but everyone was pushing, I couldn't— I had to let go. Then I heard this, this . . ." She shut her eyes and pressed on the lids, hard. "I don't know how to describe it. Like an egg cracking. But louder, like a hundred times louder. I swear I could throw up. I turned around and she wasn't there, she was just. Gone."

Didi Flynn opened her eyes and looked at me.

I said, "Do you remember where you were?"

"There." Corner of the sidewalk, where the blood trail began. "And there's this car, a blue car, and people are screaming, and banging on the hood, like, stop, *stop, now.*"

A queer smile, not directed at me, not at anyone.

"The driver didn't know she was under there," Didi said.

She began to cry.

My radio blipped; Nikki Kennedy spoke. *Any available coroner, assistance requested.*

I said to Didi, "Thank you. I know it's difficult to talk about. I'd like to ask you a couple of questions about Jasmine." I paused. "Is that okay?"

She gestured *go ahead.*

"Was Jasmine married?"

"No."

"Do you happen to have contact information for her family?"

I saw a change come over her, a hardening of the jaw. "No."

"It's important for me to find them, so that I can inform them of her passing."

She said, "We're her family."

Any available coroner, please.

"I understand," I said. "She's not married, though."

"I told you she wasn't."

"In that case, I'm going to need to speak to her parents."

"Why would you do that?"

"If Jasmine didn't have a spouse, they're next of kin."

"She never talked to them. They hated her. They made her life hell. Why do you think she left in the first place?"

"I get where you're coming from," I said.

She rolled her eyes. "Right."

"I'm asking you, please, to consider another point of view. Whatever occurred between her and them in the past—and I'm not excusing it—she's their child. They have a right to know. How they respond, that's on them."

Didi Flynn continued to shake her head in disgust.

"Think about if it were your child," I said.

She said, "I'd never treat my child like that."

Hello? Nikki said. *Anyone?*

I depressed my call button. "Coming." To Didi: "Listen, you mind if we pause for a minute."

She shrugged.

I gave her my card. "Please stay here. For Jasmine. I'll be back soon, okay?"

"Yeah, all right."

Midway across the intersection I realized that I'd forgotten to take her contact information. It was that sort of night.

I hurried back to the tape, but she had vanished.

4:23 a.m.

The two Oakland detectives were named Von Ruden and Bischoff. Von Ruden was a moose of a guy, half-eaten rolls of Tums spilling from his pockets as he interviewed a partygoer. It was Bischoff I wanted: he was the lead on Jasmine. I finished helping Nikki load the first GSW onto a gurney, then went to find him.

Nowhere in sight. I asked the patrol sergeant, who warned me that Detective Bischoff might be busy for the foreseeable future, dealing with the latest vic, at 1124 Almond.

"It's a kid," the patrol sergeant said.

I swatted air. "Fuck."

"Yuh."

"What the fuck. *In* the house?"

"Must've caught a stray. There's a hole in the basement window." He made a circle with thumb and forefinger.

"I don't understand," I said. "Why are we just finding out about this now?"

The patrol sergeant shook his head. His name was Eddie Acosta. Trim, short, brush-cut hair and a prizefighter's nose. "They're living down there in two tiny rooms, him and the mother. He's on a cot by the fridge. She heard the shots but didn't look in on him. She didn't want to wake him up."

Put that way, it didn't sound so crazy. You lived here, you heard shots.

"Some point she notices"—Acosta waggled toward the scrum of cops and cars. "She gets nervous, goes to check. Six years old."

"For God's sake."

"Yuh."

On the sidewalk fronting 1124, the main-floor tenant was giving a statement to a uniform. The mother wasn't there. They had removed her from the scene in a squad car, to a relative's, where she could claw at the inside of her mind in private.

If she'd checked on him sooner.

If she'd put him to bed in a different spot.

If she'd found another place to live.

I said, "How many goddamn rounds were fired?"

Acosta said, "Fuck if I know. Twelve? Fifteen? Real miracle is we don't have more bodies. These assholes are shooting into a crowd of people from five feet away."

"Unbelievable," I said.

Acosta made a face. To him, it was utterly believable. "Welcome to the Wild West."

"What about the vics they took to Highland?"

"One guy got grazed in the leg. He's fine. The other's gut-shot."

My hand went to my own torso instinctively, and I noticed then that I wasn't wearing my vest. I'd gotten dressed in a hurry. I hoped Amy didn't spot it hanging in the closet. She'd be pissed.

"I haven't heard anything," Acosta said, "so I assume he's still alive. Although, who the fuck knows? The night is young."

I asked about the driver of the car that had struck Jasmine Gomez.

He paged through his notepad. "Name of Meredith Klaar. She's downtown."

"Witness I spoke to said she stopped the car once she realized what was going on."

"My impression, too. She looked a mess to me."

"A mess as in upset or as in toxed?"

"I didn't talk to her myself. I believe she was Breathalyzer-negative but maybe that's wrong." Acosta glanced at the party house. "I'm gonna speculate that there was some recreational use of controlled substances happening."

Sarge.

Up the block, a uniform was waving at us.

Acosta sighed. Spoke into his shoulder. "On my way."

JASMINE GOMEZ'S CALIFORNIA driver's license had her at five foot six, a hundred and twelve pounds; brown hair and brown eyes. Born April 19, 1995. Berkeley address. The sex was listed as F, which meant that, regardless of external genitalia, she was legally a she. That's what would go on her death certificate.

They hated her.

They made her life hell.

We're her family.

Moffett came over to look. "That's her?"

I handed him the license, blurry through two layers of clear plastic—zip bag inside evidence bag. "I'm waiting on the detective before I remove. He's occupied with the decedent inside eleven-twenty-four."

He nodded. "Me and Nikki will take the GSWs and head back. I spoke to Shoops. She's about sixty minutes out. She's gonna swing by the office and pick up another van."

Simpler, in retrospect, would have been for us to use the refrigerated truck; now we had to play musical vehicles. When the first call came in, there was no way to know how many bodies we'd end up with.

Moffett said, "You can hold shit down here?"

I almost made a wisecrack; almost gave an ironic salute. *Yessir Sarge sir.* I still had a hard time thinking of him as my superior. Looking at him now it struck me how much he had aged in the last year and a half. No more butt slapping or wet willies in the locker room. Now he was somber and impatient, the skin of his jowls starting to loosen, shoulders bowed under the burden of his own authority.

I said, "I got it."

He nodded thanks.

Nikki Kennedy came over. "Ready."

Moffett said to me, "See you on the other side."

CHAPTER 4

5:09 a.m.

Three hours along, I stood at the staging area, talking to Detective Jeremy Bischoff of Oakland PD Homicide Section. Lanky, with sparse mousy hair and a 49ers tie, he seemed annoyed that I'd taken it upon myself to call the jail and request a full drug panel for Meredith Klaar.

"They're supposed to do that anyway," he said, draining his coffee.

I made vague conciliatory noises. If he wanted to stand on ceremony, I could point out that it was disrespectful of him to keep putting me off, while Jasmine Gomez continued to lie in the street. I held my tongue. I couldn't fault him for being strung out. Everyone was.

Patience and diplomacy.

I didn't apologize, either. I've been in law enforcement long enough to know that *supposed to* doesn't mean *will*. A ten-minute phone call can save a lot of future headache.

I told him about Jasmine's friend, Didi Flynn; I showed him

Jasmine's ID and said we were prepared to remove the decedent, unless he had any objections.

"Yeah, knock yourself out."

He didn't ask for Flynn's number. Either he already had it or Jasmine wasn't his priority. His mind was on the dead child.

It's natural for a person facing a swarm of horrors to sort, compare, weigh merits.

What can wait? What can't? How will it play with the brass? The public?

A young adult cut down is sad.

As sad as a first-grader, bleeding out in his bed?

What about the gut-shot, languishing on the operating table? If he didn't make it, was that harder to accept because of the wasted effort? Or easier, because, hey: We tried.

Ten thousand people die each year in Alameda County. As Bischoff jabbed at the coffeepot plunger, tipping the pot to coax out the dregs, people were dying, elsewhere. In hospice or at home or in an alley. In a thicket beside the freeway; in a motel room; surrounded by loved ones or alone.

How sad can you afford to be, right now?

Bischoff dumped his cup in the trash.

"I'll let you know about the autopsy," I said.

"Mm." He was already walking away.

NOBODY AT THE scene knew Jasmine Gomez. Nobody knew Didi Flynn. Or else they were lying and didn't want to talk to me.

The lone white flip-flop remained in the street. I bagged it, searched the area for its companion, came up empty-handed.

My phone dinged, Amy texting.

Are you ok

On days when she goes into the city to see patients, she's out of the house by eight. Otherwise she'll snooze. Rarely had I seen her awake this early by choice.

She hadn't been able to get back to sleep.

Don't worry I'm fine I wrote.

I'm watching it on tv

I hesitated before responding. Was I live? Could she see me? The news helicopter was long departed. But there were still camera crews camped behind the cordon.

You forgot your vest she wrote.

Whoops.

I know sorry

Stay safe. Ly

To my left, shrill beeps.

A Coroner's van was backing up to the barrier of black-and-whites.

Ly 2 I wrote.

The van came to a stop, and Lisa Shupfer, hair a nest, shirt bloused at one side, hopped out, frowning. She'd driven straight to the bureau from her home outside Sacramento, eighty-odd miles on four hours' sleep.

"Shitshow," she said.

Couldn't argue with that.

"Lindsey went back in her own car," she said.

"I'm going to need to do the same."

She went around to open the rear doors. Inside, on the right gurney, a small bulge, sheeted and buckled: the dead child. The victim was roughly the same age as her son. If the removal had bothered her, she gave no sign of it.

We hauled out the free gurney and wheeled it toward the tape. The uniform on duty made as if to turn us away. *One way in, one way out.* Shoops cut him a look and he immediately shrank back.

Inside the pop-up, she got down to inspect the body.

I said I hadn't performed a full exam. "Right now I just want to get her out of here."

Shoops nodded.

We placed Jasmine Gomez atop a clean set of sheets.

She felt like nothing, like the body of a bird, hollow bones and down.

We wrapped her, knotted handles. Having enough room to work required that we widen the pop-up, exposing a gap of several feet. Thinning crowds had freed up sight lines, and Amy's text had made me leery of the camera crews. We had to keep shifting the panels to ensure that nobody had a direct view of us or what they really wanted to see.

In preparation for the lift, we crouched and took a three-count. Always a precarious moment for me and my bum knee; more so when I'm paired with Shupfer, because of the eleven-inch height difference between us. When we stood, I almost toppled backward, so faint was the resistance.

We laid the body on the gurney, buckled it in, wheeled it to the van.

I loaded Jasmine in beside the boy. Shupfer retrieved the pop-up.

"Drive safe," she said, climbing behind the wheel.

It was six thirty-two in the morning.

As THE LAST coroner on scene, I went to check in with Acosta.

"I'm taking off," I said.

"You got it, brother. Merry Christmas."

"You too."

The bulk of the players along Almond Street had cleared out, leaving behind a skeleton crew. The ambulances were gone. The detectives were gone. Few onlookers remained, all but the hardest of hardcore tragedy addicts having had their fill.

Now that we'd removed Jasmine Gomez's body, the uniforms were opening up 11th; redrawing the cordon to contain the frontage of the party house; taping off the perimeter of 1124. Dew misted windowpanes and windshields and mirrors, the eastern sky crinkling with an ambivalent dawn.

On my final pass through the intersection, I detoured to hunt around for the missing flip-flop. I knew I ought to get back to the bureau—I owed it to my teammates—but it was driving me batty that I couldn't find it.

Preserving Jasmine Gomez's property: that fell to me, didn't it?

Say the car had struck her from behind. What trajectory would the flip-flop follow? What about a side impact? Say she was running; she was standing still. What did a flip-flop weigh? An ounce? It had to be close by.

I checked the bushes and the gutter.

I got down to peer beneath parked cars.

I paced the south side of 11th, craning over low, spiked iron fences.

Nothing.

My radio, still open to the common channel, began stuttering.

Uh, this is Grelling 889.

The baby-faced rookie.

Requesting immediate assistance.

Acosta's voice came on. *Copy 889. What's your twenty?*

I'm here, uh . . . There's a—I think it's, uh.

Grelling. Where the fuck are you?

I'm—uh. On the property.

Which property?

*The house. The big house. In the yard, all the way at the back.
Sir?*

He was hyperventilating, the poor bastard.

Sir, there's another body here.

Stay put Acosta said. *I'm coming.*

I started walking, too.

CHAPTER 5

Acosta and I reached the lawn at the same time.

He said, "I thought you left."

"So did I."

The entrance to the backyard was through a chain-link fence. Strategically placed bamboo created a visual barrier from the street. When I pulled open the gate, I didn't know what I was stepping into.

The property was an unholy morass of furniture, "art," and overgrowth.

Acosta radioed Grelling to describe his location as precisely as possible.

Toward the back.

"Which back?" Acosta said. "West? North?"

Silence.

"Grelling."

Um . . . west. West. Sir.

We climbed over detritus, Acosta muttering to himself. "I told that motherfucker."

"Who?"

"Von Ruden. I told him we needed to grid and search the entire yard."

"He didn't?"

"He said the street's the primary scene. Jackass."

Adding to the disarray was an infill of party trash: discarded cups, cigarette butts, tissue paper streamers, condom wrappers. My brain winced as I imagined cataloging it all. Acosta was right, but I could also understand Detective Von Ruden's thought process. To spend your night picking up a hundred thousand pieces of lint—when you had witnesses fleeing in droves, bodies cooling in the gutter, a dead child in a basement—promised a lousy return on investment.

Acosta stumbled over a cement turtle. "Man, fuck this."

A low electrical hum grew louder as we went forward. Acosta parted a bead curtain that had been nailed to a horizontal ficus branch, and we came to an area with a fire pit. Tiki torches flickered; lawn chairs lay ass-up in the weeds. Velvet ropes guided those in need toward the house, where a side entrance was marked BATH-ROOM. There was a table kitted out with DJ equipment, wires running to the source of the hum: a speaker, left on.

Acosta went over and unplugged it.

I saw his face pinch with alarm. Followed his gaze to the fire pit.

A charred human form.

I said, "Oh shit," and stepped toward it.

Stopped when I saw that it had eyes the size of hams and a foot-long purple nose.

Some kind of effigy.

Acosta cupped his mouth. "Grelling."

Muffled: "Back here, sir."

The northwest corner of the house dovetailed with the rear chain-link, forming a triangular space roughly ten yards deep. It was what I call a nowhere space—a few forgotten square feet, filled with afterthoughts. You see them everywhere, the standpipes and the transformer boxes, the cement aprons and the drainage ditches. Or rather, you don't see them. You want what's beautiful in the world. You edit out what isn't.

This particular nowhere served as overflow for the homeowner's least prized possessions. Cobwebbed bicycles. Some wooden pallets, some milk crates. Trash cans, one two three in a tidy row, backs to the siding. Wheel them out for pickup, convenient street access through the gate at the far end.

My first thought was to wonder if the flip-flop could have touched down here. It didn't seem physically possible. I started running the calculations regardless, picturing the distance to the corner. That ought to clue you to my state of mind—how much fatigue had clouded me. Only when Grelling spoke again did I notice him.

Sort of a nowhere guy, Officer Grelling.

He was standing inside the triangle, gazing as though hypnotized at a plywood shed with a slanted plastic roof. Against its side leaned gardening implements: hoe, shovel, rake. The hasp was closed, but the double doors bulged out an inch or two past parallel. On the ground nearby, a flowerpot lay tipped over.

Officer Grelling said, "I saw it and I thought . . ."

Acosta looked at him. "Yeah?"

"I thought I should call."

"Good thought," Acosta said.

Someone had placed a large, heavy object in the shed. This person had shut the doors and set the hasp, but the doors wouldn't keep closed. Maybe the hinges were loose, or the plywood had warped in the rain. They wanted to open, those doors. To prevent that, this person had placed the flowerpot in front of them, hoping it would act as a doorstop.

This person hadn't been thinking.

This person had been in a rush.

This person's plan had misfired, because the large heavy object inside the shed had shifted, either right away or eventually, of its own volition or due to the natural processes of tissue change. And when the large heavy object shifted, it pushed against the doors, hard enough to knock over the flowerpot, before the hasp caught.

The large, heavy object had once lived and breathed.

At the threshold, like a pale gibbous moon, jutted a thumb.

7:33 a.m.

Acosta went to his car to call it in. I phoned my office.

"Coroner's Bureau, Zaragoza."

"It's Clay," I said.

"Hey. Where are you?"

"I haven't left yet. Is the sergeant there? I need to talk to her."

"Yeah, hang on."

I plugged my ear against a mad babble of birdsong. The sun had risen, acid thorns of light piercing the surrounding clutter. I stood close to the shed, keeping an eye on Officer Grelling, pallid and sheened and fixated on the thumb.

I wondered how many dead bodies he had seen.

He swayed on his feet, and I snapped my fingers at him, motioning at him to back up. If he was going to keel over, I didn't want him to hit his head on the shed. He could hurt himself. He could disturb the scene.

Sergeant Paula Turnbow came on the line. "Clay? What's happening over there? Why aren't you back?"

"We caught another."

"You're shittin me," she said.

"Wish I was. But, Sarge? This looks different to me."

"Different how?"

The shed doors were barely ajar, angles and shadows prohibiting a clear look. Without knowing the actual disposition of the body, without assessing its condition, I could only describe what I saw and hope she understood.

"Okay . . ." she said. When she thinks, her voice drops a notch and loses its usual animation. "What do you need?"

"A camera, a van, and a secondary."

"How long you think you can hold out?" she asked. "We're getting crushed."

"The detective hasn't even arrived yet."

"Call me when you're ready."

"Will do."

I hung up. Grelling had turned to peer into the foliage. Nothing to see, but easier than staring at the thumb.

I said, "How'd you end up back here?"

"Huh? I was—there was a goat."

"Excuse me?"

"You know. Like." He made horns with his fingers.

"I know what a goat is," I said.

"Yeah," he said. "Sorry."

He explained that he'd just gotten through restringing the crime scene tape around the front of the property when he spotted an individual tearing up a flower bed.

"By individual," I said, "you mean 'goat.'"

"I was like, 'Yo, get out of there.'"

"Did you consider maybe they're his flowers?"

"I—no."

"All right, you caution this goat. It fails to heed."

"Yeah. I go over there, to make it stop, and it runs inside the yard."

"At which point you engaged in a foot pursuit."

"Yeah."

"Or hoof pursuit, if we're gonna be accurate. So, where's the fugitive now?"

"I don't know," he said. "I couldn't find it before I saw . . ."

He didn't finish.

Normally I'm the one trying to maintain an appropriate atmosphere in the presence of a decedent. But it had been such a long, loopy night.

I said, "Good on you, Grelling."

"Thanks." He paused. "Can I ask you something?"

"Sure."

"Do you, like, like what you do?"

"Not every minute of every day," I said. "It's still a job. But most of the time, yeah. I wouldn't do it if I didn't."

"It's not . . . I dunno."

"Weird?"

"No, not that."

"Gross? Boring?"

"Depressing," he said.

I said, "It can be."

He nodded. "I don't think I could do it."

He was staring at the thumb again.

"Well," I said, "I couldn't do your job."

Which was bullshit. I have done his job. But I thought he could use the bucking up.

We waited in silence for another twenty-five minutes.

Voices drew near, Acosta's and that of a woman.

I saw them approach in slices, between the stalks of a stand of giant sunflowers. She was medium height, with blue-black skin, elongated facial features, and hair knitted in patterned braids. She wore dove-gray slacks and silver flats, her detective's badge on a neck chain, swaying in the folds of an emerald satin blouse.

"Delilah Nwodo," she said to me, putting out her hand.

"Clay Edison."

She was assessing me in the twitchy way that people do when they're trying to hide the fact that they recognize you. It still happens to me on occasion, mostly with people my age who went to Cal and saw me play ball. It goes like this:

Step one: don't stare.

But two: don't avoid eye contact, either.

Repeat.

Detective Nwodo said, "Let's have a look."

CHAPTER 6

She shone a penlight through the cracked doors.

"And we're sure it's a real person," she said.

"As opposed to?"

"A mannequin," she said, straightening up. "I noticed some on my way in."

I'd never seen a mannequin with such a lifelike digit. But I wasn't going to rule it out, not without a look at the rest of the body. The whole yard was filled with bizarro stuff, and anything felt possible.

"Forensics?" she asked.

"They're scraping up a new team," Acosta said. "Shit's fucked today."

"It'd help to know if we need them in the first place," she said and turned to me.

"Is that okay with you?"

Nice of her to ask. Plenty of detectives say *My scene, my call.*

I said, "Long as we're careful."

Nwodo and I each photographed the area around the shed. I prefer the Nikon, but a phone will do in a pinch. The earth was hard and gravelly, inhospitable to footprints or drag marks. Hundreds of pieces of potential evidence lay within a fifty-foot radius. It was going to be a technician's nightmare.

Once we'd finished, Grelling and Acosta each took a shed door. I knelt by the threshold, ready to catch the body if it tumbled out.

Nwodo gently depressed the doors, using a pen to flip back the hasp.

Grelling and Acosta let the tension out.

The doors opened.

The body didn't move an inch.

The shed stood on a poured-concrete pad, six feet wide and four feet deep. Hand tools hung on pegs affixed to the insides of the doors. It was a dumb place to try and hide a body. Heaped sacks of potting soil and organic fertilizer left open only an eighteen-inch strip of concrete, parallel to the threshold, in which to place the decedent.

Not a mannequin.

Size and proportions suggested a female. She lay oriented with the head to the right, twisted at the waist, a position that elevated the left hip and shoulder and forced the right arm behind her. It was the tip of the right thumb that Grelling had spotted. More sacks covered the legs, neck, head, and parts of the torso. One dirty blue running shoe stuck out.

No visible blood.

No insect activity.

Manure masked any other smells.

She hadn't been there long.

We took more pictures.

A fine layer of soil dust covered the sacks. Nwodo fretted over whether to move them, scrutinizing their surfaces for hand- or fingerprints.

Acosta said he'd try to get an ETA for the forensics team.

While he stepped away to make the call, Nwodo quizzed me and Grelling on the evening's events. We did our best, but the account that emerged was fragmentary.

Acosta rejoined us. "They're telling me fifteen minutes."

"So, forty-five," Nwodo said.

"Yuh."

"We'll wait." She took out her phone. "Anyone for Scrabble?"

9:49 a.m.

I stood at the curb, waving to the approaching van.

Zaragoza pulled up and got out.

"You look like crap," he said, slinging the camera over his shoulder.

"Good morning to you, too."

We grabbed sheets and began bushwhacking through the backyard. Zaragoza told me that the office was getting deluged with calls from people who had read about the shooting on the internet or seen the morning news.

"They put our main line up on the screen," he said.

"Hell no."

"Hell yes. Turn it on and it's like 'Oakland Party Massacre.' There we are, right at the bottom. Big numbers. 'Call for information.'"

"Why would they do that?"

"Now all these people are terrified it's their kid got killed. 'I haven't seen her in six months, she's mad at me, but I know she goes to parties.' What twenty-year-old doesn't go to parties? Turnbow's pissed."

"No shit."

"She's on about we need to get them ID'd and start notifying ASAP. Like we're going slow on purpose."

"She's stressed."

"I'm stressed," he said. "You're stressed. We're all stressed."

"For ice cream," I said.

He laughed and stepped over a bongo drum.

"Anyway," I said, "allow me to point out, you're the one guy got to sleep in today."

"The baby was up at two."

"Stop fucking having babies, then."

"Please please tell that to my wife."

Forensics had removed the sacks covering the body and set them out on the ground for examination. A tech was going through the trash cans, removing the contents piece by piece. Another was dusting the gardening implements.

I stepped over to get a look at my decedent.

White female, slight build. As with Jasmine Gomez, the lack of insulating fat meant that rigor had begun to set in, evident in the clenched jaw, the hands hooked into talons.

Like Jasmine, like everyone who had died there that night, she was young.

She wasn't wearing a costume, so far as I could tell. The dirty blue shoes were an off brand. Faded black Levi's. Gray cotton sweatshirt near the same shade. She'd picked holes in the sleeves, near the cuffs, for sticking her thumbs through. Among certain demographics, it can be difficult to know if threadbare clothing signifies wealth or poverty.

On the whole her outfit seemed inadequate, given the chill.

Had she left a coat inside the house? A bag?

Had she been in the house?

Had *we* been in the house?

Zaragoza moved in a semicircle around the shed, taking flicks.

The body conformed to the concrete, her left arm thrown up over her head, leaving the inside of the wrist and a bit of forearm exposed. Needle marks.

Nwodo had asked my permission. Just plain manners to reciprocate. "Okay for us to get started?"

"Be my guest."

I spread sheets on the gravel. Zaragoza put down the camera and we crouched to ease the decedent out. Her limbs were stiff but not fully set; when we placed her on the sheet, her left arm curled back into position, like a spring-loaded doll.

Daylight revealed extensive bruising around her throat. No ligature marks apparent, although it does happen that they get lost amid other trauma. My gut told me she'd been throttled. Skull and neck unbroken, extremities intact. I detected a soft spot on the left side of her rib cage, possibly a fracture.

Turning her over, I saw outlines of finger pads in the bruises, as well as the scratch marks characteristic of an attempt to pry loose an assailant's hands. Ruptured blood vessels bloomed in her cheeks and the whites of her eyes.

Up close, her features suggested that she was of mixed race.

Her jeans were buttoned and zipped.

Her pockets were empty.

I stared at them, turned inside out like dry white tongues; no paper, no possessions, nothing to establish her personhood or validate her place in society. Of all the awful things I'd witnessed in the last eight hours, it was the sight of those pockets that got to me most. Perhaps exhaustion had finally set in. But I couldn't stop myself from imagining her final moments.

Rough hard concrete against the back.

Lazy trickle of dirt inside plastic bags.

The solitude; darkness waxing.

Behind me, the techs were discussing soil types.

Nwodo was shuffling her feet.

Zaragoza had resumed taking flicks.

I completed my preliminary exam, noting the extent and location of lividity.

We bagged and zip-tied her hands.

We covered her and knotted the sheets.

My primary concern was getting her ID'd. At the request of Forensics, Zaragoza and I hadn't searched inside the shed. Could be her wallet was tossed behind the sacks, or its contents scattered in the yard.

Other than Jasmine's friend Didi, I hadn't spoken to many witnesses.

Someone would have seen this girl, arrived with her, known her.

"Is there a guest list?" I asked.

"My guys talked to twenty, thirty people," Acosta said. "I think there was a lot more. You got to assume most of them took off after the shots."

"What about the homeowner?"

"Downtown."

"Is she under arrest?"

"Not yet."

The lead tech said he planned to empty the shed, scour the yard, search the house.

Nwodo turned to me. "Anything comes up, I'll let you know."

I believed her. I had to.

As with Bischoff, I promised to call her about the autopsy. "I can't predict how the schedule'll stack up. Hopefully no later than end of week."

She thanked me. We swapped info, and then Zaragoza and I picked up the dead woman and carried her out through the maze.

. . .

OFFICER GRELLING WAS on his knees, by a flower bed, genuflecting in the shadow of a weeping willow. After Zaragoza and I had loaded the decedent in the van, I went back to him.

"You find your suspect?" I asked.

Grelling peered up at me.

I made goat horns.

"No," he said. He gestured to the overturned earth. "Look what he did, though."

Uprooted greenery. Azaleas chewed to nubs. A black sign with white lettering had been pulled up, aluminum stakes bent, edges ragged with tooth marks. BLACK LIVES MATTER.

"You'll get him," I said.

Grelling nodded. He wasn't convinced, though, and neither was I.

CHAPTER 7

11:31 a.m.

I drove myself to the bureau and met Zaragoza in the rear lot. Over the course of the night and morning my boots had accumulated a second sole of dirt; I cleaned them on the brush scraper, and we got the gurney out and onto the scale.

The decedent weighed a hundred and five pounds.

Beneath the merciless lights of the intake bay, Zaragoza took more flicks. We left the body dressed, protocol for homicides. The pathologist would examine her clothes for evidence before removing them for the autopsy.

I called to the morgue for a tech and began filling out paperwork.

The automatic doors glided open, and Dani Botero came in, dressed in scrubs, absent her usual smirk. Without a word she fetched a fingerprint card and an ink pad. One by one I pried the decedent's fingers open, and Dani inked and rolled them. I couldn't tell what had her so subdued. The age of the victims, perhaps. Although it's an unfortunate fact that Coroner's cases are often young. Young people are disproportionately likely to die of violence.

I suspect, rather, it was the general feeling of failure, the collective guilt, that permeates the unit following any mass casualty event. Reality has gone off the rails. What did we do to get here? Why didn't we do something to prevent it?

Deep down, we know we're powerless. We're not on the front lines. And those on the front lines are pretty much powerless themselves. All of us, however, would like to imagine that we're contributing in some small way to keeping the world orderly. Then comes along a stark reminder to the contrary.

Then come the families.

Whose photos are no longer accurate. Whose calendars have acquired a hideous new holiday. Those broken apart by grief; those already broken, for whom death will provide the worst reason to mend fences. The mothers emptied, like amputees of the heart; the fathers bewildered. Sisters without confidantes and brothers missing necessary rivals.

Circles of lovers and friends, irreparably deformed.

Dani said, "I'll take it from here."

I glanced at my decedent, small, pale, silent. Went upstairs.

THE SQUAD ROOM was hectic. A phone conversation ended and the receiver went down and the ringing began again. Keyboards creaked. Lunches wilted, forgotten.

In the conference room the television was on mute. Morning news had given way to *The Price Is Right.*

Moffett was still there, working into his nineteenth straight hour. Turnbow was trying to persuade him to leave, acting offended that he hadn't.

"It's under control," she was saying.

Moffett said, "I just want to get it down while it's still fresh."

"You're not fresh, Brad. That's my point."

I went to my cubicle.

We label cases by year and number. There are exceptions: complex deaths or those involving multiple casualties, which merit their own category. The Oikos campus shooting. The Ghost Ship fire. When I sat to upload my photos, I found a newly created folder.

ALMOND STREET

I had a moment of indecision about where to put my flicks of the dead woman. Hadn't I told Turnbow that it looked different? Hadn't she agreed? The new folder already contained over four hundred pictures. I didn't want mine getting lost.

Lindsey Bagoyo said, "We're trending."

I stood up and leaned over the partition. She pointed to the edge of her computer screen, where #OaklandShooting was ninth in the Twitter rankings.

Across the room, Moffett rose, defeated, and headed for the exit.

The sergeant went back to her office. I heard the door close.

I sat down and got to work on Jasmine Gomez.

4:35 p.m.

By day's end we had made presumptive identification on four of five victims. Turnbow gathered us in the conference room to review. Somehow the television had managed to remain on; Judge Judy filled the screen with silent indignation. The sergeant switched it off and scribbled on the whiteboard.

Rebecca Ristic
Grant Hellerstein

Benjamin Felton

Jasmine Gomez

Jane Doe

In a second column she added two more names.

Oswald Schumacher

Jalen Coombs

"Housekeeping, first," Turnbow said. "Kennedy's the primary. Everything you do goes in one file, with her name on it. I don't want to get a month in and realize we can't find something cause someone hid it in the wrong place. Okay? Okay. Let's start with the GSWs."

"Rebecca Ristic, twenty-six," Bagoyo said. "Grant Hellerstein, twenty-four, her boyfriend. She's local, he's out of state. We pulled addresses but haven't notified either."

"We tried her parents' house," Zaragoza said. "Nobody answered the door."

"They might be traveling for the holidays," Turnbow said. "Which reminds me. The captain is"—a beat—"*requesting* that we get the notifications done ASAP so that they can release names to the media."

"'Requesting,'" Shupfer said.

"Call it a 'strong suggestion,'" Turnbow said.

I understood now why she'd been riding us hard. Someone was doing it to her.

"If possible," she said, "let's aim for Christmas, the latest."

"If not possible?" I asked.

"Go ahead and notify whoever you can find and we'll deal with the rest in time. Anyway it ain't practical to sit on anything."

A truth of the social media age: we as an institution could not control the flow of information.

"Who's next?" Turnbow said. "Shoops."

Shupfer said, "Benjamin Felton, six years old. Mom's Bonita Felton. OPD took her to her sister's. I'll look in on her, make sure she understands what's going on."

"Please do. I've asked for him to be autopsied first. From what it appears that'll happen Wednesday. Which, another thing, reminds me: Dr. Bronson and Dr. Lewkowicz are out till after the New Year. Dr. Park will cover the week of Christmas. Cold keeps up, we're gonna have our hands full. Expect delays. Clay, you have the ped struck."

"Jasmine Gomez," I said. "Twenty-two. Born male, so I'm pretty certain that's not the birth name. Accurint's not giving me anything for the female name, and CIB doesn't have prints on file for Alameda. She's listed as female on her driver's license. I'll ping DMV in case she filed the change with them."

"Wouldn't she have to?" Bagoyo said.

"Not if she first applied as a female," Shupfer said.

"I asked IT to pull the phone data," I said. "I'll hit the home address tomorrow."

"Fine," Turnbow said. "Jane Doe."

"Same deal, nothing local from CIB. I'm hoping they found ID after we left the scene, or someone who was at the party'll recognize her."

I tried to sound confident. Inwardly, I squirmed. I kept thinking about those empty pockets. The prospect of a Doe—a real Doe, not a twenty-four-hour blank space on a form, but a ghost that hangs around for years—turns my stomach. A person's home serves as a form of soft identification, so the fact that that she was found outside, minus the context that a residence provides, unsettled me further.

Either Turnbow didn't share my concerns or she didn't have time for hand-holding. She had moved on, tapping the names in the second column. Oswald Schumacher and Jalen Coombs. "These are the two got brought to Highland. No need to go chasing them down. If they're ours we'll hear about it sooner or later. All right," she said, erasing, "good work everyone, now get the hell to bed."

I waited till the room had cleared to say, "Sarge, about my Doe. We discussed whether to break it out into a separate file."

"We discussed that?"

"Over the phone."

"If you say so. My head's"—she spread her fingers, made an exploding sound.

"You want Advil? I have some in my desk."

"Nn . . . Okay, explain it to me again."

I reviewed the circumstances.

"Right," she said. "You did tell me that. Well, look. From my end, the important thing is that you don't isolate yourself. Because, say she is connected to the others. I'd rather you be sharing information than keeping it to yourself."

"I won't."

"Go ahead, then. Just—Clay? Stay focused."

She didn't elaborate, but I knew what she meant and that she meant well. The last time I'd wandered down a byway, I'd strayed far outside my mandate, earning myself a weeklong suspension. I accepted it without complaint. Still, my old sergeant, a guy by the name of Joe Vitti, wouldn't let it go. Any interaction, no matter how mundane, became an excuse for him to level at me some disparaging comment masquerading as wisdom.

Trust isn't given, Clay. It has to be earned.

The tension got bad enough that I'd toyed with transferring to another duty station. I might've, if he hadn't beaten me to it.

That it was Turnbow who replaced him was a lucky break. She

was a different breed, sharp and thoughtful, nuanced where Vitti was blunt, driven by a pathological aversion to disorder and waste.

I said to her now, "I'll be careful."

"All I ask," she said. "That and a couple of Advil."

7:28 p.m.

Amy said, "Hello?"

"In here."

I heard her familiar tread, its gentle clip-clop, and I pictured her long, graceful, purebred stride.

She paused before coming into the living room, as though afraid of how she'd find me. As though death were contagious.

I did in fact look half dead. Drowned in TV glow, skin blued, one foot on the sofa arm and the other on the carpet; my cheek smushed against the cushion, a hand pinned beneath me, numb; uncomfortable but doing nothing to change that.

Amy dropped her bag, slipped off her shoes, unpinned her hair and shook it out, a billow of gold. "What are you watching?"

"I have no clue."

"Can I join you?"

I curled up to accommodate her. "I didn't get a chance to start the cooking."

"It's okay."

"I know we have a lot to do."

"It's fine. The only thing that has to be done in advance is the duck, because that needs to cure. The rest we can deal with on Monday and Tuesday morning."

I started to rise. "I'll do the duck."

"Stop, please," she said, pressing me back down.

The *Modern Marvels* logo appeared on the screen, subtitled: "Avocados."

"I can't believe you're still awake," she said. She stroked my knee. "I thought for sure you'd be passed out."

"I wanted to see you."

"That's sweet."

"Also, I sat down and then I couldn't get up."

She laughed.

On the screen, a man in a lab coat caressed a Hass, rhapsodizing over essential oils.

"Seriously," Amy said, "why are you watching this."

"It's really interesting. It might be the most interesting thing I've ever seen."

"Do you want to tell me about your day?"

"I'd rather hear about yours."

I'm grateful for Amy for many reasons. Among them is that she never tells me I'm avoiding my feelings. Even when I am.

"Okay," she said, and she proceeded to talk about her patients. Not by name, of course. But the jokes they made, the wild stories they told. Piece of bad news: there'd been an overdose over the weekend.

"I'm sorry," I said.

"Thank you. He was Liz's patient, not mine. She's pretty devastated."

The screen showed rows and rows of broad green trees.

"Look how much fun we are," I said.

"Loads of fun."

"Boatloads," I said. "We're like a cruise ship of fun."

She craned to kiss me, then got up, heading for the kitchen. "Duck time."

I stretched out and shut my eyes.

CHAPTER 8

Sunday, December 23

I woke up on the couch around two a.m., draped by a blanket. Not wanting to disturb Amy, I stayed in the living room, fading in and out for another couple of hours before conceding defeat and feeling around for the remote.

Early-morning news had nothing to say about the shooting.

Neither did Steve Harvey, or TMZ, or Mike & Mike.

We had ceased to trend on Twitter.

The world had stopped to stare, then kept on going.

4:28 a.m.

At the bureau, I ducked into the locker room to change.

A shirtless Brad Moffett sat slumped on a folding chair, supported by the bulge of his own abdomen, his skin shiny and sallow.

"Morning," I said.

He acknowledged me with a grunt.

"You get any rest?"

"Some."

"How was the night?"

"Busy." He scratched at his chest. "The kid died."

"Which kid?"

"The gut-shot," he said. "Coombs. He made it through surgery but went into shock. They called a few minutes ago."

"I didn't know he was a kid."

"Like eighteen or nineteen."

That brought the body count to six.

"What about the other guy?" I asked. "Schumacher."

"The nurse told me they discharged him."

"That's good, at least."

Moffett yawned. "Yeah, I guess."

"Who's on the call?"

"Nobody yet," he said.

"All right. We'll handle it."

"It's four thirty," he said. "Why are you here?"

"I couldn't sleep."

"Mm."

"Go home," I said. "I'll make sure it's taken care of."

He nodded gratefully. "The sheet's on my desk."

"No problem. I'll sign you out."

He kept nodding but did not move, staring down at his stomach. I imagined him imagining himself with his guts blown open, a human soup bowl.

He said, "I'm a fat fuck."

He looked up at me. "When did I become such a fat fucking fuck?"

I said, "Honestly, Sergeant? I can't remember that far back."

He smiled and flipped me off.

. . .

I WASN'T THE first one from our team. Zaragoza was at his desk, typing, perhaps to atone for his lateness the previous night. Coombs's death came as news to him.

"I didn't speak to Moffett," he said. "I must've missed him on the way in. Gimme one second to finish up what I'm doing."

The phone rang. I went to take it.

"One second" turned into a minute, then five, ten. Zaragoza took a call. I fell into paperwork. Turnbow appeared at quarter to, followed by Bagoyo and Shoops soon thereafter. A new mood settled over the squad room, quiet and purposeful, free of haste, coffee mugs and cleared throats and staplers chunking. The techs arrived, chatting about their vacation plans. Carmen Woolsey had the latest issue of *Food Network Magazine* and was excited to try out a recipe for pear cardamom spice cake.

We could have been any midsized American office—the regional branch of some beverage distributor.

The phone rang, although with less urgency and frequency. People worried about their niece, their cousin, their college roommate; calling from other time zones, out of state, word of the shooting having migrated. The internet could sustain a story TV had dropped.

At ten to six I passed Moffett's desk and spied a half-completed intake sheet atop his keyboard.

"Shit," I said. "Zaragoza."

He lifted his head.

I held up the sheet. "Coombs."

"Shit," he said.

We reached Highland Hospital by six fifteen. Zaragoza backed the van up to the morgue loading bay, and we got out and buzzed for admittance.

No answer. Zaragoza jabbed the button.

Silence.

A final jab, then we gave up and walked around to the main entrance.

A clutch of Oakland uniforms hung out in the lobby, sipping coffee and shooting the shit. Zaragoza told them we were here to pick up the kid who'd died overnight. Did they happen to know who caught it?

"Try upstairs," a uniform said.

"They got the shooter in a bed," another said. "He showed up bleeding in the ER."

We thanked them and headed for the elevators.

A LINE THREE-STRONG had formed outside room 431: Detectives Bischoff and Von Ruden, and, nearest to the door, Delilah Nwodo.

"Hello again," she said.

Bischoff and Von Ruden nodded as well, although it was evident from their bleary expressions that they had no memory of me whatsoever.

Through the closed door I could hear voices, one steady, one agitated.

"Popular guy," I said.

"Oh yes," Nwodo said. "What brings you here at this fine hour?"

"Jalen Coombs," Zaragoza said, asking who owned the case.

"That'd be Ms. Muñoz," Nwodo said, thumbing at the room. "In there, as we speak."

"Taking her time, too," Bischoff said.

"First come, first served," Nwodo said.

Bischoff gestured *yeah, yeah*.

"You guys got a lotta hands in the pot," I said.

"We can totally spare the manpower," Von Ruden said. "It's one hundred percent, totally not at all how it looks."

The shooter's name was Isaiah Branch. He was nineteen years old. Around midnight, he had walked unaccompanied into the emergency room, his arm bound in a bloody T-shirt. Exam revealed an injury to his biceps consistent with a through-and-through gunshot wound. When asked about its origin, he became evasive and expressed a desire to leave the hospital.

The ER staff convinced Branch to wait. Then they called the cops.

"Hang on a sec," I said. "He's the shooter, who shot him?"

"There's a guy shooting on the other side, too," Von Ruden said. "From the party."

"Whole thing's on tape," Bischoff said. "You can watch it on YouTube."

"For real?" Zaragoza said.

"We're calling them the Sharks and the Jets," Von Ruden said. "Helps to keep em straight."

"Old school," I said.

"How we roll in Oaktown."

"Which one's which?"

"Shit, I forget," Von Ruden said. "Who's the white gang?"

"The Jets," Nwodo said.

"Okay, so that's the party people."

What about the round that hit the kid in the basement? Did they know who fired it?

Bischoff shrugged. He had swapped out his 49ers tie for Santa Clauses. "Maybe I'll find out"—he inclined toward the door, spoke in a stage whisper—"if I ever get in there."

"What we need," Von Ruden said, "is those pagers they give you, tell you when your table's ready. Like at the Cheesecake Factory?"

"What you need," Nwodo said, "is to not eat at the Cheesecake Factory."

I asked if she'd had a chance to question the homeowner about Jane Doe.

"She claims not to recognize her," Nwodo said. "'She's at a party at your house, you don't know who she is?' But she says they throw these parties twice a month. They get all kinds showing up. Strangers, plus-ones."

"They were charging admission," Von Ruden said.

"That doesn't sound legal," Zaragoza said.

"Least of her problems," Bischoff said.

"What about the driver on my ped struck?" I asked him. "Meredith Klaar."

I saw it dawn on him, then, who I was.

"Negative for everything," he said. "Except maybe being a shitty driver."

Plus scared out of her mind. "Get a chance, send me a copy of her statement?"

Before he could acknowledge the request, the door opened and a woman with cinnamon hair and a belt badge—Detective Muñoz, presumably—stepped out carrying a gunshot residue kit.

She said, "He says it wasn't him doing the shooting."

The other detectives reacted with predictable disdain.

"Also, he knows Jalen Coombs," she said. "They're friends going back to third grade. That much I think he's telling the truth. He lost his shit when I told him Coombs was dead."

"If he's not the shooter, then Coombs was," Bischoff said.

"According to him, no. He won't say who else was with them, though."

"Right," Von Ruden said. "I guess bullets are magically appearing from thin air."

"Where's he been the last twenty-four hours?" Bischoff asked.

"Ask him yourself," Muñoz said. "Maybe you'll do better."

Nwodo's turn. She started into the room.

"You mind if I tag along?" I asked.

Probably I should've cleared it with Zaragoza first. We had a body to remove. But I didn't want to miss my chance. Maybe Isaiah Branch had seen what happened to Jane Doe—or to Jasmine Gomez. I doubted Bischoff would ask; he and Von Ruden were interested in Branch as a perp, not as a witness.

Nwodo eyed me briefly. "No," she said, "I don't mind."

I looked to Zaragoza. He shrugged. He introduced himself to Muñoz and they went off to confer about Jalen Coombs. Von Ruden was popping a Tums. Bischoff checked his watch and let out a strained sigh.

7:19 a.m.

Isaiah Branch lay on his side, hugging a pillow, his uninjured arm cuffed to the bed rail. In the corner sat a uniform, swiping at his phone: right, right, right, left, right.

Nwodo pulled a chair close to the bed. "Hey there."

Soft voice. Soothing.

Isaiah sat up, rubbing red eyes. He was rangy and handsome, with a hi-top fade and a small metal stud in his lower lip. The neck of his hospital gown drooped. Seeing me, he ducked down, glaring, projecting an air I knew well: young male, excruciatingly aware of his own naïveté, desperate to hide it.

"I already told her," he said. "I don't know anything else."

"Whoa, whoa," Nwodo said. "I haven't even introduced myself yet. I'm Detective Nwodo. This is Deputy Edison."

I raised a friendly hand. "Hi."

"All right," Isaiah said, speaking to Nwodo. "I get how it works."

She said, "How's it work?"

"The white lady runs out of steam, she sends you in."

Nwodo smiled. "Look, Isaiah, let's make this quick. I don't care who you shot."

"I didn't shoot—"

"Great. Then we don't have to talk about it. What I want to know about is this girl."

He hesitated, then glanced at Nwodo's phone, a photo of Jane Doe, framed tight to her face.

"Recognize her?" Nwodo said.

He chuffed. "Some Sarah."

He meant some generic white girl.

"She's dead, if that matters," I said.

Isaiah flinched. "Doesn't mean I know who she is."

"That's fine," Nwodo said, putting the phone away. "But I want you to listen carefully, cause I'm going to share some information that might be of interest to you."

She rested a hand on the bed rail and leaned in. "Me, personally? I'm not asking you about the shooting. The second I walk out of here, though, there are two more detectives waiting in the hall who plan to do exactly that. You stop talking to me, you start talking to them. And I hate to tell you this, but between you and me, they have some stuff that'll make you shit your pants. For example."

He was looking at her, now.

"There's a video," she said.

His mouth opened a fraction of an inch.

"Yeah," she said, nodding. "Somebody got the whole thing on camera." She raised her eyebrows at me. "Crazy, right?"

"Technology," I said.

"I told you," Isaiah said, "I didn't *do* anything."

"I believe you," Nwodo said.

"I don't care if you believe me or not. That's the truth. You have a video, fine. That's what you'll see."

"Isaiah." That same mothering tone, so at odds with the content of her words. "Hang on. Let me explain something that you might not realize. You ever heard of the felony murder rule? You know what that is? It says it doesn't matter whether you're the one who pulled the trigger. You were there. You went over there with them. That makes you part of everything that happens next. You understand? It means they can arrest you for murder."

I couldn't tell how serious she was. I had no idea what they had on him. But she was doing a terrific job of selling the danger he was in. And her concern for him. Isaiah looked rattled as hell.

"That's bullshit," he said.

"It's the law," Nwodo said.

I said, "She's right."

"My advice to you," she said, "this point forward, Isaiah, you need to think about yourself. You need to protect yourself. Anything you do to help me, that's going to help you, when it's your turn to stand in front of the judge. But the offer isn't good forever."

Out in the hall, new voices. *Excuse us, please.*

Isaiah's eyes went to the door.

"It's good right now," Nwodo said, speeding up. "So if you did see her, if you know anything about what happened to her, it's in your best interest to tell me that."

I could hear Von Ruden saying *If you could just give us a few more minutes.*

Isaiah? Are you in there?

Ma'am—

"Now," Nwodo said, "while you still have the opportunity to affect your future."

The door flipped open and a middle-aged black couple entered.

"That's enough," the man said.

"Sorry," Nwodo said. "You are?"

"His parents," the woman said. "And he is not talking to you anymore."

Isaiah started to open his mouth.

"You be quiet," the woman said. To Nwodo: "Did you hear me? We're done."

"All due respect, ma'am, he's not a minor."

"Isaiah," the man said, "tell the detective you're done talking and you want a lawyer."

Isaiah said, "But I didn't do—"

"Shut up," the woman said, "and repeat what your father said."

A beat.

Isaiah Branch said, "I want a lawyer."

CHAPTER 9

Down at the morgue, Zaragoza was waiting for an orderly to complete the release form on Jalen Coombs. I recounted what had happened upstairs.

"He's all *I ain't scared of nothing*," I said, "but man, you should've seen his face when Mom and Dad walked in. You could basically hear his asshole pinch shut."

Zaragoza laughed.

"Von Ruden and Bischoff were pissed," I said. "They didn't get to talk to him."

"Early bird gets the worm." He squinted through reinforced glass into the cramped office where the orderly sat, mousing. "Muñoz said the family was around. I'm going to see if I can find them."

A few minutes later, the orderly emerged with a clipboard for me to sign. He and I transferred Jalen Coombs's body onto a gurney and loaded it into the van. The orderly retrieved a clear plastic bag crammed with Coombs's possessions, those items removed from him or fallen off in the course of his ambulance ride, intubation, surgery, and death.

A phone. A wallet. A thin gold necklace.

Bloody clothes; a bloodstained pair of Jordans.

I sat on the van's rear bumper, staring at the shoes and thinking about my brother. We'd bike to the Bay Fair Mall and stand before the display wall at Foot Locker like pilgrims at a shrine. New Jordans ran a hundred fifty bucks.

My father would laugh. For sneakers? Worn out in three months? Forget it.

We begged. Threatened. Tried to explain: these weren't any old sneakers; these were *Michael Jordan's sneakers*. The significance was lost on him. He tossed us the classifieds.

The first and only pair we ever got—we got them at the same time, we had to, or there would be blood—were the XVs. My grandmother paid for them, a joint Christmas-birthday present for each of us.

Ugly shoes. Laces sheathed in waffle fabric, an odd foreskin-like overhang at the top. Bad shoes, too, baggy in the mid-foot. Get crossed up in them and you'd turn an ankle.

We didn't care. Good enough for MJ. Good enough for us. I was fifteen and chose white and dark blue. Luke took black and red. It didn't take three months till they had holes.

The morgue door kicked wide.

"They're gone," Zaragoza said. "Nurse said they left around five thirty."

I could tell he felt guilty. We'd run late, and as a result, he'd blown a chance to be present for them, to offer them solace in the form of information, a lifeline of red tape to grab hold of amid the upheaval.

We drove to the bureau, intaked Jalen Coombs, handed him off to Sully. Zaragoza sat at his desk to track down the Coombs family, and I sat at mine to search for Jane Doe.

. . .

IF YOU LIVE in the great state of California and you're a licensed accountant, your fingerprints are on record. The same goes if you're a registered nurse, a veterinarian, or a psychologist. A termite inspector. A geologist. Clergy. If you coach Little League or sell real estate, you've had to submit your prints.

If you train guide dogs for the blind, and you die unexpectedly, and nobody can say who you are—I, or someone like me, will look up your fingerprints.

If you've been incarcerated, your fingerprints are on record.

Applicants for a California driver's license must give a thumbprint.

Jane Doe was not any of these people.

Things get trickier once you cross state lines. No comprehensive clearinghouse for fingerprint data exists. Some states take prints for a license. Others use a different biometric marker. A few don't bother at all. The military sits in its own hermetic box. The FBI's Integrated Automated Fingerprint Identification System holds a hundred million sets of prints acquired over decades from criminals, civil servants, firearms owners, terrorists. That's a lot of fingers, but it's not everyone, not even close.

As an American, leery of Big Brother, I'm glad.

As a coroner, it annoys me to no end.

Another wrinkle: not every person who dies in the great state of California *lives* in the great state of California, or, for that matter, in the United States of America. A healthy chunk of our great state's gross domestic product derives from tourism, and while plenty of those tourists arrive from Nevada, Arizona, or domestic points farther afield, an enormous number step off planes from China, Japan, Brazil, Denmark, India, Lithuania, Djibouti, or anyplace in the wide world where people still dream. Which is to say, everywhere.

And which is to say nothing about the substantial number of Californians who cross the border, but not as tourists; who live here, but not quite as residents; who do their utmost not to end up in the system, and for whom getting in touch with the authorities sits down near the bottom of the to-do list, sandwiched between *gouge out own eyes* and *munch turds*.

She could be anyone.

I'd submitted Jasmine Gomez's prints as well, hoping I might get back a record with her birth name. No local hit there, either.

I replied to CIB, asking them to expand the search radius for both sets of prints.

I wrote to forensic IT, asking when I could expect the data from Jasmine's phone.

The homeowner of the Victorian was named Rhiannon Cooke. According to her Facebook page, the theme of the party was *Winter Solstice: Howl at the Moon!! Wear costumes that reflect your Inner Creature. Ten bucks at the door. DJ Fooye spinning. Cash bar.*

Browsing the list of RSVPs, I couldn't distinguish between genuine attendees and those who had promised but failed to show. Nor did the list account for anyone who'd dropped by spontaneously. Over seven hundred people had reacted to the post, many of them after the fact: friends airing their grief in public; internet strangers compelled to share their two cents.

How many of these folks could I realistically track down on my own?

What were the odds they knew Jane Doe?

To test the waters, I picked a handful of distinctive-sounding names and looked up their home phone numbers. I reached two live people. I asked if they had a female friend who'd gone to the party and was still unaccounted for. I got one *no* and one *maybe* that became a *no* when I described Jane Doe's clothing.

I then had to spend ten minutes politely deflecting their questions.

For all I knew, it was Jane Doe's date who had killed her. If by some fluke I stumbled across him, he'd never talk to me.

I googled the video the detectives had mentioned.

They'd led me to expect a single hit. Instead I got hundreds, hosted on a variety of platforms: YouTube, Instagram, Vimeo, WorldStarHipHop. Confounding the search results were clips ripped from local TV news, as well as a slew of videos of unrelated shootings. The sheer number implied a depressing appetite for cheap thrills.

Oakland provided plenty of fodder.

Street-corner shootings. Midday shootings. Front-yard shootings. Drive-bys.

I plugged in my headphones.

Most of the footage from the night in question showed the party itself, prior to the shooting. The atmosphere was raucous. The DJ was a bearded white guy in a tux; projection screens ran berserk with trippy animations. Young people mugged for the camera, spilling drinks, howling on cue. They looked happy. They looked ignorant.

I hit PAUSE, scanned the faces.

No Jane Doe.

I clicked a link for "DEADLY Oakland party 12/21."

Close-up of a human shape writhing in flames.

A spike of adrenaline, before I remembered the effigy with the purple nose.

The camera zoomed out, panned along a ring of partygoers holding hands around the fire pit, singing and jumping and landing out of sync.

I let the video run to the end.

The promised deadliness never materialized.

No Jane Doe.

I clicked the next link, and the next, and the next.

No Jane Doe.

Jasmine Gomez, on the other hand, made several guest appearances. Her popularity, I reckoned, had to do with the costume. Aside from the robes and the mechanical wings, she had on a goofy plastic halo, attached to a headband. Missing, by the time I got to her. But of course there would be one.

I should've inferred that on my own. What else had I missed?

I watched her strike a pose, draw down the chain at her side.

The effect was dramatic: fully spread, the wings measured a good five feet, tip to tip. The audience cheered, and Jasmine took a bow.

You made that? Yourself? Rad. Hey, check this out. Do it again.

She was happy to oblige.

Eventually I came to a video two minutes and seventeen seconds long, uploaded by a YouTube user named yeoldejeff22 and titled "Okaland shoot out." The errant letter, along with the flood of noise, had caused it to sink down in the search results.

I clicked.

It opened without prelude, the fight already in progress. The perspective put the cameraman on the lawn of the Victorian, twenty or thirty feet back from the street, filming through the crowd.

The Sharks and the Jets, Von Ruden had called them; and indeed, the action had a flat, theatrical quality to it. Insults bounced back and forth like a discordant round. Houses in the background possessed the depth of a painted scrim.

At around the forty-five-second mark, the cameraman moved up to get a better vantage, and the leads came into focus.

The Sharks were three young men. Two—Isaiah Branch and Jalen Coombs—were black. The third Shark was Asian. He was out front, puffing his chest. Cross talk muddled his words, though the subtext was clear enough. Angry young male.

The Jets were harder to define. If you counted everyone massed on the opposite side, it seemed like a pretty unfair fight. But two stood out. Rhiannon Cooke I recognized from her Facebook page. She wore a silver lamé jumpsuit, her hair dyed purple and pink and shellacked into a helmet. Beside her was a lean, shaggy guy with thick glasses and a red knit beanie, feinting and bobbing like a buoy.

What's your fuckin problem.

The camera moved shakily over the crowd.

Taut, disgruntled, restless, jeering.

Asshole.

Get the fuck out of here, asshole.

Fuck off.

The mob, starting to flex like a single unit, to chant.

Fuck off fuck off fuck off.

A bottle came flying, shattered on the sidewalk.

The camera rolled back to center stage, where the Asian guy and the guy in the beanie were up in each other's faces, shouting. Jalen Coombs was restraining the Asian guy. Isaiah Branch, in turn, was tugging on Coombs: *Let's go.*

At the 1:47 mark, several things happened in quick succession.

The Asian guy surged forward.

His shirt rode up, revealing the butt of a gun.

The man in the beanie recoiled, grabbing at the small of his back.

A shot rang out.

Pandemonium.

An eruption of screams crackled my eardrums; I lunged to lower the volume. The camera jerked as its operator attempted to flee, filling the screen with a nauseating barrage of pixels and blobs and streaks. *Fuck oh fuck.* He couldn't get anywhere, he was trapped, colliding with other bodies, elbows thrown, shoving. *Fuck oh God oh my God fuck.* Seven dense seconds of this and then, at 1:54, the real shooting began: a series of quick, overlapping claps.

I had to lower the volume again.

It's worse, somehow, when it's happening off screen.

At 2:06 the cameraman got free and broke up the middle of the street, arms pumping, the world dark scribbles.

I could hear metallic smacks: car doors. I could hear tires.

Three more shots.

The camera fell, scraped along the sidewalk, landed facing up.

Sky. Cloud. Stars.

One shot.

A giant hand came down to retrieve the camera.

I caught a glimpse of him as he leaned over.

He was white, with a beard.

Two more shots.

The clip broke off.

I rewound to the beginning and slowed playback to a quarter speed, examining the gallery of faces that surfaced and submerged in the patchy streetlight.

I thought I saw Grant Hellerstein, the male GSW.

No Jane Doe.

It was difficult to say who'd opened fire. The camera was moving nonstop, hungry for drama. In yeoldejeff22, we had ourselves a regular auteur.

I saw Isaiah Branch pulling at his friend's sleeve.

I saw the Asian guy rise up, enraged.

The guy in the beanie, galvanized.

No Jane Doe.

It made sense. We'd found her in the backyard, not the street.

Four possibilities, then.

She'd been killed and stuck in the shed at some point prior to the party.

She'd been killed and stuck in the shed at some point *during* the party.

She'd died simultaneous with the shooting.

Possibility four, the most chilling: she'd died after the shooting, in the intervening seven-plus hours before Grelling found her, while the neighborhood was crawling with cops.

"Shit is messed up." Zaragoza was staring over my shoulder at the screen.

I took off my headphones. "I'm not so sure Isaiah Branch was lying. He's not holding a gun, far as I can see. Neither is Coombs."

He smiled quizzically. What business was it of mine?

Turnbow's voice in my ear, chiding. *Stay focused.*

"D'you read the comments?" Zaragoza asked.

"Do I want to?"

"Depends," he said. "Have you already met your recommended daily allowance for human awfulness?"

He went off to get coffee.

Against my better judgment, I scrolled down.

In thirty-six hours, the video had garnered fifty-eight thousand views, and almost as many opinions.

The problem, see, was a culture that glorified violence.

No. The problem was gentrification and a shortage of affordable housing, when you started kicking people out of a neighborhood that had been theirs for decades.

Could we not forget that these are REAL people, they're my FRIENDS, please don't hijack this to push your own agenda?

Who was kicking anyone out?

What else could you call it when you let greedy developers come in, and rents doubled and tripled overnight?

It's called the free market.

THESE ARE MY FRIENDS.

It was an Italian neighborhood originally.

Actually it was German.

Are you a fucking idiot, no one has the "right" to live anywhere.

It was African American and had been since World War II.

Did you know anything, anything at all, about history?

The problem was you'd never read a book other than Harry Potter.

Could everyone PLEASE PLEASE PLEASE try to remember that we were talking about a dead child, this is a TRAGEDY, we get nowhere playing THE BLAME GAME.

Your the idiot.

Animals with no value for human life.

Not sure what you mean by "animals" other than oh yes you're straight up nazi.

The problem was guns.

The problem was millenial entitlement.

The problem was cultural appropriation.

*you're

Can you PLEASE PLEASE DON'T WRITE IN ALL CAPS CAUSE IT'S ANNOYING AF?

Ever heard of the Second Amendment, shitbag?

The problem was cis white male privilege.

The problem was that neither side is listening to the other.

The problem was that not each side is worth listening to.

The problem was you.

You, motherfucker.

You.

2:41 p.m.

The address on Jasmine Gomez's license belonged to an LGBTQ+ community center, a converted Craftsman home on Telegraph Avenue, half a mile south of the Berkeley campus. Rainbow-colored letters screwed to the eave spelled out THE HARBOR; a sign in the front window declared it to be a SAFE SPACE. A young man with a pencil mustache answered my knock and admitted me to a musty, paneled foyer.

I asked for the person in charge.

He invited me to have a seat and went to the reception desk in the parlor.

While he called, I wandered into the adjoining room, shabby but comfortable, with a magazine rack and mismatched chairs that exuded a faint smell of sweat. The bulletin board advertised meetings and support groups. Some were aimed at the general public: grief, Al-Anon. Others felt more niche. Married and/or once-married bisexual men 35 to 50. Middle Eastern queer femmes. Partners of the non-conforming.

"Can I help you."

A woman in her late twenties was coming down the stairs. She had ruddy skin and auburn hair in a pixie cut. She introduced herself as Greer Unger, one of the co-directors. I gave her my card and asked if we could speak in private, and she brought me up to her office on the second floor, at the end of a long hallway lined with a bald runner. Beside a potted fern, a white noise machine burbled, masking the conversations taking place behind closed doors.

She gave me a chair and went to her desk. Slogan posters and Native American art scaled the walls.

I said, "I'm going to ask you to keep what I'm about to tell you confidential. It's part of an ongoing investigation, and not public yet. Can you make me that assurance, please?"

"Not until I've heard what it is."

"It's about Jasmine Gomez," I said.

No reaction.

"Do you know her?"

"I can't answer that."

I said, "Jasmine passed away over the weekend."

Greer Unger shut her eyes. "Oh God." She opened them and met mine. "Was she killed?"

Her assumption took me aback. "Is there a reason you'd think that?"

"Yes. Because people like Jasmine get hurt. What happened?"

"What I can tell you is that we're looking into it. I'm sorry I can't be more specific. Right now I'm trying to get in touch with her family. That's the first step."

"I can't help you there. I've never met them."

"Jasmine never mentioned their names?"

"No."

"What about her own name?"

Greer Unger screwed up her mouth. "Excuse me?"

"Before she was Jasmine," I said. "What did she go by?"

"You're asking me to deadname."

"What—I'm not sure what that means."

"Referring to someone by a name they've abandoned is a form of transphobia."

"You understand that that's not my intention."

"Even so," Greer said, "it can be a deeply traumatic experience for the individual."

"Jasmine is deceased," I said.

"That's all well and good, but it's not her I'm thinking of. Say I tell you and it gets out. People come here seeking support they can't get elsewhere. For many of them, we're a last resort. You're asking me to violate Jasmine's privacy, then turn around and tell them they're safe."

"It won't get out. You have my word."

She shook her head. "Sorry."

"I'm not—judging, or—"

"That's kind of you," she said. "Not to judge."

Silence.

I said, "What I want is to take care of Jasmine, and to make sure she gets a proper burial. To do that, it's imperative that I speak to her family."

"I told you, I don't know them."

"Maybe we can narrow it down, some. Did she come from the Bay Area, originally?"

Greer shook her head. *No* or *No comment.*

"On her license she listed this as her home address. Was she living here?"

"We don't provide residential facilities."

"Was she out on the street?" I asked.

"From time to time."

"What about when not?"

She had broken eye contact. "I'm sorry, but I'm going to need to consult with my colleagues before we continue this conversation."

She stood, shoving her hips out like a gunslinger. "Take care. Officer."

On my way out, I stopped to scan the corkboard. Homeless trans youth 16–21 met on Monday nights at eight. I tore off a tab.

The receptionist passed by with a mug of tea. "FYI, there's no groups tomorrow."

"Right," I said. "When do they start up again?"

"After the New Year."

"Thanks very much."

The receptionist said, "Have a nice holiday."

I wished him the same.

CHAPTER 10

Monday, December 24

Before Amy and I started dating, I wasn't much of a cook, and while I defer to her expertise in the kitchen, I don't think it's boasting to say I've learned a lot in the last year and a half. I enjoy myself, anyway. An antidote to the job.

The smells are nice smells.

The instructions are clear, the quantities measurable.

The meat doesn't have a family.

AMY SAID, "MINCE me a shallot, please?"

"Yes, Chef."

"And take the pie dough out of the freezer."

"Yes, Chef."

"I prefer Doctor."

"Yes, Dr. Chef."

Minestrone, garlic mashed potatoes, roasted root vegetables, butternut squash ravioli, beef potpie, duck confit; soda bread with caraway seeds and raisins; chocolate chestnut soufflé. A scattershot menu, reflecting the dearth of firm holiday traditions on either side. Amy's father comes from a long line of Jewish atheists. Her mother, herself a marvelous cook, comes from a long line of Italian atheists. My family cooked a little more often than we went to church, but we didn't do either very often or very well. I grew up on boxed mac-n-cheese, peanut butter sandwiches, and Sunday-morning *SportsCenter.*

The quantity of food reflected Amy's strategy for conflict deterrence. Our parents were meeting for the first time. Mouths busy chewing couldn't argue.

"Yours are fine," I said, crosscutting. "It's mine we've got to worry about."

She unwrapped the dough and set it on the counter to thaw. "I just want everyone to get along."

I said, "By 'everyone' you mean me and Luke."

"I'm expressing a general sense of optimism."

"I'm going to say it one last time," I said.

"Clay—"

"We didn't have to invite him."

"He's your brother."

"And?"

"And he's your *brother.*"

"All I'm saying, if you're trying to limit the number of variables, he's first to go."

In the four months since Luke's release from prison, I'd seen him face-to-face half a dozen times. One obstacle was my schedule: I worked odd hours, and in my free time I often felt too wiped to do much more than watch TV. I suppose if I felt highly motivated, I could've invited him to watch TV with me.

I didn't feel highly motivated. That was the main obstacle.

"It sounds like he's happy at his job," Amy said.

"You talked to him?"

"He called to ask if he could bring anything."

"I didn't know he had your number."

"I assume your mom gave it to him," she said.

"I didn't know *she* had your number."

"Anyhoo," she said, stirring soup. "I told him we're set."

"Pretty sure the only thing he knows how to make is meth brownies."

"Clay."

"All right, all right."

Beneath our laughter lay a fundamental difference in how we each viewed the world. Psychologists believe people can change. They have to, or else what's the point of psychology? The opposite is true for law enforcement. We rely on the principle that people tend to make the same stupid mistakes, over and over.

"Do you think," Amy said, "they're expecting us to announce that we're engaged?"

"You know, it hadn't crossed my mind till you said it. But— yeah, I bet they are."

"Should we disappoint them early?"

"Like at the door? Take their coats. *We're not engaged.*"

She snickered.

I went to the fridge for butter. "Or," I said, "we don't have to."

"Have to what."

"Disappoint them."

I had my back to her and wasn't sure what her silence meant. Then I faced her and still wasn't sure.

She stared at me, the ladle loose in her fingers. "Did you just propose to me?"

"I think I did."

She stepped to the cutting board and picked up the knife.

"Are you—eh. Amy?"

She took an unpeeled shallot, halved it width-wise, cut a quarter-inch slice. Poked out the middle sections to form a floppy ring.

"Try again," she said, giving me the shallot ring.

"Amy—"

"Ah ah ah."

I knelt down. "Amy Sandek, will you marry me?"

She extended her hand.

6:28 p.m.

We agreed not to tell them right away; we agreed not to tell them at all, unless it felt right, which would be mutually confirmed in private.

When evening arrived, we were giddy with our shared secret.

Her parents arrived a couple minutes early. My parents arrived a couple minutes late. Introductions were made, drinks poured, small talk kindled. Amy and I steered them toward topics of mutual interest. Sports for my mom and her dad. The housing market for her mom and my dad.

Once the conversations had left the shore, wobbling, but afloat, we escaped to the kitchen to finish getting ready.

"So far, so good," she whispered.

"We should tell them now," I said, taking down bowls. "While everyone's still happy."

"Let's eat first."

I glanced at the microwave clock. Five to seven. "You told Luke six thirty, right?"

The doorbell rang.

Covering the distance to the door in a few long strides, I reached for the knob, bracing myself for the usual minor shock.

Fourteen months and half an inch separate Luke from me. He

looks like me, too, if you edit out the effects of hard living on his skin, hair, and teeth. For years he had a goatee, which helped. But he shaved it off after his release, and seeing him now is like staring into a dirty mirror.

I opened the door.

A woman said, "Hello."

She was white, with curly brown hair and round black eyes, mildly heavyset, wearing a fringed print skirt and an embroidered peasant blouse. Short, maybe five-one. Pressed up close behind her, Luke looked like he was sprouting out of the top of her head. A mutant sapling in a too-small pot.

"You must be Clay," she said. "I'm Andrea."

She stepped over the threshold to wrap me in a hug. Strong perfume, tickling my nose. "It's so wonderful to meet you."

Luke smiled. "Nice shirt, dude."

From the living room, my mother said, "Hi, honey. Come on in."

Andrea remained clutching me, her face nuzzled in my armpit. I was doing my best not to sneeze. Luke sidled past, clapping me on the shoulder as he went.

I heard Amy say, "No problem at all, let me just grab another place setting."

"This is so special," Andrea said. She held me at arm's length. "So, so special."

OVER SOUP, THERESA Sandek said, "So how did you two meet?"

Andrea and Luke exchanged a smile.

"I took her class," he said, reaching for her hand. "She was my teacher. Is."

"At—" Theresa began, before stopping.

"Please," Andrea said. "There's nothing to be ashamed of. Yes, at the prison."

Paul Sandek asked what she taught.

"Mindfulness."

"I think it's terrific that they offer that," Paul said.

"For sure," Andrea said. "I feel a mindful approach can benefit everyone. But there aren't too many groups of people who need it more than the incarcerated."

"She wasn't incarcerated," Luke said. "Just to be clear."

"I volunteer."

"She drives from Salinas," Luke said. "Two hours."

"Wow," Theresa said. "That's commitment."

"It's important work," Andrea said.

"Soup's delicious," my father said.

"Thank you," Amy said.

"And how long," Theresa said, "have you done that?"

"Practiced?" Andrea said. "Or taught at Pleasant Valley?"

"Either. Both."

"Eight years practice, teaching for three."

"Andrea works as a trauma counselor," my mother said.

"How lovely," Theresa said.

"I'm not sure I'd call it lovely," Andrea said.

"No, of course not. I should've said—"

"Important," Paul said.

"Yes, important," Theresa said.

"It's healing," Andrea said.

"You two have a lot in common," Luke said to Amy. "Career-wise."

Amy smiled. "I'm sure we do."

"Well," I said.

Everyone looked at me.

"I mean," I said. I looked at Andrea. "What kind of degree do you have?"

Amy began reaching for bowls. "Anyone for seconds?"

"I'm asking," I said, "cause Amy went to grad school. She has a PhD. I'm not sure what it takes to become a trauma counselor."

"There's a certification," Andrea said.

"Uh-huh," I said. "Like, are we talking online, or—"

"Honey, can you give me a hand with these, please?" Amy said.

"Actually, Clay," Andrea said, "from what I understand, it's not that different from what you do."

"I'll get it," my father said, standing.

"No no no no no, not allowed." Amy smiled. "Honey."

I took Luke's bowl. "Save room."

WHEN WE WERE alone in the kitchen, Amy said, "Stop it."

"I'm not going to sit there and let them pretend she's your peer."

"Yes, you are," she whispered, pouring soufflé batter, "because I've been cooking for three days, and because she's not doing anything wrong."

"It doesn't bother you? How smug she is?"

"No, it doesn't, and if I don't care, you shouldn't, either."

"She shouldn't even be here."

She wiped her hands on her apron and handed me the platter of duck. "I love you. Don't be an asshole."

AT THE TABLE, Luke was talking about his job in the stockroom at the San Leandro Walmart.

"It's temporary," my mother said.

"I don't mind," Luke said. "I'm in there at three a.m., it's kinda nice. Quiet."

"Tell them the big news," Andrea said.

Luke grinned. "Which one."

"He's playing basketball again."

"Coaching, more like," Luke said.

"Good for you," Paul said. "Where at?"

"Late-night league."

"For high-risk youth," Andrea said. "It helps keep them off the street."

"What a wonderful idea," Theresa said.

"We meet at McClymonds," Luke said. "You should come with us sometime."

Realizing he was talking to me, I laughed, shook my head. "Yeah."

"A real baller? They'd love it. They'll eat it up."

"College baller," I said, reaching for the bread basket. "Anyhow I'm asleep."

"It's not every night, just Tuesdays and Saturdays."

"They start each game with a ten-minute meditation," Andrea said.

"That part was her idea," Luke said.

"Have you ever thought of giving it a try?" Andrea asked me.

"Basketball?" I said.

"Meditation."

"It really helps," Luke said. "Like with your knee."

"Nothing can help that," I said.

"I think what Luke is saying," Andrea said, "is that a mindful approach can help you live with, and in, the present, including fully experiencing the moment-by-moment reality of your body. Is that right?"

"Totally," Luke said.

"I do live with it," I said.

"That's the idea," Andrea said. "Since you are already living with it, regardless."

"Or like with job stress," Luke said.

"I'm fine," I said.

"It's important to have an outlet," Andrea said.

Paul said, "Am I misremembering, Clay, or were you planning

on taking a woodworking class? I seem to recall Amy saying something about that."

I nodded. "Or blacksmithing, I haven't decided yet."

"Blacksmithing," Theresa said. "How *fun*."

"Where's this?" my father said.

"Urban Foundry. I have to see what they're offering in the spring."

"Blacksmithing sounds like an excellent outlet," Paul said. "All that *wham, bam*!"

Andrea said to me, "There was that shooting a few nights ago. Were you there?"

"I was."

"It must be difficult."

"For the victims and their families it is."

"You're a victim, too, though. Maybe not *the* victim, but *a* victim."

"I try not to think of it that way."

"It's interesting that you feel there's a correct way to think about it."

I shrugged, called to the kitchen: "Honey? You okay in there?"

"Right out," Amy called.

"You seem reluctant to talk about it," Andrea said.

"I can't," I said. "It's an open case."

"What's the other big news?" my father said.

Amy emerged balancing mashed potatoes in one hand, ravioli in the other. She passed them down opposite sides of the table. "What big news?"

Andrea looked at Luke.

"You tell them," he said.

"We'll tell them together," she said.

"Okay," he said.

Andrea said, "We're getting married."

A beat. Then everyone came alive at once: my mother tented her hands over her mouth, and Paul said, "Wow," and my father leaned over to shake Luke's hand, and Amy looked at her mother, who was touching Andrea's arm and saying "Congratulations" while Andrea sat there, beaming, soaking it in.

I shook a large dollop of potatoes onto my plate. "Congratulations."

"Thanks," Luke said.

"When's the big day?"

Luke made a *who knows* face. "We're not there yet. Her lease is up in March, then she'll move and we'll figure it out from there."

"We're just enjoying this moment, right now," Andrea said.

"As well you should," my father said.

"Don't wait too long, though," my mother said.

Amy sat down. She was staring at the tablecloth, her mouth pinned shut, and I felt a crazy bolt of rage. I tried to meet her eye, to let her know that I saw her hurt and was ready to start throwing punches in her defense. To show this usurping clown and my fool of a brother what was what.

Then I realized that Amy was in fact struggling not to laugh.

Across the table, Andrea was telling Paul and Theresa about how strange it was going to be for her, leaving Salinas, where she had grown up and spent her entire life. My father announced that everything was delicious, amazing, delicious. My mother eyed my brother and me, ready to jump in and separate the dogs.

I handed Luke the mashed potatoes. "I'm happy for you."

"Thanks, man. I appreciate it. Thanks again for having us."

"Our pleasure."

"It'd be cool, though," he said. "To play sometime."

There was a sincerity in his voice. An alien warmth.

Do people change?

"Maybe," I said.

"Awesome."

Andrea sniffed at the ravioli. "Are these gluten-free?"

DISHES SOAKING, LEFTOVERS in foil, Amy and I sank down on the sofa.

"Well," she said, leaning against me. "Andrea seems nice."

I laughed.

"I'm glad we waited to say anything," she said.

"Right, we wouldn't want to upstage her on her special day."

"Very special."

"So so *so* special."

"You know," Amy said, "I'm wondering if I misunderstood Luke."

"How's that."

"When he called. Maybe he asked if he could bring some*one*. Not something."

"That's a generous interpretation."

"I try."

"What was so funny before?" I asked.

"When . . . ? Oh," she said. "The look on your face."

"*My* face?"

"Like you showed up to prom and your best friend had on the same dress."

"Is that it."

"Pretty much."

"Marcia Marcia *Marcia*."

She laughed.

"'We're just living in the moment, for a moment, momentarily.'"

I sat up. "What's it like for him, having to listen to that shit all the time?"

"Obviously it works for him."

"That is the last thing he needs. Literally *the last* thing *any* addict needs is more living in the moment. He needs to do the opposite of that. He needs to think *ahead*. Living only in the moment is why you blow a red light at double the speed limit."

"He did that because he was high."

"Is there a difference?" I paused. "You're going to tell me I'm wrong?"

"I'm going to point out that you only get this way around him."

"I know, it's ridiculous."

"On the other hand," she said, "it's refreshing to see you get irrationally angry once in a while."

"It's been a hard week."

She nodded.

"You think I should take up meditation?" I said.

"I think you should do what makes you happy."

"You make me happy," I said.

She kissed me.

I said, "Do what makes me happy? So I should do you."

"Har har."

I shifted to kiss her neck. "You walked right into that."

She said, "Ugh. I'm full of potatoes."

Her chest; her neck again. "Yes, Chef."

"Fair warning," she said. Her body moved against mine, her fingers sliding through my hair. "I'm going to burp in your mouth."

"Yes, Chef. Right away."

CHAPTER 11

Five days post-shooting, an official narrative had begun to gel, the case chopped into manageable portions and repackaged for public consumption.

We had served notification to Rebecca Ristic and Grant Hellerstein's families, and the names of both victims were released to the press. Jalen Coombs, nineteen, a resident of West Oakland, was identified as the third victim. A fourth victim, run down by a car, remained unnamed, pending notification. Also unnamed was a six-year-old boy.

The mayor of Oakland was "heartbroken and outraged." She called for frank and open dialogue, a conversation that would help us get to the core of these tragic events and allow us to move forward as a community and heal. As always, the people of Oakland were strong, unafraid, unified.

A memorial vigil was scheduled for Saturday evening, in Lafayette Square.

The chief of police decried the brazenness of the shooters and empathized with the pain of the victims and their families. Thanks to the timely efforts of the men and women of OPD, one suspect was already in custody.

That the cops hadn't solicited the public for information regarding other suspects—declining to release names, sketches, or descriptions—signaled to me that they had a decent idea of who they wanted. No reason to tip anyone off.

The media made no mention of Jane Doe in the shed.

Lying in the cooler, anonymous, a secret kept by an unlucky few.

Lodged in my consciousness like a rusty nail.

Meanwhile our office was gearing up for a countywide hangover. As Turnbow had predicted, the plummeting temperature had already brought about three exposure deaths, two homeless men and an ill, elderly woman whose heat had cut out.

Another homicide: a Christmas-morning dispute over a PlayStation, resolved with a kitchen knife. I had to admit that my own family looked pretty benign by comparison.

New Year's, with its regular spate of car accidents, loomed.

Most wonderful time of the year.

The logjam had spread across the entire system, which meant that my request for missing persons reports—white female, age sixteen to thirty—was taking even longer than usual.

Benjamin Felton and Grant Hellerstein had been autopsied on Christmas Eve. Rebecca Ristic and Jalen Coombs were scheduled for today. Tomorrow was my big day, with Jasmine Gomez in the morning and Jane Doe in the afternoon.

I called Delilah Nwodo to let her know.

"I'll be there," she said.

"Thanks for bringing me along the other day."

"No problem."

"Look, I don't know how you feel about these things, but my thinking is you and I shouldn't waste time conducting parallel investigations."

"Uh-huh," she said.

"I'm just putting it on the record that I plan to let you know what I find."

"And you expect me to do the same for you."

"Not expecting," I said. "Asking."

"What've you got so far?"

"So far? Nothing."

"So far, this sounds like a bad deal for me."

"It might appear that way for the moment," I said. "Consider me an investment."

She said, "I'll see you tomorrow."

I called Detective Bischoff about the Jasmine Gomez autopsy. He didn't pick up.

Thursday, December 27

7:01 a.m.

Standing at the morgue viewing station, I watched through the glass as the pathologist dried his hands on a wad of paper towels. Maggie Garcia, the tech, arranged instruments on a metal tray. A wall-mounted flat-screen displayed an overhead view of Jasmine Gomez's wrapped body, a hyperreal echo of the physical body, lying on the nearest table.

Dr. Park spoke through the intercom: "He's not here yet?"

He meant Bischoff.

I pressed the intercom button. "I'm not sure if he's coming."

"We'll go ahead and get started," Park said.

Garcia switched on the recorder.

"The date of the autopsy is Thursday, December twenty-seventh, twenty eighteen," Park said. "The time is seven oh three in the morning. I am Dr. Simon G. Park. Assisting me is technician Margaret Garcia. The body is presented in a white sheet."

Garcia and Park unknotted the sheet and opened it.

On the flat-screen, the fabric parted, and Jasmine Gomez surfaced—a kind of anti-birth. I saw the dirty angel's costume, every shred and granule in high definition. I saw her face, a misery of flesh.

"At the time of examination, the body is clothed in a white . . ." Park paused. "Robe."

Seeing him struggle to identify the item strapped to Jasmine's back, I tapped the glass.

Park glanced over.

I made a flapping motion.

"Attached to the body is a set of mechanical wings," Park said.

He described the damage to the outfit, noting the stains and rips in detail. It took a while. Simon Park had a well-deserved reputation for thoroughness. Maggie appeared relieved when the time came to cut the clothes off.

Having talked and thought about Jasmine as female, I found it jarring to see the naked genitals, lolling against a scrawny gray thigh. Park's narration, delivered in a neutral monotone, likewise landed odd on the ear.

"The body is that of a normally developed, undernourished white or Hispanic male measuring sixty-six inches in length and weighing one hundred nine pounds. Appearance is consistent with the offered age of twenty-three years."

I listened to Park catalog Jasmine's exterior. The hair on the head, thirteen inches long and brown. Skin. Dehydration had caused black bristles to crop up along the upper lip and jawline. Lividity. Eyes and teeth. Scars and markings, piercings and tattoos.

The condition of the pubic hair, recently shaved. Chafing around the groin and thighs, caused by the compression shorts.

The disrupted symmetry of the skull. Shards of plastic embedded in the scalp: traces of the missing halo. Three fingernails stripped off.

Maggie Garcia reached for the circular saw.

The whine started up.

A question my colleagues and I get asked a lot is *How do you want to die?* As though we have any say in the matter; as though we've got Death's private line on speed dial. I understand the curiosity as a form of anxiety, the flipside of another common question: *What's the worst way to die?*

I don't have a ready answer for either one.

Whatever happens to me, though, I don't want to be a Coroner's case.

I waved to Maggie, indicating that I was going upstairs to get some work done. She nodded and continued opening Jasmine's head.

DETECTIVE BISCHOFF HAD yet to forward me a copy of Meredith Klaar's statement. Nor had he replied to my follow-up emails. For form's sake, I sent him another polite reminder, then looked up her home number and called her myself, unsurprised to get a voicemail. I could imagine she was under siege.

Lisa Shupfer entered the squad room and took her place opposite me. I didn't ask where she'd been. I didn't need to: it was her third visit to check on Benjamin Felton's mother, Bonita, since the night of the shooting. At this point, I doubted they were covering much new ground. But as brusque as Shoops can be at the office, there's no one better in the field, in a situation like that, when the questions have run out, and nothing remains but the unthinkable tomorrow.

I tossed her a small package of pretzels.

She tore it open with an appreciative nod.

My direct line rang.

"Coroner's Bureau, Edison."

"This is Didi Flynn. I think we met before."

The friend who'd gone to the party with Jasmine. "Hi, Ms. Flynn. Yeah, it's me you talked to. Thanks for getting in touch."

"I was reading what they wrote," she said. "I don't understand. They didn't say anything about Jasmine."

"Sorry," I said. "You were reading what?"

"*SFGate*," she said. "Like, what the fuck?"

Good question. "Do you have the specific article handy?"

She gave me the title. I found it, scanned as she went on: "It's not right. They don't say anything about her. It's like she doesn't exist."

I said, "It mentions a victim struck by a car. Second-to-last paragraph."

"That's all it says, 'victim.' She has a name."

"We ask the media not to publicize the information before we've had a chance to notify next of kin. That's so they hear it from us, first. So far I haven't been able to reach her family. Once I do, we'll release it."

"Where is she?" Didi Flynn asked. "What's happening to her?"

On a steel slab. Her face peeled back. Her brain on a scale. Her chest butterflied.

"Right now, she's with us," I said.

"How much longer?"

"That depends on what the family decides."

"We want to have a service."

"You should," I said. "Absolutely."

"We can't. Not without her there. What kind of service is that? That's just, I don't know. Sitting in a room."

"I get where you're coming from. But there's nothing says you need to wait for her to be buried to remember her—to celebrate her."

Didi gave an irritated honk. "How does that even make sense?"

"If you want to expedite the process, it'd help to find out where her family's at."

"I told you, I don't know."

"Right. The thing is, I'm having a little trouble, because she's not in the system under Jasmine. If she had another name, for example, I could search for that."

Silence.

I said, "Can you tell me where Jasmine was living?"

"I don't know."

Silly lie. They'd gone to the party together. Jasmine had left Didi her money and phone to hold. Didi wanted to organize a memorial service. She didn't know where Jasmine lived?

Calling someone out on the spot seldom gets them to cooperate. Mostly, they get angry and double down. "Her license gives an address on Telegraph that belongs to a place called The Harbor. I spoke to a woman there, Greer Unger."

"I don't know her."

More bullshit. "She told me Jasmine spent some time on the street."

Several beats.

"Ms. Flynn?"

"I guess."

"Was she staying with you?"

"No."

"Not currently, or not ever?"

"It wasn't like that," she said. "We weren't, like, together."

"I meant more like, she's your friend, she needs a place to crash."

No reply.

"Ms. Flynn, I ask because legally I have to secure her possessions. Since you two were close"—so close that you claim ignorance of her address—"I thought you might be holding items for her."

"I gave you everything I have," she said.

"Okay. Thanks, then. I'll go back to Greer and see what she has to say."

Another silence.

"Kevin," she said.

"Pardon me?"

"That's it."

I said, "Her birth name was Kevin?"

She made a sound of assent.

"Same last name?"

"I think so."

"Do you know where her family's at?" I asked. "Are they local?"

"L.A. I really don't know where."

"Okay. Great. I appreciate it. This helps a lot. You're doing right by Jasmine."

"Can you do it, now," she said. "Release her?"

"There are a few steps, procedurally. Let's say this, okay? Let me speak to the family and take their temperature."

She didn't answer.

I said, "You're doing the right thing."

She hung up.

GUESS HOW MANY people are named Kevin Gomez?

I'll wait while you go google it.

Okay. Now guess how many of them reside in the Los Angeles metro area.

That's how I spent my lunch break.

12:54 p.m.

For my next autopsy, I met Detective Nwodo in the lobby. She was nicely dressed but looked tired. Carrying a scratched Warriors travel mug—her sixth cup of the day, she said. Less than twenty-four hours had elapsed since our most recent phone conversation. In that time, she'd caught another murder, this one gang-related.

I offered her a free refill.

She shook her head. "Not unless you want me on the slab."

Unlocking a side door, I led her past the transcriptionist's office, the pathologists' offices, the break room where Bagoyo sat watching Dr. Oz extol the virtues of turmeric for joint health. A second locked door opened onto the morgue viewing platform.

We stepped into a rectangle of sterile light, Nwodo sipping her coffee.

Buzzing quiet. Warm odor of stale carpet.

A sunken body beneath sheets. On the table; on the flat-screen.

Dani Botero entered the morgue and headed to the sink to wash her hands.

While we waited for Dr. Park, Nwodo and I chatted about the status of the other investigations. They were still debating what to do with Isaiah Branch. The options ranged from nothing all the way up to charging him with murder. To a certain extent it depended on what he and his friends had intended when they rang Rhiannon Cooke's doorbell; whether he knew his companion was carrying a firearm. It also depended on how much pressure they wanted to put on him.

"It's the shooter they want," she said.

"They have a name yet?"

"Tuan Trang. Another childhood friend of him and Coombs. Getaway car's his. Witnesses picked him out from a photo array."

Park entered the morgue.

The shooter from the party—the murderous Jet—was named Dane Jankowski. Nwodo confirmed that he was the shaggy guy on the tape, wearing the red beanie.

Like Trang, he had a record, handful of drug arrests, one for misdemeanor battery.

Like Trang, he'd gone to ground.

The killers differed in their choice of handgun. Sixteen casings recovered; two different calibers, .38 and 9mm. Based on the tape and a relatively intact slug pulled from Grant Hellerstein's body, it appeared that the latter belonged to Trang.

I remembered Patrol Sergeant Acosta: *Real miracle is we don't have more bodies.* Packed crowd, sixteen rounds, four casualties, not counting Jane Doe or Jasmine.

Grant Hellerstein, Rebecca Ristic, Jalen Coombs. Little Benjamin Felton.

"The kid," I said. "Any idea whose shot that was?"

Nwodo shook her head. "Bullet's all fucked up."

"Charge em both," I said.

"Probably."

The intercom blipped. Park said, "Shall we begin?"

Dani Botero turned on the recorder.

"The date of the autopsy is Thursday, December twenty-seventh, twenty eighteen. The time is one oh eight in the afternoon. I am Dr. Simon G. Park. Assisting me is technician Daniella Botero. The body is presented in a white sheet . . ."

Compared with Jasmine Gomez's outfit, Jane Doe's was straightforward, and Park went into less detail. Grease stains and ground-in dirt suggested that the items had not been recently laundered, although he noted the possibility of transfer from the sacks of fertilizer.

Before undressing her, they removed the paper bags from her hands to take fingernail clippings. Park used trauma shears to cut away the clothes, and Dani piled them, along with the old blue running shoes, on a rolling steel table.

"The body is that of a normally developed, well-nourished white or Asian female, possibly of mixed race, measuring sixty-one inches in length and weighing ninety-nine pounds, with an estimated age ranging between eighteen and thirty years."

The surface of Jane Doe's body spoke to an unquiet life, with more downs than ups. The needle marks I'd previously noted on the exposed portion of her wrist continued along both arms. Park had called her well nourished, but that was a relative term; ribs and hip bones poked out. Fine white lines laced the tops of her thighs. Self-harm scars.

The soft spot I'd felt in her rib cage corresponded to a bruise, yellow-green and heart-shaped. Her scalp was bruised, too. Numerous smaller cuts and abrasions marked her chin, knuckles, the insides of her wrists.

The centerpiece was the throat, with its lurid palette of violets and reds. Swollen tissue above and below the level of compression gave the neck a slight hourglass shape.

Strangling someone with your hands requires determination. You have to maintain an iron grip for several minutes, all while they claw and punch and buck and kick. During the dissection of the neck, Park ticked off the structures destroyed, wholly or in part: larynx, thyroid cartilage, cricoid cartilage, hyoid bone.

Determination, and fury.

Nwodo sighed.

I glanced at her. Not impatience she was expressing. Just soul weariness, at the monstrous things people do to each other.

Park incised a Y into the abdomen.

Two broken ribs.

Dani Botero reached for gardening shears to open the sternum.

A crunching sound came through the intercom.

I lowered the volume and pulled over a couple of chairs.

Nwodo said, "How was your Christmas?"

"Not bad," I said. "Yours? Do anything fun?"

"My father roasted a pig in the backyard," she said. "He does it every year."

"Sounds like a party."

"Oh, it is."

"My girlfriend and I cooked for our families. My brother brought his fiancée."

"That's nice."

"Would've been," I said, "if he'd told me she was coming. Or that he had a fiancée."

Nwodo smiled.

The heart. The lungs. Everything Park observed supported manual strangulation as the cause of death. The blunt impact that had broken the ribs and caused the bruise could have come from being struck, from being pushed into a railing, from a fall.

There were few other conclusions, and nothing probative to Jane Doe's identity. As the autopsy dragged on, Nwodo began to slump, first forward, then back, her leg jiggling with excess energy, her hands clenched together as if to contain her growing disappointment.

She was hoping for a revelation. We both were.

Dani Botero took tissue and tox samples.

Maybe something helpful there.

We'd know one way or another in a few weeks.

After two and a half hours, they began to sew the chest cavity back up.

Nwodo said she was leaving. I walked her out to the lobby.

"I've been thinking about your offer," she said. "Share and share alike? There's a vigil this weekend. Remembering the victims."

"I heard about that."

"They're expecting a crowd," she said. "It might be interesting to see who shows up."

"Might help to have a second pair of eyes."

"Wouldn't hurt," she said. She sounded relaxed. She'd expected the offer.

We shook hands.

"Six thirty," she said. "Text me when you get there."

"Will do. I'll be coming straight from work."

She clucked her tongue. "Change first."

CHAPTER 12

4:58 p.m.

I was in the locker room, ready to step into the shower, when the door opened and Zaragoza stuck his head in.

"Dani needs to talk to you."

"Tell her I'll be out in a few."

"Clay," Dani yelled. "You gotta come see this."

I yanked the curtain around my naked lower half. "What the hell, dude."

"I'm not looking."

"Can you please get out?"

"Hurry up."

I dried off, pulled on clothes, and went out to the intake bay. Dani Botero had a camera around her neck and was hopping from foot to foot, grinning. "Come on."

I followed her into the morgue, to the area where they'd autopsied Jane Doe, now scrubbed clean. "What am I looking at?"

Like a game-show hostess, Dani swept her hands toward the

rolling steel table. The ruined clothes, folded and sealed inside an evidence bag. Old blue running shoes.

Beside them, two rubber-banded stacks of credit cards.

Dani said, "She kept them in her shoes. Under the insoles. I went to bag them and the inside of the left one was kinda sticking up."

She curtsied. "Ta-*da*."

I looked at her. "You."

She tilted her head.

"Are awesome."

She smiled and handed me a box of gloves.

Each stack measured about a quarter of an inch thick, seven or eight cards' worth. It couldn't have been comfortable, walking around with that underfoot.

Living on the street. Sleeping arrangements uncertain.

Associating with people she feared might cause her harm.

She wasn't wrong, there. Someone *had* harmed her.

But not for her money.

Or he didn't know where she kept it.

Or he ran out of time.

I picked up the first stack. The topmost card was a Visa.

"Catherine Myers," I read.

It was like stepping through a doorway.

It was like I could see, or breathe, for the first time in days.

I removed the rubber band. In a perfect world, Catherine Myers's driver's license would be in there.

I dealt the cards out in a row.

Three more Visas. Three Mastercards. An Amex.

I picked up a second Visa. "Hold on." Not Catherine Myers. "Beth Green."

The next card in the deck, a Mastercard: "Frances Ann Flatt."

Dani Botero said, "Oh snap."

. . .

Sixteen cards.

Sixteen names.

No license.

I called Amy.

"Hi," she said. "I'm just about to order dinner. Is Thai okay?"

"I'm going to be late," I said.

I called Delilah Nwodo. She didn't answer, so I texted her, and emailed as well. The subject heading was *your investment pays off*.

I hunched in my chair, staring at the screen.

Column of numbers.

Column of names.

Off the top of my head, I could think of several ways to obtain a credit card for fraudulent purposes.

You could remove it from another's possession by force. I had a hard time picturing ninety-nine-pound Jane Doe as a mugger.

Pickpocket, then. Straight out of Dickens.

Easier and safer was to clone it. Maybe she worked as a server at a restaurant. *Did you enjoy your meal? Lemme run that for you. Be right back.*

You could open an account in someone else's real name. Purchase a trove of account data from a black-market vendor. Pull random names off the internet.

You could open an account in a fake name.

Surely there were other new and exciting methods. No species on earth outdoes humans for innovation, especially when it comes to stealing other people's shit.

A column of numbers; a column of names.

If the names did in fact refer to real, flesh-and-blood individuals, I faced the same hurdle that I had with Jasmine/Kevin Gomez: the Big World Problem.

You want to believe there can exist but one Frances Ann Flatt or

Dara Kenilworth or Karla-with-a-K Abruzzo. But it's a big world. Statistics will kick your ass, every time.

Without a second data point, a name is close to meaningless.

Still, some names are rarer than others. I skipped Beth Green and Catherine Myers and Jessica Chen and googled Frances Ann Flatt.

And got a hit.

Assuming I had the correct person—the gods owed me that much—she lived in Seattle, was fifty-one years old, and worked as a statistician for the University of Washington.

Her LinkedIn profile showed a woman most assuredly not the dead one in our freezer.

Accurint delivered a home phone number.

No answer.

I left a message.

Emboldened by my early success, I tried Leah Horvuth next.

Two hits: forty-nine-year-old English professor in Raleigh, North Carolina. Thirty-four-year-old veterinarian in Connecticut.

And so on.

It's a Big World.

I picked up the phone.

7:37 p.m.

My optimism was fast evaporating.

In addition to Big World issues, I was running into a much more banal hurdle: nobody would talk to me.

I'd made two dozen calls, to points flung throughout the continental U.S., managing to reach four people, all of whom had hung up on me within thirty seconds.

Makes sense. Stranger calls you up. At night. Blocked number.

Claiming to be law enforcement, some department you've never heard of.

Yes, hi, ma'am. May I speak with you about an issue regarding your credit cards?

Click.

Sergeant Brad Moffett sauntered by, pausing to chuck me on the shoulder. "No authorization for OT. Go home."

I told him what Dani had discovered, showed him the list, shared my frustration.

He said, "Go home."

I wasn't going to solve it, in one evening, at my desk. But I felt wired.

He added, "Take that as an order."

"You're really power-tripping," I said.

"Believe it."

"Ten more minutes," I said. "Two more calls."

"Whichever comes first."

I started to reach for the receiver, but paused.

I was going about this backward.

Concentrating on the names, when it was the card numbers that mattered.

Contact the credit card companies and request account data.

Address. Phone. Social Security number.

In all likelihood the information would turn out to be bogus. Worth a try, though, especially given my inability to persuade people I wasn't running a scam myself.

Plus it provided a welcome excuse to stop for the day. Business hours were over.

I stood up, my stomach rumbling at the thought of reheated Thai. Poor Amy. I still hadn't had a chance to shower.

Friday, December 28

11:45 a.m.

Modern police work often requires obtaining information from cellphone carriers, financial service providers, social media. How helpful they are depends on the prevailing legal mood, which in turn depends on how scared we are as a nation—that is, how recently we've had a terror attack. Privacy versus security. At minimum they want a warrant.

Again: as an American, I'm glad.

As an investigator?

Sixteen credit cards, with sixteen names, issued by sixteen different companies?

It was like I'd handed my morning to Kafka: *Do your worst.*

I finished my call with Capital One.

Once the appropriate paperwork had been filed, reviewed, and processed, I could expect a response within eight to twelve weeks.

My ear throbbed from the pressure of the receiver. I'd started out on speaker, but after several hours on hold, the doodly-doodly-doo music had begun to drive my co-workers insane. Sully hurled crumpled Post-its at me. Maggie Garcia threatened to file a harassment complaint.

At lunchtime I announced that I was stepping out and got a round of applause.

TIME TO DEAL with facts at hand.

Meredith Klaar lived in Emeryville, a small city sandwiched between Berkeley and Oakland, shaped like a price gun and adjacent to the Bay. For decades it had languished, as local industry faltered and collapsed, warehouses emptied out, and factories went quiet. Eventually the free market had its say. First came the cafés, followed by small-scale residential projects. The short hop to San

Francisco made the location attractive to start-ups and their employees fleeing crushing rents. A city council friendly to developers didn't hurt.

Now the area boasted condos and an Ikea, corporate headquarters, an outdoor mall, and a perpetually crowded Target. Making Emeryville the very model of a high-density, mixed-use urban environment, available today, starting at seven hundred dollars a square foot.

Exiting the freeway, I passed a homeless encampment big as a baseball diamond.

The mid-rise Meredith Klaar called home had underground parking, a fitness center, a doorman who signed me in and buzzed me up. Her unit, a fourth-floor studio, faced away from the water. She answered my knock with the lights off and the blinds drawn, bracing her foot against the bottom of the door while she examined my ID.

She said, "Come in."

She was in her early twenties, medium height and whittled, with a gamin face and flat brown hair tipped electric blue. Gray sweatpants made an incongruous pairing—as if she'd made a last-ditch attempt to infuse color into her life, only to change her mind and give up.

Just a studio. Nice, though, for someone so young. Maybe family money. Maybe the first time her life hadn't gone as expected.

The interior smelled of old takeout. Everywhere lay evidence of a neat person who'd temporarily lost control. The bed was made, but the duvet was askew and throw pillows were scattered on the floor. Houseplants fainted. A kitchen bag, overflowing and yoked to a drawer pull, dangled helpless as a hanged man.

I said, "May I turn on a light?"

Nodding, she pulled herself cross-legged on the bed. I switched on an Ikea halogen and rolled an Ikea desk chair over.

People under stress don't always process well. I reiterated that I was from the Coroner, was there to gather facts, to gain a fuller picture of what had happened last Saturday night. I understood things had been pretty chaotic and that a week had gone by. Her memory might not be perfect. I asked her to do her best. I encouraged her to take her time.

Meredith Klaar wrung spidery hands. "I killed her. That's what happened. I don't know what else there is to say. I don't understand why I have to keep answering these same questions. What's the point? Can we please just get it over with?"

I said, "What is it you want to get over with?"

"This," she said. "Whatever you're going to do to me. I'm not telling you I didn't do it. I have never said that, not one time. I did it. Okay? *I did it.* Don't you think this is kind of, I don't know. Inefficient?"

"I'm sure you've spoken to a lot of people, last couple days."

A crazed, high-pitched laugh spurted out of her.

"I've never been so popular in my life," she said.

A second burst of laughter and then she sucked in air to smother herself, glancing at me in abject terror. "I'm sorry."

"It's okay."

"I don't know why I said that," she said. "I didn't mean it. I'm sorry."

"It's fine," I said.

"I'm sorry," she said a third time, and she began to weep.

With a lurch toward the nightstand she grabbed a tissue box, one of many strewn about. A clear plastic wastebasket brimmed with used tissues; empty boxes mobbed the table, the floor, lurked half hidden behind a guitar on a stand. On the kitchenette counter, reinforcements: two more six-packs of boxes, one of them started into, shrink wrap puckered like an open wound.

Meredith Klaar yanked one, two, three tissues from the box in her hand. She blew her nose, mopped her eyes, clutched in her palm a sodden white fruit. She had peach-colored nails and a sprinkling of freckles across the bridge of her sunburnt nose. On the wall behind her was a calendar: Twelve Months of Yosemite.

I said, "I'm not here to judge you."

Which is a thing we say. It's one of our lies. Because I am there to judge you, if not precisely in terms of guilt or innocence. Even pity is a form of judgment, after all.

She sat there and wept and I could feel the wretchedness coming off her like decay, and I thought of the others like her I have known, inadvertent killers, sleepwalking through life, mimicking normalcy, their souls bent double under an invisible burden.

Meredith Klaar's mouth opened, and her jaw slid forward, and she heaved with impatience, as though I had proven myself an awful disappointment: I refused to judge her when she wanted to be judged. Compared with the damnation she was levying against herself, mine would've been a welcome distraction.

"I'm actually a good driver," she said.

I nodded.

"I've never ever had a ticket. I've never gotten behind the wheel drunk. I've never had an accident. Before I got my job I was driving for Uber. My rating is something like four point nine. You understand? That's—it doesn't happen."

"I believe you."

"No," she said, her agitation rising. "You need to understand. I hit her *because* I was trying to be careful. Okay? I was trying to look in ten directions at once. That's what . . . I am not a reckless person. The opposite. You can ask anyone."

I said, "Who should I ask?"

She put her eyes down. Her hands twisted, slowly annihilating the tissue. When she next spoke it was close to inaudible.

"Anyone," she said.

I asked where her car had been parked.

"Near the corner."

"Which corner?"

She hesitated.

I gave her my notepad and my pen. "Can you draw it for me, please? Where you were, and what you remember."

I watched her carefully scribe the lines of the street, the position of her Camry, the path she had taken. She drew an asterisk at the point of impact, three quick uniform strokes. She handed the pad back to me. What she had drawn corresponded to the tire marks I had noted at the scene, including the jump onto the curb.

I asked how she'd heard about the party.

"Online."

"You went with a friend, or . . ."

She bound two fingers in a Kleenex rope. "I was alone."

"Do you recall how much you might've had to drink, prior?"

"I didn't have anything. I had to drive home."

"What about the gunshots? You remember hearing them?"

She went quiet for a ten-count, blinking. Then the words came tumbling out: in the backyard. Away from the dancing. That's where she was, when the shots went off. Curled up in a deck chair, nursing her solitude, toying with getting herself a beer. Yeah, she had to drive. But she felt lame. She didn't have to drink it. Just to have something in her hand, give the impression that she was occupied and not a completely pathetic loser.

Finding the bar deserted, she realized that the majority of the partygoers had migrated toward the front yard. She hadn't noticed, she was in her own head, she got like that from time to time, more than was good for her.

She followed the current, ended up on the front lawn. She went up on her toes to see what the fuss was about. Next thing she knew she was running. It seemed the correct thing to do. Everyone else was.

"Did you witness any of the shots going off?"

". . . no. I don't think so. No."

"So by the time you got to your car, the shooting was over."

"I don't remember. There may have been more. I don't know. I can't . . ."

Once again she lapsed into silence.

I said, "Were you scared of getting shot?"

She looked at me. "I wish I had been."

BEFORE I LEFT she asked me to turn off the lights.

Down at the curb, I sat in my car, collecting my thoughts.

When it comes to determining the manner of death, intent is irrelevant. The coroner's definition of homicide is death at the hand of another. Jasmine Gomez had died as a result of actions taken by Meredith Klaar.

But that's a ways to go from determining criminal liability. I'm far too familiar—personally familiar—with the section of the penal code that deals with vehicular manslaughter. To qualify, you have to show negligence. Texting, or speeding, or ignoring stop signs. Intoxication makes it worse.

Other circumstances mitigate, one of which is the perception that you're in imminent danger. To my mind, a shoot-out was about the best example imaginable. I had a hard time believing you could convince twelve people otherwise. If I were Meredith Klaar's lawyer, I'd play the YouTube video in court. Failing that, I'd wash the blue out of her hair, put her in a drab dress, stick her up on the stand, and let her cry.

And while I'm not a lawyer, I do have a feel for how district attorneys think. I could see little upside to pursuing a criminal charge, and plenty of pitfalls. Simpler to leave the parties to hash out their grievances in civil court.

My phone rattled in the cup holder.

Luke.

Personally familiar.

"Hey," I said. "What's going on?"

"Not much," he said. "You?"

"Working."

"Cool," he said. "Hey, so, first off, thanks for dinner."

A torrent of sarcastic responses rushed into my throat. I held back, thinking of something Amy had said to me while we lay in bed together on Christmas Eve.

Believe in him when you can.

She dealt with addicts, day in and day out, could calibrate her expectations. More important, she didn't bring her entire family history to the table.

Whereas I found it hard to lower the bar for Luke. I knew. He couldn't lean on the standard environmental excuses. We weren't rich, but we weren't poor. My parents weren't perfect, but they weren't reality-show-bad.

It had been my environment, too.

He'd made his choices and the rest of us had to live with them.

Do it for you Amy said. Her hand on my heart. *Not for him.*

I said to Luke, "You're welcome."

"Andrea really enjoyed meeting you guys," he said.

I forced the words: "Us too."

"She's very sensitive," he said. "You know? To the way people are? So when she feels a connection, it means a lot."

"I'm glad."

"So, yeah. Good food, too. I didn't know you could cook."

"Amy's the master. I'm the student."

"Shit, man. Look at us, all domesticated." He laughed. "Anyhow, I told the kids about you. They're hella excited."

"Which kids."

"Late-night ball."

"You told them I was coming?"

"I mean." He paused. "You don't have to."

"I do, now. Cause if I don't, that makes me the asshole."

"Come on, man. Chill out."

"Look, you want me to do you favors, that's fine. Ask. But wait for the answer."

"All right," he said. "I'm sorry."

Believe him. When you can.

I rubbed one eye. "Remind me when you play."

"We have a game this Saturday."

"I have work the next day."

"Yeah, no problem. What about Tuesday?"

"New Year's Day?"

"Most definitely. That's the whole point, man. Keep em busy."

"I might be able to. I have to check with Amy."

"Okay. Awesome. We start at eight."

"The game, or the meditation?"

Luke laughed. "Why? You want to meditate?"

"Not really."

"Telling you, dude," he said. "Changed my life. Changes it every day."

I rang off and started the engine. In the middle of San Pablo Avenue, on the median, a man sat hunchbacked on a folding stool, brandishing a sign that said WILL WRESTLE U 4 BEER. Without meaning to—I was staring into space—I made eye contact with him, and he bounded up, wiping off his jeans, making *come here* gestures that could have been cheerful, or hostile, or both. The line's not always clear.

CHAPTER 13

There's nothing particularly wrong with Lafayette Square, but there's not much to recommend it, either. Westerly downtown, a lumpy grass rectangle, tot lot and bus stop, morose conifers dully envious of the skyscrapers that loom blocks away.

Not the neighborhood of the shooting. Not a hub of civic life. Why choose it for the vigil? As my high school coach used to say: *Ain't no ability like availability.*

Several nonprofits had attached their names to the event, along with a real estate developer and an HMO, tragedy creating strange and opportunistic bedfellows. Sponsorship took the form of a PA setup and a vinyl banner that read OAKLAND STRONG, paralyzed in the sharp, slack air.

Short memories and low temperatures had suppressed turnout: I estimated fifty people, mostly white, an even gender split. The overlap with the party attendees had to be significant. Scruffy ectomorphs in bike helmets, chin straps waggling as they sipped canned beer. Girlfriends side-hugged to ward off the chill. They complained about jobs. They made New Year's plans. The mood was more anticipatory than somber, like the rootless lull that descends after an opening act vacates the stage.

I'd come early, wanting to get the lay of the land.

I joined the line formed in front of a picnic table. A woman was distributing votive candles and matchbooks branded with the name of a popular downtown brewhouse.

"Please wait," she said, filling my hand. "We're all going to light together."

I took my candle and matches, and retreated to the shadow of a solitary palm tree.

At twenty past Nwodo arrived, dressed in track pants, running shoes, a navy bomber jacket with a screen-printed lion.

She plucked at my Cal sweatshirt. "Nice disguise."

While we waited, I updated her on my progress with Jane Doe's credit cards. "I pinged a buddy in cyber-crimes. He basically laughed at me. They get a hundred calls a day for that kind of thing."

"How's their solve rate?"

"I didn't think it was polite to ask. Meanwhile, warrants are in the mail."

"Look at you," she said, smiling faintly.

"Like I said: an investment."

"You're a regular walking, talking 401(k)."

I laughed.

Nwodo told me that forensics from around the shed was proving unhelpful. There was simply too much crap to single out any one item as evidentiary. They had latent fingerprints to last a lifetime. Same went for the interior of the house.

"I was thinking of asking my sergeant for permission to release Jane Doe's photo to the press," I said.

Nwodo shook her head. "I already asked. Permission denied."

As a rule, we avoid publishing pictures of decedents, and almost never so early in the investigation. But this was a bigger-than-usual mess. I'd figured the brass might loosen up.

I said, "Even for an unidentified vic?"

"Even. Maybe especially. I think they're scared of being accused of Pretty White Girl syndrome."

"That's bananas."

Nwodo shrugged.

I said, "If that's their issue, why'd they put Bischoff on the Felton murder?"

"Instead of the black lady detective, you mean."

"Yeah."

A dry smile. "Who's gonna look better solving it?"

I got what she was implying. OPD needed to rehab their image, and a white man toiling around the clock to bring the killer of a black child to justice provided more PR punch than a black-on-black solve.

"You are a cynical bastard," I said.

"Among my finer qualities."

By five minutes past official start time, the crowd had doubled in size, bodies continuing to collect at the edges.

"What are they waiting for?" I asked.

A ripple passed over the park.

"That," Nwodo said, pointing.

The mayor. She'd driven up in her own car, accompanied by a single aide in the passenger seat. No City Hall posse. No security. Too arm's-length, too police-state, contra her down-to-earth woman-of-the-people image. With a photographer trailing in her wake, she clasped elbows and inclined her head, her features fluid, intelligently gauging the need in each pair of eyes and reacting accordingly.

Now wistful, now encouraging.

She took the stage and lowered the microphone. "Thank you, everyone, for coming. We're going to get started. Reverend."

A black man in a clerical outfit stepped forward. "Thank you, Mayor. We come together tonight, in the depths of winter, to warm one another. We celebrate, and commemorate, young lives."

Nwodo and I split up, circulating, attuned to anyone who didn't fit in, who'd come alone or who held himself apart, who appeared skittish, whose demeanor betrayed excessive morbid curiosity or a noteworthy lack thereof.

"Let us make no mistake. Their loss is a loss for our whole community."

Arms linking. Torsos swaying in response to the rhythm of the words. The concert vibe persisted: the majority of the audience had their phones up, a ghostly ocean of blue light. There was a professional film crew, too, a young man prowling the periphery with a camera on his shoulder, while an older man limped behind, holding the boom and whispering instructions into his ear.

"And yet, while we do not deny the tragedy, forgetting neither the individuals nor the void left by their departure, let us also acknowledge their power, their vast and beautiful power, to unite us."

I slid between peacoats and overshirts, whispering *excuse me,* drawing glares.

"People will try to tell you that this is about one group or another," the minister said. "They will tell you that it is about us versus them. Black versus white. Rich or poor. Friends, I stand before you and I say: refuse to accept that. Don't let the ignorance that leads to hatred come into your heart. Banish it. Banish it, and reach out to your neighbor."

He turned the mike over to the mayor.

"Thank you, Reverend, for those inspiring words. Lucy, if you'd like to . . ."

The candle-distributing woman stepped forward. "Thanks, Mayor."

Lucy Candle-Giver wanted to let everyone know that a Go-FundMe had been established to benefit the victims' families. Donations could also be made to a memorial fund with the Greater Oakland Harmony Project, which supported musical education in the public schools, which was something she hoped we could all get behind.

I began moving up to the front of the crowd at a snail's pace.

Before they lit, Lucy Candle-Giver was going to read the names of the victims, followed by a minute of silence. If we wouldn't mind putting away our phones, please.

She unfolded a piece of paper; I could hear it crinkling nervously through the speaker, hear her tremulous exhale as she bent to the mike, too close. When she spoke Rebecca Ristic's name, it belched out, overloud and distorted. A collective flinch.

"Grant Hellerstein," she said.

From various quarters came weeping, in soft pulses.

"Jalen Coombs."

How many people were here for Jalen Coombs?

I thought about his bloody sneakers.

I thought about my brother.

I wondered if Jalen Coombs had a brother; if they ever fought over shoes.

Looking around for Nwodo, I spotted her stationed along the opposite edge of the crowd. She was tracking the progress of the film crew: the director with his hand on the cameraman's back, urging him to get closer, closer. I couldn't tell if she was suspicious or simply put off by their lack of tact.

Lucy Candle-Giver said, "Jasmine Gomez."

I shouldn't have been as surprised as I was. One week out, we had yet to release her name. You couldn't prevent people from talking, though.

Nevertheless it felt like a violation. Her family remained out of reach.

I waited for the announcement of Benjamin Felton's name.

Nothing. Either they didn't know it, or they'd decided to exercise restraint when it came to a child.

"If you'll please get out your candles."

Lighters sparked. Matches scraped. I held mine in my hands but didn't light.

The mayor angled toward the mike. "Careful, please, everyone."

An ivory glow seeped up, filling in colors, carving out cheekbones and eye sockets. It was beautiful and also frightening, as though the earth itself had caught fire.

"Silence, please," Lucy said.

Up front, five or six bodies deep, I noticed a man in a denim jacket.

Whereas most folks were holding still, with their heads bowed, his was on a swivel, swinging left and right like a harried weather vane; like he was expecting a punch from any of four compass points.

Unshaven throat; untidy fringe of hair.

Red beanie.

Same as the shooter in the video. Dane Jankowski.

Big World.

But.

How many guys in need of a haircut?

Who own red beanies?

In the East Bay?

With a close interest in the events on Almond Street?

I pocketed the candle and matches, got out my phone, thumbed on the camera.

The man glanced over his shoulder.

I snapped a photo.

Too blurry.

I edged up to try again. People were shooting me dirty looks, muttering: *Douche.* Meanwhile I was counting down, the minute bleeding away, to be followed by the breakup of the crowd, disorder, opportunity lost.

The guy glanced back again. I tapped the screen.

This time the image came out crisp.

With hurried, numb fingers I texted the picture to Nwodo. *Shooter?*

I looked up.

The guy had wrenched around to stare at me.

He started shouldering his way out of the crowd.

The minute of silence came to an end.

Over the mike, Lucy Candle-Giver said, "Thank you. Reverend?"

Without benefit of amplification, the minister began to sing "Amazing Grace."

The guy in the beanie cleared the crowd and started across the lawn toward 11th.

I followed, dialing Nwodo. When she answered, I heard the hymn in the background, buzzy and desynced to the sound receding at my back.

"He's moving," I said. "Eleventh toward Jefferson."

"Hang on, I can't hear you. Hang on."

A scrape; the call cut out.

Reaching the end of the block, the man hopped down to cross against the red.

All else failed, I could cite him for jaywalking.

I fixed the distance between us, advancing along the hollowed-out street. Behind me the singing dwindled. We passed a parking lot stripped bare; passed an office worker striding in the opposite direction. In their nowhere spaces—in architectural crannies, atop hot exhaust grates—the homeless lay swathed in cardboard.

The guy had his hands in his jean pockets and was moving with deliberation, not fast, not slow, just a dude walking, not a person of interest.

He might be armed. Very possible. He'd brought a gun to a party whose guest list leaned more NPR than NRA. You had to wonder what his friends made of him.

Classic Dane! Ha ha ha.

Now that he was wanted for murder?

I don't carry an off-duty firearm.

I'd come without my vest. I was trying to blend in.

Was I imagining it: a bulge at the small of his back?

I strained to see.

The phone in my hand, blank.

Where was Nwodo?

We were without backup.

If she couldn't find me or reach me in time, I was without any backup whatsoever.

I'd given the guy a healthy head start. If he jumped into a vehicle, I'd lose him.

A bicycle, I'd lose him.

I walked faster.

The phone shook.

"Where are you?" Nwodo said. She was breathing hard.

"Clay."

"*Where* are you?"

Grasping her confusion, I said, "Clay Street. By the convention center. Eastbound."

"Any sense of where he's going?"

A gust tunneled through. The man leaned into it and picked up his pace. I matched him, my bad knee starting to stiffen. "BART, maybe."

"There's an entrance on Eleventh," she said. "I'm gonna cut him off. Stay on the line."

It's a long block to Broadway. I sped up to a jog, pulling within twenty yards. Leg nausea coming on: bones grinding, tendons and cartilage getting shy, curling up.

Fifty feet from the corner he reached into his back pocket for his wallet. I could see him fiddling with it, taking out his BART pass.

As he moved to replace his wallet, he checked behind and saw me gaining ground.

He took off.

I shouted into the phone: "Coming your way."

Up ahead Nwodo appeared from around a raised marble plaza. We had him sandwiched. But I had spoken too soon, or too loudly, alerting him to her presence; she had revealed herself too readily; and the fifty feet of play enabled him to veer across the street, toward the Marriott, the frontage of which sits at an angle, a short-cut that collapsed our advantage.

"Stop," Nwodo yelled.

We converged on Broadway, running side by side.

He banked to the right, like he meant to turn down 10th, then juked back along Broadway, passing a series of quaint storefronts, Victorian façades restored or reimagined. Downtown was having a moment, it would have its moment any moment, Oakland was the City of the Future, look at all the excitement it had to offer.

Asshole. Stop.

My long loping stride, hampered by the retching sensation in my knee, wild protestations lighting up my nervous system. The fuck did he think he was going?

I assume he didn't realize there was a police station, two blocks ahead.

Or perhaps he did: he bolted left, across six empty lanes, down 9th.

We rounded the bend, Nwodo pumping her fists. She tucked her head down and then, with an astounding burst of physical impatience, an unspoken *Enough of this shit,* she exploded ahead like a funny car, leaving me goggling at her sudden disappearance, one instant beside me and in the next a shrinking silhouette, eating up the gap.

He felt the heat on his back.

He had barely enough time to turn around before she caught him by the neck and gave him a nice hard sideways shove, a bit of encouragement that, combined with his own momentum, pitched him face-first into the roll-shuttered entrance to a Vietnamese market.

He caromed off, reeling backward, tripping over his own feet, one eye scrunched in bafflement and mouth a black tunnel, whirling and flailing to remain vertical, and just as it seemed as though he might right himself, as his mind began to embrace the fantastic hope that he could still get away; as his waist began to corkscrew and his arms to seek freedom; it was right about that moment that I caught up, and, lowering my shoulder, crushed into his midsection.

Hit through the guy. That's what football coaches tell linemen. Make the object of your wrath not the opponent but a space two feet behind him. Hit that.

Never my game, football. Still, good advice is good advice.

Down we went, tracing a steep and vicious curve, like the line of a fourth-rate economy in free fall. His body reached the pavement first, followed by his head, damp crack and then silence. For a second I worried I'd hurt him badly. Then I felt his limbs fluttering beneath me, his breath humid on my face.

Nwodo was right away by my side. Together we rolled him onto his stomach.

"Shit," he moaned. "Oh God."

"You got a gun on you?" Nwodo said.

"God. Shit."

"Shut up. You got a gun?"

"Shit . . ."

She patted him down. No gun. He did have a pocketknife in his boot. She tossed it aside. He was clutching his BART pass in his right hand and his wallet in his left. He hadn't had a chance to put them away. I had to give him props for hanging on.

Nwodo pried the wallet from him and took out his license.

She flipped it around to show me. She leaned over, smiling, to look him in the eye. "How's it going, Dane."

THE POLICE STATION was two blocks away.

It took twenty minutes for a cruiser to arrive.

By then Dane Jankowsi had recovered enough of his wits to start bitching.

"I'm gonna sue you fuckers."

He was lying on the sidewalk. I had my foot on his back. Nwodo had lit the votive candle and placed it on the ground nearby.

"Go right ahead," she said.

"Both of you. Fuckin police brutality."

"Tsk," I said. "It's terrible."

"Keep your hands behind your head," Nwodo said.

"It fuckin *hurts*," Jankowski said. "You hit me."

"I believe it was the ground did that," Nwodo said.

"The shutter," I said.

"That too."

"You see how he tripped?" I said.

"Oh yeah," Nwodo said. "Clumsy."

"Fuck you both."

"That's very original, I've never heard that one." She looked at me. "You ever heard that one before?"

"Nope," I said. "You should copyright that shit."

"*Fuck you.*"

"Where's your gun, Dane?" Nwodo asked.

"I don't have any gun."

"You ditch it? Where you been staying, this last week?"

He did not reply.

"Don't be stupid," Nwodo said. "Either way, you're going down."

A black-and-white pulled up.

"Last chance," Nwodo said. "Where's the gun at?"

Jankowski cursed and spat. The uniforms tossed him into the cruiser, where he gave up the posturing and heaped against the door.

"Well," Nwodo said, cricking her neck, "that was fun."

"We'll see how I feel in the morning." I looked at her. "You got jets."

"Nah. You're just slow."

We shared a chuckle.

I hesitated, then said, "The film crew."

She nodded. "I'll check it out."

She didn't appear offended by my suggestion. We were still basking in the glow of a shared win. I almost offered to help her out. But that felt a step too far.

"Listen," I said, "it might be best, when you write this whole thing up, I'm not part of the story."

"Why's that."

"From a jurisdictional point of view."

"Not cause you don't want to get sued."

"They never do."

"I don't know," she said. "He seemed pretty mad."

"Yeah, cause you embarrassed him," I said. "Anyhow, take my word. I don't need it getting back to my boss that I'm out running around chasing people down."

A plastic bag rattled along the street.

"While conducting surveillance," Nwodo said, "I observed an individual acting in a suspicious manner. A closer look revealed that this individual was identical with Dane Jankowski, whose face I recognized from the BOLO. I pursued the suspect, and when he did not yield to my requests to stop, I detained him, subduing him in accordance with department-sanctioned guidelines for the use of force."

"I appreciate it."

She nodded and left to talk to the uniforms.

I went home to ice my knee.

CHAPTER 14

Tuesday, January 1

7:36 p.m.

Funny: my knee felt fine, that night and over the next few days. Better than usual, in fact, less junky. I mentioned to Amy I might take up sprinting.

"That's definitely the logical conclusion," she said.

"I was reading that short bursts of intense exercise are easier on the joints than prolonged low-intensity activity."

"Reading where."

"Online."

"Mm," she said.

"I feel like you're not supporting me in my fitness journey." I scooped rice. "You should have seen her, though. It was unbelievable. Like we're in a video game and she powers up. *Foooosh.*"

"It's cute that you have a crush on her."

"What I am," I said, "is an admirer of human achievement and athletic prowess."

"Is she hot? You make her sound hot."

"She's pretty hot."

"Is she taken? Should we set her up with someone?"

"No ring, but I don't know."

"Boys or girls?"

"Why would I know that?"

"Well, try and find out."

"I can't do that. That's super awkward."

Amy smiled, checked the oven clock. "What time are you supposed to be there?"

"Eight."

"Stay safe, okay?"

"Luke? He's not going to do anything to me."

"I meant driving around there."

She was one to talk. Her clinic is located in the Tenderloin. The sidewalk outside the building is a syringe graveyard.

I stood up, wiped my mouth, kissed the top of her head. "Love you."

"You too."

McClymonds High School sits at the base of a seedy triangle defined by San Pablo, Peralta, and Grand. Crossing the parking lot, I saw the gymnasium lights burning. No dribbling or yelling that I could hear, though, and it was a white silence that greeted me as I walked the hall, feeling the riven linoleum through my sneakers.

Taped to the gym doors, a paper sign, Luke's floppy handwriting.

Late Nite Ball

The door let out a loud pop, and several of the bodies spread out on the hardwood twitched. That's how I knew they weren't dead. For all appearances, I'd stumbled upon a massacre: thirteen black adolescent males, flat on their backs in a circle, and sitting cross-legged at the top, the keystone, my brother.

He smiled at me and put a finger to his lips.

One boy had risen up on his elbows to stare. Luke motioned for him to lie down. After a wary moment, he did.

"Just keep riding the waves of your breath," Luke said.

His voice was unrecognizable.

I tiptoed to the grandstand.

"What's on your mind now?" Luke said. "Where has it gone?"

The boys were fourteen or fifteen years old, but in their limp vulnerability, I perceived them as younger. Absent the rolled shoulders, the bulletproof carapace of indifference.

"Wherever it's got to, that's okay," Luke said. "Look at it. Hold it in your attention. Breathe with it, and accept it. And then, without judging yourself, let it go, and bring your attention back to your breath."

In that short span—without any real attempt on my part—I found myself lulled, tuned to the sensations percolating around me: the green shriek of the indoor floods; floorboards ticking, whir and wheeze; sweet ancient sweat. My own paced inhalations, growing shorter and shallower, until a chime lanced the stillness.

I sat up, blinking, alert.

The high warble faded to nothing. Again Luke touched the bells together.

The boys began to stir.

The third chime disappeared into chatter and the eager chirp of sneakers. Somebody lugged over a decrepit ball cart, and the air began to vibrate with thuds.

Luke tucked the bells in a drawstring bag and ambled over to me.

"You came," he said.

"I said I would."

He squeezed my shoulder. "Right on."

Cupping his mouth, he called: "Okay. Let's get warm."

. . .

NORMALLY THEY PLAYED for three hours, broken up by occasional drills. Seeing as they had an authentic baller in their midst, Luke asked me to spend a few minutes talking to them first, describing what it takes to compete at the highest level.

I wasn't far into my thumbnail autobiography before a runty kid in a Kevin Durant jersey raised his hand and asked who I had played for.

"Cal Bears," I said.

"Ain't no Bears."

"It's Division One."

The boy huffed derisively. "You said the *highest level*."

Luke said, "He went to the Final Four."

The degree of shit not given was impressive.

"You know what," I said, clapping, "I think we're good here."

THEY RAN FIVE on five, three waiting for next, knees treadling like a row of sewing machines. Luke acted as coach and referee, dashing up and down the sideline, leaping in to adjudicate a burgeoning altercation, pinwheeling his skinny leglike arms and exhorting them to pass, pass, find the open man.

He settled a traveling call and trotted over to join me on the bench.

We watched mini-Durant jack up a three-pointer from six feet behind the line.

Cries of *airball*.

"Swear to God," Luke said. "What's with all the threes?"

"It's the Steph Curry effect," I said.

"Okay, but they *pass*, too. That's what makes it beautiful to watch."

His attention to teamwork amused me. The Luke I knew and played against was a notorious hog.

Later we ran them through some layup drills, rebounding drills, passing drills. When Luke told them to line up for most-in-a-row, protest broke out.

"I don't want to hear it," he said.

A stocky boy lay down on the floor.

"Marcus," Luke said. "Up."

"I'm tired."

"You can't make free throws when you're tired, you lose. Up."

Marcus got up. He made a big production of it, flopping his limbs around, but he did it.

First to shoot hit four without a miss. His successor made three; a couple of kids managed five. Six was the number to beat when Marcus stepped to the line. Under a barrage of mockery, he calmly drilled eight straight before clanging one off the back iron.

"Told you," he said. "Tired."

"Yo Division One."

Kevin Durant had retrieved the rebound and was addressing me.

He tossed me the ball.

I said, "It's been a while, guys."

"Bitch shut up and shoot."

"Hey," Luke said. "No."

The speaker rolled his eyes.

I came forward, spun the ball in my palms.

My first attempt muddled its way in. I was shooting from a cold start. But once out of the gate, I relaxed and found my stroke.

Two, three. Five. Seven.

"Shit."

Eight.

"Division *One*."

Nine.

"*Shit*."

I figured ten was a good place to stop, but Luke waved: *Keep going.*

I ended up with seventeen.

The boys had fallen silent.

"Respect," Marcus said.

AFTER THE BOYS had gone; after they'd cleaned up, and filed out, bumping Luke's fist, one by one—*Coach, Coach, Coach*—after a cavernous hush took up residence in the rafters, like some exhausted giant settling in to hibernate; my brother and I sat inches apart, surveying the vacant waxed floor, soldiers returned to their beachhead, half a century on.

Luke said, "You missed on purpose."

I shrugged. "You want us to be here all night?"

He laughed. "For the record," he said, and said no more.

Summer evenings in Siempre Verde Park, playing till sundown, our friends drifting off to dinner, till it was just the two of us, heedless, bashing against each other, wet shirts heavy as leather. The stars came out and we shot free throws in the dark. Most-in-a-row.

Forty-three my best.

Forty-five his.

I nodded slightly, conceded slightly.

One ball had gone overlooked and was crouching in a pile of orange agility cones. I pushed up on my knees and went to retrieve it. "You do a good job with them."

"Thanks."

I walked to the top of the key, hitched, put up a fadeaway fifteen-footer.

Brick.

Luke sprang up, corralling the rebound near the baseline for a turnaround three.

Net.

The ball was hopping around, low to the ground, excited.

We both moved. I got there first and looped out to half-court. When I faced him, he was waiting for me, feet planted, palms at ten and two, shifting his hips easily. I swung back and forth, prodding the space between us. He knew better than to fall for it; he knew all my tricks.

I knew his tricks, too.

"It's late," I said.

He nodded. Terms unspoken, same as ever, game to eleven by ones and twos.

He met me at the arc, resisting me with a forearm against my back, heels dug in, our fighting waltz.

Familiar patterns, slower, wearier. Compensating for battle scars, handicaps self-inflicted or accidental. It occurred to me—as I turned at the block, banked it high and in—that those are two of the five manners of death.

"One–nothing," I said.

Eleven by ones and twos, and when we tied at ten, game to fifteen, because winner had to win by two. These rules live in you forever.

I hit a two.

He hit a two.

Game to twenty-one.

I held his shirt.

He sank an elbow in my ribs.

To twenty-five.

Backing him down, bumping him to create space. He darted in to strip me cleanly, recovering the loose ball at the weak-side wing, where he paused, scissoring his legs, licking at a wolfish smile. Twenty-three all. He could win with a two. A long two was well within his range.

We both knew. We had the math in our bones. I closed on him.

He initiated the cascade of movements I expected: right thigh sagging inward five or so degrees, a fractional collapse that reverses to explode through the hips. Well before he reaches an apex, the ball is up and back and out of reach. He shoots out of the top of his head. It's next to impossible to defend, because by the time you react and get your own hands up you're eighteen inches too late.

I'd watched him do it ten thousand times before my tenth birthday.

In every aspect of our lives, I outstripped him: I excelled in school, I was reflexively polite, simpatico with adults. In the one arena that counted to us, the game, he got by on natural gifts. I had to work. I'd worked so hard that eventually I destroyed my own body.

Luke did nothing, I did too much, and those were our downfalls. It made him ungovernable and me a clockwork. He knew what I would do and I knew that he knew and yet I did it anyway, because he had victory sewn up unless I acted to stop him, now.

He sagged.

I scrambled, my arm outstretched, seeing him through the gap between thumb and forefinger, the webbing stretched taut.

He did nothing. Drew down, sneakers screwed to the hardwood, and I sailed past, grabbing at air, leaving him a clear path to the basket.

After you, sir.

He took two lazy dribbles into the lane and tossed up a finger roll.

"Twenty-four twenty-three," he said.

On the next out he inexplicably went for the winner from far.

No, wrong: explicably. Luke in a nutshell. Maximum unnecessary drama.

The ball traced overhead against the glare.

I exhaled. God exhaled.

Iron.

I hauled in the rebound and we traded positions.

"Dead at twenty-five," I said.

He pounded his thighs, unsympathetic.

"I mean it," I said. "I need to get home."

He waved assent, and I hunkered to plot my attack. But his mouth was still jawing.

I propped the ball on my hip and gawked at him. "What was that?"

"Huh?"

"What did you say."

"I didn't say anything."

I started to laugh. "Did you really just do that? Call me a pussy?"

"I don't know what you're talking about, man."

Still laughing, I shook my head, slammed the ball once, twice. "All right."

He stood up, aggrieved. "Are we playing or not?"

My answer was to barrel down the lane, knocking him on his ass. He slid to a stop under the basket as the ball fell through the net and landed in his lap.

"You want a foul?" I said.

"No."

"You sure?"

He bowled the ball to me and got up. "Twenty-four all."

I checked it to him, hard.

He checked it back, harder.

Game point. The prudent play: back him down again, use my weight and strength. He'd left prison thirty pounds lighter. I reversed, and he squared in anticipation, falling against me bodily, draping me. I could feel his heart clubbing at my spine.

I made a sharp strong-side cut.

No surprises. In our bones. He began his lateral slide.

Too slow. He'd lost a step.

His eyes chased the ball as it left my hands, preparing for a rebound that never came.

The shot peaked, paused, and dropped through the cylinder with a nylon kiss.

How I made it, I'll never know.

Because I'd lost a step, too. On my way up, my foot caught on his shin, pitching me forward to an off-center landing.

Electric shock, patella to groin.

Luke turned in a circle, looking for me, ready to demand game to thirty-one. He seemed surprised to find me curled up on the pine, breathless and agonized, knee pulled into my stomach.

HE KEPT APOLOGIZING as he helped me out.

"Not your fault," I said.

Except for my car, the parking lot was deserted. He'd taken the bus.

I told him to get in.

For the duration of the drive to San Leandro, Luke fidgeted, alternately staring out the window and glancing at me, his expression meek. I'd racked the seat way back so I could work the pedals with my right leg fully extended. I could bend the joint, although the surrounding tissue had begun to balloon with hot fluid.

One of the downsides of a morgue education is the ability to picture your own anatomical processes with revolting precision.

Luke apologized again.

"Forget it," I said, pulling to the curb outside our parents' house.

"Thanks for the ride," he said.

"Sure."

"Let me know what the doctor says," he said.

I nodded curtly.

He hesitated with his thumb on the seatbelt release.

I said, "I really gotta—"

"Yeah yeah yeah. Yeah. Sorry."

I watched him slink up the porch, like a teenager out past curfew. But he was a grown man. We both were. Allegedly.

I throttled the ignition as hard as I could.

CHAPTER 15

Saturday, January 5

A sprain. Not a tear.

Four to six weeks, light duty.

I would've preferred to get hurt arresting Dane Jankowski. That, at least, would've spared me the ordeal of having to explain myself to my sergeant. What could I say that wouldn't sound absurd?

But . . . he called me a pussy.

"I'm gonna have you sign one of those contracts," Turnbow said. She was standing at my cubicle, admiring the aluminum scaffolding that ran the length of my leg. "'No waterskiing in the off-season.'"

"Call my agent." I tugged down my pant cuff. "I'm sorry, Sarge."

"Tell me you won, at least."

"By one point."

Dani Botero breathed *crowd goes wild* noises.

Turnbow turned to inspect the mosaic of windows open on my computer screen.

Jane Doe narrative.

Missing persons reports.

Spreadsheet, sixteen credit card numbers, sixteen names.

"Silver lining," she said. "You got plenty of time."

I'D IGNORED THE seven women with common-sounding names. Now I started plugging them into Accurint, triggering an avalanche of hits.

Jessica Chen. Beth Green. Include every variant of Catherine or Kathy or Cathie or Kate Myers, and in California alone you had forty-three people.

Plenty of time.

Nothing but.

Carmen Woolsey shook crumbs from her big witchy skirt, pausing en route to the coffee station to offer me some.

"Please," I said. "Thank you."

When she brought it to me, Sully clucked her tongue. "This how it's gonna be."

"How's that."

"Us waiting on you, hand and foot?"

With a guilty laugh, I sat back, blowing on the cup.

Tell me you won, at least.

Packed inside the sergeant's words, her real question: *Was it worth it?*

My mind replayed Amy's words from Christmas dinner.

You only get this way around him.

We are who we are in relation to others.

Without a second data point, a name is close to meaningless.

But a name, in relation to others, is itself a data point.

I started searching the names in pairs.

Your search—"Karla Abruzzo" "Frances Ann Flatt"—did not match any documents.

Your search—"Karla Abruzzo" "Dara Kenilworth"—did not match any documents.

I worked systematically, keeping track of the failed combinations.

Your search—"Dara Kenilworth" "Kelly Doran"—did not match any documents.

Despite *no* after *no,* I felt charged up, intent, in contrast with the day sluggishly unwinding outside. Noncommittal rain pricked the windows. The phone burped and bleeped while around the room idle chatter skated. Lindsey Bagoyo's church was running a children's clothing drive. Best *Real Housewives* franchise, by consensus: New York. Though Maggie Garcia made a strong case for Atlanta.

How do you watch that garbage, Shupfer wanted to know.

How do you not, Dani Botero countered.

Your search—"Dara Kenilworth" "Lainie Pedersen"—did not match any documents.

Two funerals had taken place while I was out of the office, Rebecca Ristic and Jalen Coombs. Grant Hellerstein's body was in transit to his family in Upper Michigan. Benjamin Felton's funeral was scheduled for the coming week.

Your search—"Dara Kenilworth" "Catherine Myers"—did not match any (goddamn) *documents.*

My ears pricked up: Zaragoza, behind the partition, saying, "They got him?"

"A week ago," Bagoyo said. "It's like, how come they don't call and tell us that?"

"Got who?" Sully asked.

"Come on, dude," Bagoyo said. "You call me when you have a problem. You think I don't like good news? I have to get it from the internet?"

"That's us," Shupfer said. "The bad news brigade."

"Got *who,*" Sully said.

"Shooter from the party," Zaragoza said.

"Nice."

Did you really think that your search—"Leah Horvuth" "Kelly Doran"—would match any documents? Sucker.

With Dane Jankowski's name floating around, people had begun pulling apart his social media, poring over every photo and comment and trying to mold them into a coherent political position that could then be used as evidence for their own beliefs.

Bagoyo said, "He showed up to the rally thingy."

"Moron," Sully said.

"Thank God for morons," Shupfer said.

Your search—"Leah Horvuth" "Beth Green"—hahahaha.

My coffee was stone-cold. I'd tried fifty-four combinations. Karla-with-a-K Abruzzo was out of the running, as were Dara Kenilworth and Lainie Pedersen.

As far as Leah Horvuth was concerned, my attitude was: Screw you, Leah Horvuth. What have you done for me lately?

On my fifty-fifth attempt I typed "Leah Horvuth" "Catherine Myers" and pressed ENTER.

The browser crowded with words; a tingle crowded on the surface of my skin.

Hits.

Twenty-nine of them.

Leah Horvuth, I take it all back.

THE FIRST LINK led to a San Francisco arts website—a theater review, several years old.

Bringing Up Baby in a New Era

How do you tell your children that the world has gone mad?

This is the question at the heart of playwright Leah Horvuth's new black comedy, which opens Thursday at Hidden City Theatre.

Plot summary: two women huddle together in a bomb shelter. It's never made clear if there is an actual bomb to shelter from. End of plot summary. The reviewer flagged the play's "heavy-handed parallels to *Godot*." He preferred the younger actress. Directing for the Articulate Apes Company, Catherine Myers had chosen to emphasize the script's surreal elements over "apocalypse shop-talk of fallout and MRE expiration dates." Tickets cost $38 and could be purchased by calling the box office.

The remainder of the links were archived listings for the same show.

I searched for "Catherine Myers" "Articulate Apes."

The troupe's website listed Cathie Myers as a co–artistic director. A native of San Francisco, she held an MFA in theater arts from Yale University.

I opened Accurint.

In San Francisco proper, there were two people with that exact spelling of the name. Age sixty-eight, residing in the Sunset; age fifty-one, residing in the Mission.

Like the critic, I preferred the younger woman.

"Hello?"

"Ms. Myers?"

"Yes?"

"This is Deputy Edison with the Alameda County Sheriff's Office. Am I catching you at an okay time?"

"Sorry," she said. Pleasant enough; unguarded. "You said Alameda?"

"Yes, ma'am, county sheriff. Are you Cathie Myers the director?"

"I'm sorry, what's this about?"

Defenses starting to rise.

I restated my credentials. "It's about an identification. I'm trying to verify that I have the correct person. I was wondering if I might be able to come by and have a brief word with you. Nothing to worry about. Routine inquiry."

"Regarding what? What does that mean? You're making me nervous."

"Please don't be. It's nothing major. Please feel free to call my office and verify."

A beat. "What was that badge number again?"

I gave it to her. "Would this afternoon work for you?"

"I have rehearsal at six."

"I'll make sure we're done well before. Thanks. You're still on Capp Street?"

"Yes."

"I'll be there in a couple of hours. Thanks again."

I grabbed my crutch and hobbled toward the exit.

Dani Botero yelled, "It lives!"

2:14 p.m.

The orthopedist had fixed the brace at thirty degrees, an angle intended to permit most everyday functions. I raced to the edge of San Francisco in twenty minutes, then crawled along for half an hour to reach the 101 North, squirming in my seat, tapping at the gas, ankle starting to tire. By the time I made it to Mission Street and found parking, everything from the waist down pounded like a disco.

I climbed out of the car and steadied myself against a lamppost, catching my breath against the pain, buffeted by whiffs of rancid fryer oil and off-key Spanish oozing from a storefront evangelical church. Outside a head shop, men in rotted garments perched curbside, watching a sun-scorched woman delight over the squashed remains of a mouse. She slapped the pavement with her bare palms, shrieking *Inside out! Inside out!*

I dry-swallowed four ibuprofen and set off.

CATHERINE MYERS LIVED, mercifully, on the ground-floor unit of a begrimed row house. She answered the door with the chain on. Protuberant green eyes peered out from beneath an overhang of sapped gray hair. She was white, thin-lipped, wearing a black leather motorcycle jacket over a loose Hawaiian-print dress and brown Uggs.

"Deputy Edison," I said. "We spoke on the phone."

My smile did nothing to relax her. Neither did the uniform or the crutch. Maybe she took them for props. The home invasion specialist doth protest too much.

She kept the chain on, took her time comparing me to my ID. A Yorkshire terrier padded up behind her and cocked its head to one side.

"There's a café on Van Ness and Twenty-First," she said, shoving the badge back at me. "Five minutes."

SHE BROUGHT THE dog. It trod circles beneath the table before bedding down at her feet.

I showed her a color copy of the credit card in her name, a Wells Fargo Cash Wise Visa. "Our department recovered it, along with several other fraudulent cards."

"Why would you think this is me? As opposed to any other Catherine Myers."

I took out a copy of the Credit One Bank Platinum Visa issued to Leah Horvuth.

That unsettled her more than her own card had. She tucked her hands in her lap, frowning. "Does Leah know about this?"

"I haven't been able to reach her. I could use help finding the right contact information. When did you last speak to her?"

"A while. Two or three years, I think."

"After your show closed."

A chary smile. "That's how you found me."

I nodded.

"It didn't end well." She reached down to scratch the dog's head. "Different visions."

"How did you two connect in the first place?"

"Leah? I've known her since I was nine. We went to school together."

Big red neon letters: data point. "Where was that?"

"Watermark."

She spoke the name like it was something everyone knew, or ought to.

"Sorry, I'm not familiar."

"It's near Tomales. In Marin."

"Is that where you're from?"

"Me? Oh no. I grew up in the city. Leah . . . I think she's from Texas, originally."

"A boarding school."

"In a manner of speaking." Cathie Myers squinted at the cards. "What am I supposed to do about this? Is it going to screw up my credit?"

"I'd call the bank."

She sighed. "What a nightmare."

"You never opened an account with Wells Fargo."

"No."

"Never received a statement, a renewal notice."

"Never. I'll sign an affidavit, or whatever. This has nothing to do with me."

"Can you think of a way someone might've gotten ahold of your information?"

"I mean, I've had cards stolen before," she said. "This is the first time the police showed up."

She flipped the page facedown. "They don't send cops for identity theft. What's going on here, really?"

"Ms. Myers, I have a few other names I'd like you to look at, and tell me if you recognize any of them."

I watched as she ran down the list.

She said, "Karla, she was with us."

"At Watermark."

She nodded.

"Any idea where she is now?"

"None."

"Does the school have your information on file?"

"Of course not," she said.

"If you gave them a donation, for example."

"I don't give them money," she said. "I don't have money to give, and if I did, I'd have other priorities. It was forty years ago. I was only there for a little while before I left. I haven't had a thing to do with them since."

"You stayed in touch with Leah."

"She's my friend," Cathie Myers said, frowning again. "That's separate."

I wondered how different two artistic visions had to be to ruin a four-decade friendship. "What about the others?"

With an air of disdain she resumed scanning the list. "Her I don't know. Not her, either. Kelly Doran—we had a Kelly, but her last name was Modigliani. Like the painter. I don't know the rest of them. I told you, I was only there briefly. Can you please tell me what's going on?"

"If you don't mind," I said, "there's one more thing I'd like you to look at."

When photographing decedents for the purpose of obtaining identification, we try to arrange their features in the plainest, most inoffensive way possible. There's a question of respect and another of effectiveness: you're more apt to recognize a face when not distracted by an agonized expression.

It's not always practical. Nobody looks normal with a caved-in skull or a bullet hole through the eye.

The challenge with Jane Doe had been framing. Too tight and you lost a sense of scale. Too wide and the bruised throat came into view. I'd aimed for the sweet spot in the middle, but you could still see dry scratches, the unnatural looseness around the eyes.

Cathie Myers said, "I don't know her."

"You're sure."

"I've never seen her in my life."

"Okay." I put the photo away and began gathering my things. "Thanks."

She was staring at me, gray bangs quivering. "Who is she?"

"We haven't been able to identify her."

Her eyes returned to the spot on the table where the photograph had lain, as if to claw back its memory. She was putting it together. "That's who stole my identity?"

I said, "There's no reason to assume it bears directly on you."

"Well, sorry, but, it's my name, so I think it does."

"Thanks for your time, Ms. Myers."

"Wait a second." She started out of her chair, uprooting the dog, who began hopping around, pawing at her calf. "Hello? Hang on, please. You can't just drop this on me and leave. Excuse me."

I gave another useless smile. "If I learn more, I'll be in touch."

CHAPTER 16

Sunday, January 6

8:50 a.m.

The Watermark School was closed for winter break. The office would reopen on Monday, January 7. If I wished to leave a message, I should feel free to do so after the beep. Otherwise, I could submit a request through the contact form available at www dot the watermark school dot com. Please be advised that it could take several weeks to receive a reply. Thank you very much.

The school's homepage was basic and sunny, all primary colors and rounded fonts. A slideshow boasted healthy-looking children, ranging in age from five to the mid-teens. They hiked. They played saxophone. They stood in an emerald glade, painting in watercolors. Dewy-eyed they encircled a teacher, who displayed the monarch butterfly cradled in his palm.

They planted in the school garden, they harvested the vegetables, they chopped those vegetables for soup.

They—

I squinted.

They welded?

There she was, a little girl kneeling amid a hail of golden sparks and hot dripping slag, a helmet obscuring her face. Along her skinny nape lay a shank of hair secured with a Hello Kitty barrette. She swam inside her protective leather jacket, shoulders landing at her elbows. Made to guess, I would've put her at no older than nine.

The image dissolved as the next slide faded in: an adolescent boy, lazing in a hay cart, ukulele in hand and mouth open in a yodel.

Near the top of the screen, superimposed on a graphic of silhouetted trees, the school motto:

Independence — Curiosity — Responsibility

I moused up to ABOUT US.

Since its establishment in 1951, the Watermark School has continually blazed trails in progressive education.

The operating principle, I gathered, was that children are happiest and learn best when left alone to do as they please.

Watermark enforced no formal grade structure; classes were offered, but there was no requirement to attend them; boys and girls lived in co-ed dormitories. These and other unusual policies emerged from the pedagogical theories of the school's founder, an Englishman named Conrad Erasmus Buntley.

To a great extent, Buntley *was* Watermark, and the history page read like a tribute to him—a creation myth, presented in heroic terms. Born into extreme poverty, he was an autodidact, illiterate to the age of ten. He'd worked as a printer's devil, a merchant seaman, and an actor before discovering Jungian analysis and making several pilgrimages to Switzerland.

Buntley endorsed what he called "teaching the whole child," arguing that human growth had far more to do with what happened outside the classroom than in.

Today these ideas are commonplace, having been co-opted and diluted by the educational mainstream. When C. E. Buntley introduced them, however, they provoked controversy and, often, fierce resistance.

Dusty black-and-whites of Buntley accompanied the text. Slope-shouldered, in rumpled tweeds, he munched the stem of a meerschaum pipe, his smile giving forth a pile of smudged, jostling teeth. Combed across his pate, like vapor trails, were two white wisps; in the next photo the hair flew out on end as he swung an ax, shirtsleeves rolled to the elbows. Rigorous physical labor played an important role in the Buntley worldview.

"As nutritious soil is to the flower," he wrote, "so is the health of the body to the mind."

There was a heavy emphasis on self-reliance, although its precise flavor differed from the stuff I'd read in high school, Emerson and Thoreau. C. E. Buntley's argument emerged from a pragmatic observation: children were, at heart, selfish.

"One may claim, with some measure of truth, that all mankind shares this egotistical aspect. However, it is most pronounced in the young, for whom hands of the clock hold no sway. Past and future do not exist; there is only the eternal present, which is to say, the desire of the mind in the moment. One may as well cry at the rising tide as fight against this tendency. Therefore we do not fight it. We allow it to exist. Only in freedom will the child come to integrate both halves of the personality, the Shadow and the Light."

Perhaps the most radical of Buntley's beliefs was the notion that each member of the community, regardless of age or station, must have an equal say in the creation and enforcement of school rules.

Watermark is an ongoing experiment in true democracy, where everyone—staff and students alike—shares in rights and responsibilities. Most famously, the whole school gathers once a week for Town Hall. Motions are proposed, grievances aired, and consequences meted out according to the standard of one person, one vote. At Town Hall, a child of six holds the same power and the same obligations as a teacher of thirty years' experience. Thus, every Watermark citizen learns diplomacy, integrity, and fairness.

An inset showed a grave young boy in a Thomas the Tank Engine T-shirt, cross-legged on a Persian rug, his hand aloft.

I'd asked Cathie Myers: *A boarding school?*

In a manner of speaking.

I navigated to the photo galleries, looking for Jane Doe or a younger version of her. The pictures didn't adhere to any organizational scheme; no dates, captions, or names.

One gallery showed off the students' handiwork. Shaker-style furniture, watercolors, ceramics. The images linked out to a store where you could buy these very items, each accompanied by a handwritten artist's statement. Food for sale, too: sauerkraut, pickles, and jam. All profits went back to the school.

I tried the FACULTY tab.

No staff photos; no departmental rosters, just a general description of what sort of person taught at Watermark.

For teachers accustomed to more traditional educational hier-
archies, the experience of genuine equality with students can
prove a challenge at first . . .

A sublink to EMPLOYMENT OPPORTUNITIES informed the curious that none, at present, were available.

Other than C. E. Buntley, I found only one other person named,
the current principal, Camille Buntley. She wasn't explicitly called
out as C.E.'s daughter. No need, once you saw her photo. Both
shared the same cake-wedge nose; the same rhomboid forehead
like the broad front of a mansard roof. She posed against a tree
trunk, noon sun pushing cubist shadows down her face and flatten-
ing an insurrection of hennaed curls.

I clicked back, skimming the first few pages' worth of Google
search results.

The elder Buntley had his own Wikipedia page, its contents
lifted from the Watermark website.

There were reviews from school ratings sites; the place consis-
tently received five out of five stars.

The online student creative writing journal, last updated in
2013.

A piece in the *Marin Independent Journal* about Watermark's
fiftieth anniversary, in 2001, was pure puff.

The rest of the results trailed off into iterative garbage, the internet doing what it does best: cannibalizing itself, then vomiting
itself back out at ten times the volume.

I called Nwodo.

She said, "Interesting." Her tone was hard to read.

I said, "It's about a two-hour drive out there. I don't think my
knee can handle it."

"You want me to drive you."

"Don't tell me you don't want to come."

"No-go for the next day or so," she said. "I caught a new one down Fruitvale."

"I saw that," I said. Another shooting; property of C shift. "Tuesday, then."

"I didn't think you worked Tuesdays."

"I don't, technically."

"Didn't think your office covered Marin, either."

"We don't."

"Technically," she said.

"That's right."

A beat.

She said, "I'll pick you up."

FORENSIC IT HAD news for me regarding Jasmine Gomez's cell. I went upstairs to talk to the tech.

"First off," he said, "you need to realize, this is a Samsung SPH-i500."

"Okay."

"From two thousand three."

He waited.

I said, "Old."

"In phone years, ancient. To be honest I can't understand why anyone would still be carrying it around, aside from sentimental value."

"Or they can't afford a new one."

"Well, sure," he said. "That too."

His name was Craig. He was fortyish, with a red goatee and one of those braided-leather belts.

"Anyway," he said, leaning back in his chair, "we don't have a cable for it. And it's not like I can go to, I dunno, RadioShack. I mean, these things are living at the bottom of a landfill. I had to get one off eBay. So that took a few days. I go to plug it in, it's been switched off for so long that the battery won't hold a charge. So *now* I have to get a new battery, too. Seller in Minsk. Expedited shipping."

He made these feats sound comparable to unearthing and translating the Rosetta Stone.

"Great," I said. "I really appreciate it."

"Here's the thing," he said.

The *thing* is never a good thing.

"The thing is," he said, "it's a, kind of a quirk, of this particular model, that when you swap out the battery, it wipes the user data."

I stared at him.

"Yeah," he said. "So, I mean, you can appreciate why they stopped making that model." He shook his head in disbelief. "I mean, talk about a design flaw."

"Everything's gone," I said.

"Well, not exactly. I mean, I know how important this is to you."

"It's not gone."

"No," he said. "It's *gone*. Yeah. But, it's just not—I was able to use ZombieFile to recover some of it. Here's the thing, though."

"Another thing."

"The thing is," Craig said, "ZombieFile isn't compatible with that OS. That OS is from two thousand three. In operating system years, that's—"

"Ancient."

"Prehistoric. They stopped issuing patches for it in two thousand nine. And it's not like the developer who wrote ZombieFile had it in mind."

I said, "Is the data gone, or not?"

He turned to his computer and clicked open a file.

A pane of gibberish appeared.

"So," he said, "yeah."

He appeared to realize then that I was on crutches. "Did you want to, like, sit down?"

ARMED WITH CATHIE Myers's name, I managed to persuade Leah Horvuth not to hang up on me. She confirmed that she had attended Watermark; like her former friend and collaborator, she had been enrolled briefly, between the ages of eight and ten. I emailed her a scan of the credit card in her name along with a photo of Jane Doe. She didn't recognize either, though she discerned my purpose almost instantly.

"Oh God," she said.

I said, "I'm going to ask you to delete both files, please, and empty the trash on your computer."

"Yes," she said. "I'll—okay."

"Thank you. You mind doing it now, please?"

"Okay . . ." Faint clicking; an electronic crinkle. "Okay, I did it."

"Thank you. As I told Ms. Myers, in our view, you don't need to be concerned for your safety. Though you might want to run a credit check."

"I don't understand," Leah Horvuth said. "What's this have to do with the school?"

"We're exploring various possibilities."

She exhaled. "She looks so young."

I said, "You did delete the photo."

"Yes, I—it's just a—it's upsetting, to . . ." She paused. "How is Cathie, by the way?"

"She seemed fine," I said.

"I should call her," she said. "I was sorry about the way we parted."

"I'm sure she'd appreciate that. One thing we didn't discuss in detail was her time at Watermark. I got the impression it wasn't totally positive for her."

"Well, it's not for everyone, that's for sure."

"Did something happen to her while she was there?"

"Something inappropriate, you mean."

"If my victim was a student, anything I can learn would be help-ful."

"I never had anything happen to me. If Cathie did, she never mentioned it. I suppose it's possible. Ninety percent of the time, we were unsupervised. Anything's possible," she said, "when nobody's watching."

Monday, January 7

7:55 p.m.

Five minutes prior to the start of the weekly support group for homeless trans youth, I clomped up the steps to The Harbor, lean-ing heavily on the handrail. Nobody answered my knock, and I peered through a leaded sidelight window at the gloomy parlor. The receptionist's desk was unattended.

I hobbled down off the porch and peered upward. The second-story windows were glossed black.

I lifted my foot, shifting weight as I rechecked the tab of paper, wrinkled and soft from two weeks in my wallet. I had the correct time, the correct night. Maybe the group had been canceled, or hadn't yet resumed following the holidays.

To my left, a pair of figures approached, shouldering close to-gether.

Clad in ill-fitting clothes, toting colossal knapsacks, they had the stooped shuffling gait of people desperate to avoid attention. I watched them pivot off the sidewalk and disappear down the side of the building.

I went over to look.

A concrete footpath led through a gate, where a deck joined The Harbor to a second house, larger and set back from the street. Visually the two structures had little in common, making it easy to mistake them as unconnected.

The shades of the second house were drawn, thin frames of canary-colored light leaking from a room on the top floor. At a west-facing entrance, I encountered a mechanical five-button lock.

I rang the bell.

Above me, the shade flapped back.

Footsteps descended. The door cracked.

"Can I help you."

The speaker was a trans woman, rawboned and olive-skinned and tall enough to look down at me. She assessed me with mistrust, hugging the inside edge of the door with her torso in case she needed to slam it.

I said, "I'm here for the meeting."

She said nothing.

I offered her the torn flyer tab as evidence of my sincerity. She didn't take it.

"I don't know you," she said.

"I spoke to Greer," I said.

True enough. I had spoken to her.

"Wait here."

Five minutes passed, ten.

I rang again, then began knocking. Not loudly, but persistently.

From behind me came the squeal of the gate.

Greer Unger stepped onto the deck and planted herself on an islet of starlight.

"This is private property," she said. "You need to leave."

"I thought your groups were open to the public."

"You're not the public."

"Did you speak to your colleagues?"

"What?"

"You said you needed to speak to them before you could talk to me."

"No. I haven't."

"It's been two weeks," I said. "I've been calling you."

"Maybe take a hint."

I hadn't heard a car pull up. I glanced around. "You live close by?"

"That's none of your business. Now please go."

"I've been able to get a general sense of where Jasmine's from."

"Great. Then you don't need me."

"It's not enough to find her family. I'm telling you, because I want you to understand that I've tried to do this without asking you to violate your obligations."

"Ask me or don't. I have no intention of complying."

"I get that you have your duties. One of mine is to take custody of Jasmine's property. I don't know if she was living here or what, but if I have reason to suspect that you're holding back items that belong to her, I can get a court order. I can—hang on. Hang on. I'm not saying I'm going to do that. I'm saying we—you and I—are on the same side here. We're trying to do what's best for Jasmine. We may disagree about how to get there. I believe you when you tell me you're concerned for her privacy. I'm asking you to consider her dignity, too."

"Privacy," she said, "is one hundred percent non-negotiable."

Her gaze had strayed, and I became aware that the door to the second building was ajar, the tall trans woman leaning out, other figures lurking behind her, watching and listening.

Greer Unger raised her voice. "Safety is non-negotiable. Now I'm asking you, once and for all, to get the fuck out of here. Or, yeah, I'll call the cops, and I don't care how 'funny' you might think that is."

I said, "Have a good night."

Greer Unger wasn't done with me. She followed me as I limped down the footpath to the sidewalk. I started toward my car, and she continued to follow me.

"Chrissake," I said, "I'm going."

She said, "Twenty-five-oh-five Dana. Drive there. Take the long way."

TWENTY-FIVE-OH-FIVE DANA was around the block. Heeding her instructions, I went past, to Ellsworth, and came back up Dwight, arriving to find her waiting for me out front.

She lived in a third-floor walk-up. We took the steps at a glacial pace.

I said, "That was for show, back there?"

"I meant every word. I'm not doing this for you."

"That's fine."

"I'm glad it's fine," she said.

I sighed. Two more flights to go.

The place was in many respects a twin to her office, albeit a couple degrees more intense. Tapestries bedecked the walls, interspersed with left-wing iconography. Hard to miss the poster that read SAVE A PIG, EAT A COP.

An ornate oaken hutch huddled in the corner. With its curlicues and scrolls, it looked out of place and vaguely ashamed, like a waiter at an orgy. Glassware and crockery occupied half the cabinetry; the other half had been given over to books.

On the table, dinner for one, rice and beans, rusting over.

"Must be nice," I said, "being able to walk to work."

"Sit down," she said, waving at a spavined sofa and heading for the bedroom.

I limped to the hutch. More books lined its counter, wrinkled paperbacks on gender theory, paperback erotic fiction, some newer-looking fantasy novels.

Greer Unger came back clutching a grungy hiking backpack in both arms. She stopped and shot me an icy look.

"Sorry," I said. "I'm always interested in what people read."

She left the backpack against the arm of the sofa and took a seat at the dining table, mashing at the food in an attempt to revive her appetite.

I eased onto the sofa, put on gloves, and tugged open the backpack.

Topmost was a quarter-full packet of white faux feathers, identical to those Jasmine had used to make her angel's wings.

Greer Unger said, "I had a friend build the frame."

"I saw the video. Pretty amazing."

A tiny smile. Fondness at the memory. Or contempt for me.

I asked Greer if she'd been at the party.

She shook her head. "I was getting over a cold."

Setting the feathers on the floor, I began excavating the backpack, a layer at a time. Socks. Padded bras. Panties, rolled into candles; compression shorts.

"I wasn't lying," Greer said. "I don't know the first thing about her family. She made a clean break."

I nodded.

"Who'd you speak to," she said.

"Sorry?"

"You said you figured out where she's from."

"Didi Flynn told me."

"Ah."

"You know her."

"I do."

She didn't seem inclined to elaborate. In our phone conversation, Didi had denied knowing Greer. I'd interpreted that as an attempt to run interference, but now I wondered if other emotions were in play—rivalry, for instance.

"How long was Jasmine staying with you?" I asked.

"Just a few weeks. The guy she was living with kicked her out." She took in a forkful. "Par for the course."

"You think he'd be able to help me find her parents?"

"I seriously doubt it."

"You know his name?"

"Adam? Aaron? Something like that. I think he's a truck driver, or a bus driver. He was abusive. Jasmine told me he once pointed a shotgun at her."

I recalled Greer's immediate reaction to the news of Jasmine's death.

Was she killed?

"So, yeah," Greer said. "I don't think she was bringing him home for Thanksgiving."

I'd emptied most of the bag to reach the lowest stratum. Money. Bottle of prescription painkillers. Widening the drawstring mouth, I peered inside.

Not a totally clean break.

Pressed flat against the nylon sidewall was a sandwich bag containing snapshots.

I took out the bag and held it up.

Greer reacted with surprise, putting down her fork and coming over.

Jasmine, circa twelve, in a red satin ball gown and a golden wig. She hadn't yet perfected her feminine self: nascent puberty had given her a fleecy mustache, and her chest was sunken. She laughed, waving a wand in the direction of the camera. Indoor shot, blast of flash. I studied the background for distinguishing details. Nothing.

Next: a photo booth strip, snipped in half, leaving two frames of Jasmine and a young girl. Mid-teens. Jasmine had begun to shave. She had begun to grow her hair out. She had discovered eyeliner. They both had. They made kissy faces. No way to identify the second girl.

Next: Jasmine, not as Jasmine, but as Kevin. Boxy jeans. Shapeless T-shirt. No makeup. Aside from the long hair, she read as masculine. Actually, context rendered the long hair masculine, too—bringing out bone structure, calling attention to the breadth of the shoulders.

Beside him, three or four years older, a young man in a khaki Marine Corps service uniform.

They stood close together, grinning.

Brothers.

At one point, at least, they loved each other.

And now?

They made her life hell.

I asked Greer if she knew either the girl from the photo strip or the Marine.

She shook her head.

"Did he mention having a brother?"

"No. *She* didn't."

I didn't bother to correct myself. She was never going to like me.

I unfolded the last item in the sandwich bag, a piece of high-gloss paper, ragged at one edge. A yearbook page, decorated with inside jokes, wishes for a good summer, appeals to keep in touch. To Kevin Gomez's senior portrait someone—perhaps Kevin himself—had added gigantic breasts in purple ink.

Of greater interest to me were the names of his classmates.

Data points.

I repacked the bag. When I stood up to heft it, I nearly tipped over.

"God," Greer said. She'd grabbed my sleeve instinctively. Now she withdrew, as if she had touched something unclean and could still feel its webby residue. "Give it here."

She threw the bag on her back and we left the apartment.

On the landing I paused to adjust my crutch. "I appreciate the help."

She said, "Would you really have gotten a court order?"

"I don't know. Would you really have called the cops?"

Greer Unger burst into laughter.

CHAPTER 17

Tuesday, January 8

5:58 a.m.

A silver BMW coupe slowed outside my building, and I stepped from the lobby into a chill, clinging mist. Delilah Nwodo leaned to push wide the passenger door. "You okay?"

"All good." I pressed on the little bar to urge the seat back; it complied unhurriedly, with a smug hum. Unzipping my fleece, I slotted the crutch in the backseat and stretched out on the heated leather.

In the cup holders were two gas-station coffees. "Bless you," I said.

The car glided north along 580, the radio murmuring Top 40. A viscid gray dawn climbed over the hills. On the San Rafael Bridge, the wet air ripened into rain, and we reached the Marin Peninsula under a full-blown downpour. The blocks of San Quentin Prison squatted between damp humps of dun and mustard, a square jaw confronting the Bay. I'd never been inside. Not for work. Luke had served his time down south.

Nwodo noticed me staring. "Million-dollar view," she said.

"Rent-controlled," I said.

"All your friends live nearby."

"I smell an opportunity."

"Somebody call Zillow," she said.

Two routes took us where we needed to go, up through Petaluma, or out toward Point Reyes. Nwodo opted for the latter, and we pushed coastward through a briny slime.

Bay Area folk are jealous of their territory, the rich buffet of color and texture packed into its confines. Today gave few reasons to brag. A dank duochrome prevailed, matte silver and green-black, curled fog strangling the pines. Nwodo seemed to enjoy driving. Her smooth hands worked the wheel with ease, taking one hairpin after another, under the sporadic flare of opposing headlights: commuters, sleep-addled, bound for San Francisco. We startled them; they weren't used to anyone coming their way; they jerked their wheels, ducking the center stripe.

Before we retreated inland, I caught, through two blades of stone, the briefest glimpse of the ocean. Kamikaze whitecaps, jagged gray shelves in languid collision, warfare incessant and soundless through the glass, until the abrupt contours of the land drew a curtain.

Misnamed, the Pacific.

I pressed myself down into the seat, rubbing the humid, pebbled leather, seeking the substrate beneath me. Even as we plunged into the valley, a green, corrugated womb, I could feel the sea shouting behind us, drunk, dissatisfied, swinging its fists and demanding a sacrifice. In my nostrils lingered a primal stink, of iodine, and blood; of life forever putrefying, waking only to die again.

Approaching the northern edge of the county, where Marin bled into Sonoma, the road cast off a spur, then another, contracting to a pitted fire route that dropped between slabs of bedrock and moss. Signs of civilization grew fewer and farther between; redwoods rose up like a broken bower. GPS showed the campus as a scarlet balloon drifting over a lake of pale green, until the system gave up on us at last, its computerized voice falling silent as though chastened.

A weatherworn sign appeared on the shoulder.

The Watermark School

2.2 miles

Nwodo eased off the asphalt and into the trees.

The car bounced over stones and furrows, through mud and puddles, slewing in melting vehicle tracks. The rain had stopped. Scant light penetrated the upper canopy, only to tangle in Spanish moss.

A landscape of negative space, wraithed and unfathomable. Nostalgic appeal for Buntley, the Englishman? Any minute now I expected a swarm of giggling wood nymphs to dart out, bewitching us, sowing mischief, grafting animal heads onto our bodies.

I cracked my window, taking in the mingled scent of leaf rot and living pine. I thought I could still smell the sea, too, and its indelible violence.

"*Shit.*"

My heel slammed into the footwell; pain flared up my leg. Nwodo had stomped the brake and was hunched over the steering wheel, wheezing through parted lips.

In the middle of the road was a young girl.

Ten years old, towheaded and bony, she crouched down, the hem of her white nightgown slopping in the muck. Only the poor driving conditions and color of the fabric had saved her from being struck. As it was, not more than three or four yards separated the BMW's bumper from her frail, folded body.

Whatever she had been doing—examining an insect, scrawling with a stick—she stopped now and gazed back at us with a lacerating directness. She stood, opening her arms, as if to claim ownership of the world. Light shone through the thin gown. Naked beneath.

She turned and fled barefoot into the glare.

My heart was racing, my knee aflame. Through the open window I could hear the tick and drip of the forest. "Jesus."

Muttering, Nwodo released the brake.

We rolled forward.

A gap opened in the trees, delivering us into a muddy turnabout, beyond which sprawled the trough of the valley, clear-cut and open to the sky. Strewn along its length was a series of short clapboard structures. Their colors had faded to varying degrees under the cyclical beating of sun and moisture. Most had been outfitted with rooftop solar panels; one sprouted a satellite dish. Blocky wooden signposts indicated the way to the music room, sport court, kitchen, dining room, garden—destinations accessible via wending paths of mismatched brick and stone.

We parked the car and got out amid a cottony stillness.

The girl in the nightgown had vanished.

No signs of any children.

Of anyone.

Nwodo said, "They're not back from break yet?"

A rebuke. *You dragged me out here for what?*

Tire marks crisscrossed the clearing. Students recently dropped off. "The answering machine said yesterday."

A flash of blond caught our eyes.

Nwodo and I followed.

The girl stayed just ahead of us, a suggestion of movement, a trail of muddy footprints on the pavers. Past the dormitories; past the kiln.

Not much thought had been given to master planning. The layout felt alternately claustrophobic and yawning, weeds surging unchecked to exploit the vacuum. I humped along, perspiring inside my fleece, fingers grazing the ax-bitten surface of a chopping block as we sidestepped a listing eight-foot stack of firewood, carelessly tarped.

Before us lay a long, low structure with a curved top: a Quonset hut, painted zinc white and hugging the ground, like some enormous surfacing earthworm.

Above the entrance hung a sheet metal sign with raised lettering.

MEETING HALL

The footprints ended at the double doors.

From inside came a woman's voice.

Nwodo went ahead. I hurried after.

The interior of the hut was a single open space, fifty feet wide and twice as long, dazzlingly lit by hundred-watt bulbs that drooped from the ceiling on thick, black cables. What appeared to be the entire student body was present, sitting on benches or beanbag chairs or lolling on the floor in nests of pillows. Heads draped in laps. A stew of shoelaces and denim coagulated around a central dais made of unvarnished pine.

There couldn't have been more than a hundred of them. But I felt like I'd run up against a billion-headed beast. And silent, so silent, an underwater pressure that threatened to stave in my eardrums.

You'd think it was impossible for that many children to keep that quiet, especially given that the ceiling was a giant acoustic reflector.

A very few faces turned toward us, bored or curious. But most of them remained focused on the speaker.

Not a woman; a prepubescent boy. Elevenish, bespectacled, with unruly black hair. He paced the dais, fingers woven behind his back, holding forth in a piercing voice.

"It isn't fair," he said. "Why should the rest of us have to suffer just cause she read some retarded book? If she—"

"It's not a *book*."

The interruption came courtesy of a toothy girl the same age, slouched on a stool at the edge of the dais like a boxer between rounds.

"It's a *study*," she said, sitting up, "in a *scientific journal*."

Completing the triangle was a second girl, presiding at a lectern. She clapped a gavel, her ponytail swinging.

"The chair reminds you that you had your turn," she said, fixing the toothy girl with an admonishing eye. "Thomas has the floor."

The toothy girl sulked.

"You may continue," the chair said to the boy. "But please don't use the word *retarded* or the chair will be forced to take away your time."

A snicker arose, was instantly and sternly quashed.

"Three minutes," the chair said.

Thomas said, "As I was saying . . ."

At issue was a proposed ban of white sugar in the school kitchen, based on a study in a nutrition journal. Thomas opposed it. He had yet to get to his reasons before Nwodo nudged me.

Across the room, the girl in the nightgown was whispering into the ear of a woman with dark-red hair who sat on a beige papasan, balancing a child on each knee.

The principal, Camille Buntley.

Her gaze trained on Nwodo and me. It was then that I realized that she wasn't the only adult present. There were others, five or six in total, mixed in among the younger bodies and faces. I'd failed to notice them because they were so vastly outnumbered, like pennies packed in a barrel of sand.

Except for Camille, they appeared quite young themselves, snuggled up against their smaller neighbors. A woman with close-cropped hair lay on her stomach, kicking bare feet behind her, wiggling her toes. A man in a purple down vest and rimless glasses sat knees-to-chest, occupying less space than his natural bulk demanded.

I saw them now because it was they, the adults, who'd taken notice of us, while the kids stayed riveted to the scene playing out onstage.

Camille freed herself and headed toward us, keeping close to the wall.

An iPhone alarm sounded.

Ponytail Chairperson rapped the lectern solemnly. "Time."

Kids clapped, a group of boys Thomas's age providing most of the enthusiasm.

He bowed, exited the dais, and hopped onto an open stool.

"The chair requests a motion to bring the question to a vote."

"Motion" came a voice.

"Seconded" came another.

"The motion carries. We will now proceed to a vote. All in favor."

Arms swayed.

The teachers rose to assist with the tally.

"Please keep your hand up till you've been counted," the chair said.

Camille drew near, finger to her lips.

We stepped outside.

I heard *all opposed* and then the doors swung shut.

THE AIR WAS newly brittle, summoning a twinge in my knee. Camille Buntley faced us with a searching smile. She wore green corduroy pants, a Fair Isle sweater, hiking boots caked with dried mud.

She said, "You must be lost."

Nwodo frowned.

I said, "Ms. Buntley?"

"I'm Camille, yes. You are?"

Nwodo said, "Police," and produced her ID.

Camille scanned it, then mine. The sudden appearance of law enforcement sets most people on edge, but she returned the cards to us and gave a placid nod.

She said, "This way, please."

Her office was on the south side of the campus, in a clapboard structure slightly larger than the others. She beckoned us through a dim foyer, the floorboards moist and soft underfoot, into an overwarm room that stank of pine resin.

There was a Navajo rug, askew, and a porcelain pedestal sink. Furniture comprised a motley assortment of spindly tables and flabby armchairs backed against tongue-and-groove paneling, painted brown. Loose paper covered a small writing desk—placed not centrally, as you'd expect, but off to one side.

No barriers here. Open communication. Everyone an equal.

Beside a snuffling potbelly stove hung the portrait of C. E. Buntley that appeared on the website: the Man Himself, tweeds, pipe, teeth. Here the photograph looked old and oddly shrunken, rippling behind smudged glass.

Nwodo said, "You might want to know that one of your students was playing in the middle of the road."

"Which student?"

"The one who came to give you a heads-up."

"Althea." As if the name cleared up any confusion, made everything okay.

"I almost hit her with my car."

Camille knocked her boots against the stove, molting brown flakes.

"It was very close," Nwodo said.

Camille motioned for us to sit.

I pulled a chair up to the desk. Nwodo remained standing a moment before doing the same, her shoulders aggressively cantilevered over her knees. Beneath her outward calm, she was wrestling with the urge to grab Camille Buntley by the ears and wring sense into her idiot head.

I found the principal's nonchalance no less bizarre. We'd come within feet of killing one of her charges.

The pages on the desktop were bills—septic, water—several of them stamped PAST DUE. Invoice from a company called We-B-Klean, with a logo that looked like a cross between a vacuum cleaner and a Formula One car. Mold in Eden? Seeing me staring, Camille swept the paper into a stack and slipped it in the drawer, taking her seat and folding complacent hands on the desktop.

"She wasn't dressed for the weather, either," Nwodo said. "Althea."

Camille Buntley tilted her head. "She looked dressed to me."

"It's fifty degrees outside."

"I'm sure if she felt cold, she would put on more clothes."

"She was playing," Nwodo said, "in the *road.*"

Camille Buntley smiled patiently. "I understand why you'd think of it like that."

"How do you think of it."

"You were driving in her play space," Camille Buntley said. "One could just as easily describe it that way, yes?"

She spoke with a light shimmery accent, delicate ornamentations atop the *r*'s and *l*'s. According to the website, she'd been a student at Watermark, then a teacher, before taking over after her father's death. Her preternatural ease made me wonder how often she stepped foot outside the valley.

"Come to think," she said, "that might be a *more* accurate description. This is her home. She has every right to be here, or there, or wherever she wants to be. You, on the other hand, are a visitor. I'm not sure what entitles you to dictate where she plays."

Before Nwodo could respond, I said, "We were surprised, is all. To us it looked pretty dangerous."

"Children are less fragile, and more capable, than people give them credit for."

Nwodo's lips pursed. Then she nodded. *Fine, be a fucking imbecile.*

I put the list of credit cards on the desk. "Are you familiar with these people?"

"May I ask why you'd like to know?"

"Routine inquiry."

"I'm sorry, but you'll have to try harder than that."

Our game plan, worked out over the course of the drive, was to proceed obliquely, avoid accusations. Already it felt too late for that.

I said, "These are individuals who've recently had their personal information compromised. The connection between them, we believe, is that they went to school here. We were hoping you could help us confirm."

Camille Buntley still hadn't touched the page. "Personal information."

"Birthdays. Social Security numbers. Things of that nature."

"You keep student records," Nwodo said.

"Of course," Camille said.

"How far back do they go?"

"I couldn't say. It's not as though I sit around reading them for fun. A fair ways, I imagine."

"Who has access?"

"Access?"

"Do you keep them on computer," Nwodo asked, "or on paper?"

"There's a room," Camille said.

"Who has the key?"

"No one. It's not locked."

"Anyone can walk in and take a file?"

"In theory, I suppose. No one would. It's against the rules. You find that hard to believe."

"I think you have a remarkable amount of faith in your students," Nwodo said.

"I do, indeed."

I said, "Be that as it may, someone did take the information."

"And you know this because . . ."

"It was used to open fraudulent credit cards," Nwodo said.

"I see. And you're assuming that the perpetrator is a member of our community."

"Not necessarily," I said. "It could be an outsider."

Camille said, "We don't get many of those."

She was helping our case, without intending to. Nwodo smiled. The smile all detectives get when a corner is turned.

Camille Buntley said, "If you suspect one of the children, you could try asking them directly. In my experience that's the fastest way to find out the answer to a question. I don't see what a bunch of papers is going to tell you."

I glanced at Nwodo, who gave a little shrug.

New game plan. Kick it up.

She placed a printed photo of Jane Doe atop the list.

"This is the individual we believe took the information," she said.

Blank, stony, Camille Buntley sat; but I could sense a seismic shift taking place.

The earth sliding away beneath her, the world howling on its axis.

Comprehension, spreading through her like an ink stain.

Who we were and why we had come here.

Why the young woman in the photograph had cheeks the color of fish belly.

I also understood. I saw, now, subtle commonalities of facial structure between the two women, each a distortion of the other.

What we'd done, throwing down the picture, had been a strike of brutal efficiency.

Camille Buntley emitted a short, mechanical rasp, gears grinding before finding their mesh.

With savage energy she leapt up and bounded to the sink, snatching an oxidized copper kettle from the floor. Twisting open the tap, she gazed at the kettle intently as it filled; changing her mind, she tipped it violently down the drain, droplets spattering the wall, her sleeves, glistening on her shirtfront like birdshot.

She set the kettle in the sink with a ping and fell into her chair, gripping the photograph so hard that tremors streaked through the paper. Beneath her eyes shone watery red crescents; a mad, pinched smile seized her mouth.

"Ms. Buntley," I said. "May I?"

Camille balked, then released the photo to me.

She turned to stare at the list of names, regarding it as one would an enemy.

"Well," she said, "but it's ridiculous. I mean, it's absurd. Winnie couldn't possibly know any of these people. They're well before her time."

"Winnie," I said.

"Do you understand?" Her plummy voice had gone shrill. "It's absurd. So you can just take that nonsense and get rid of it now, right now."

I put the list in my pocket.

A raucous thrum had arisen outside the building.

Squeals, pleas, childish laughter.

Life, resumed.

"Pretty name," I said. "Winnie."

Camille bowed her head.

I said, "Is it short for something?"

"Wynemah."

"I don't think I've ever heard that before."

"It's Miwok," Camille said. "'Female chief.' They were the indigenous tribe around here. Did you know that?"

She sounded hungry for a chance to teach.

I shook my head.

"They still are," Camille said. "We had a school tradition, we used to build a bark shelter. We haven't done that in a while. I forget why we stopped. Anyway. It felt appropriate, because of that, and we liked the way it sounded. Of course it gave her fits when she was little, because she had trouble with her *w*'s. For the longest time she couldn't pronounce it."

She laughed. "Imagine that? She's running around with her hands in the air, yelling *Vinnie*, like I've given birth to an Italian grocer, and all the while I have to sit there, watching her and wondering to myself, *My God, what have I done.*"

CHAPTER 18

amille Buntley's reaction to learning that her daughter had been murdered was no more or less coherent than any of the reactions I've encountered over the years.

She was fine, thank you.

She didn't need a moment. Would a moment change anything? Go ahead and ask your questions.

Not Buntley; Winnie Ozawa.

For her father, Mickey Ozawa. An artist in batik and linocut prints.

May 5, 1997. A hundred yards away, in fact, in the infirmary.

Mickey? Gone. He died when Winnie was eight.

Beyond that, there wasn't much Camille could provide. No idea as to Winnie's current address. No knowledge if Winnie was ever married. Though she considered it unlikely. Always a free spirit.

She couldn't attest to her daughter's recent mental or physical health.

"We haven't seen each other for close to two years."

I explained the procedure for releasing Winnie's body.

I provided my contact information.

And with that, my job was pretty much done.

I had identified the decedent.

I had notified the next of kin.

I turned to Nwodo.

Her demeanor had softened, now that she realized she was dealing not with a petty bureaucrat but a bereft mother.

She said, "Ms. Buntley, first off allow me to say I'm sorry for your loss. I will do everything in my power to find the person who did this."

Camille tugged at the neckline of her sweater.

"Let's back up," Nwodo said. "You said you last saw Winnie two years ago."

"More like eighteen months. Around her birthday."

"And at that time, where was she living?"

"I don't know."

"Was she local?"

"Did I not just tell you? I don't know."

"What if we go back a little further? What was the last point you did have knowledge of her address?"

Small shake of the head. Not resistance so much as reluctance to admit more ignorance.

Nwodo said, "I'm trying to get a sense of the time line, understand what Winnie was doing, who she might have associated with." A beat. "To establish a context."

Camille Buntley tugged at her sweater.

She said, "I can't stand it in here."

She stood up. "I'm going for a walk."

WE EMERGED INTO a landscape transformed: children, far and wide, galloping through the underbrush, conspiring by a culvert, at work or play, in groups or alone, filling the valley with a vivid vibration. The frenzy made a startling counterpoint to the hush of the meeting hall, as if a valve had been opened, pent-up energy whooshing out.

We followed Camille Buntley.

She maintained a brisk clip, bounding from paver to paver, automatically avoiding the wobbly ones. Through an open door, I spied a small, undistinguished classroom, a sueded chalkboard and sloppy bookcases. A group of middle schoolers occupied a circular table, engaging in an animated discussion. Observing them from a respectful distance was the teacher with the rimless glasses. He leaned against the wall, legs kicked out and ankles crossed, finger-combing his beard, content not to interfere. On the board was written ROMANTIC ERA and JOHN KEATS 1795–1821. That was as much as I caught before we moved on.

Those kids were among the few who had chosen the indoors. Most everyone else was busy running or playing or building or destroying. It was a spectacular amount of activity, very little of which conformed to what most people would call school.

I'd read the website, knew the Watermark philosophy, but words failed to capture the sweating, panting reality. An adolescent girl knelt on a stump, reading to a gaggle of six-year-olds who kept interrupting her to rewrite the story. Thomas the orator led his pals in the vivisection of a bicycle.

In the garden, an irregularly shaped bed enclosed by chicken wire, two teenage girls, one thin, one obese, leaned on their shovels. The tops of winter vegetables shot from the soil: neon streaks of chard, cabbages mustering like a line of tiny green tanks.

Camille Buntley strode along, waving, bellowing encouragement, indifferent to whether we were keeping up. A small boy ran up to throw his arms around her knees. She tousled his hair, gently pried him loose, and sent him on his way with a pat on the bottom.

At a building marked WOODSHOP she paused to catch her

breath. We'd reached the outermost limit of the cleared area. The path had ended. Beyond it, forest gloom.

Camille plunged across the tree line.

I heaved after her, swinging my crutch like a scythe.

Her pace never slackened as she pressed on, throwing her bandy legs over fallen logs, batting aside licorice ferns that spewed from cracks in swollen bedrock. Amid the somber palette, spectral flashes: bone-white trilliums, like shrouds hung out to dry; slimed fungus caps with their noxious green-gray taunt.

Mud sucked at my feet. I was beginning to lag.

Nwodo glanced back.

I waved her on.

Soon I'd lost sight of them both.

My father teaches science and math, and when I was growing up he would periodically remember his own sons, raised in the suburbs, weaned on video games. With a guilty pang he'd shove us into the Subaru and drive us to some outlying regional park for a forced march in nature. I suppose I ought to be grateful. We hated it. We bitched and moaned while he quizzed us on the flowers and the birds.

Crashing through a thicket of California buckthorn, I had an uncomfortable and familiar thought: left to my own devices, I'd die out here.

I caught up to the two of them at the base of a towering redwood that forked as it rose, forming a massive, shaggy candelabra.

To my eye, nothing about the spot merited a filthy, half-mile pilgrimage. Within a hundred yards stood three dozen equally impressive trees.

Yet it was clear that in Camille's mind, we'd arrived. The air around her had settled palpably. I could no longer hear the man-made tumult of the students. In its place was a cryptic murmur, hidden things feasting and growing, biding their time.

I leaned on my crutch, the ground spongy beneath.

Camille knelt, scooped up bark, sifted it through her fingers. "She was never really mine, of course. I know that."

A flat tune she was singing—all business.

Nwodo looked to me. Was this normal?

I shrugged. No such thing.

"She told me she had to leave," Camille said, "or else she'd end up like me. I don't think she meant to be quite so harsh. Still. It hurt."

Nwodo said, "Like you how?"

"Here." Camille tilted her head back, raising palms to the canopy. "Stuck."

It occurred to me that she had chosen this spot precisely for its anonymity.

"That's how you see yourself," I said.

"Me? No. Never. I was happy to take over. I had years to get used to the idea. My father was sick for a long time, and senile toward the end. For all intents and purposes, I was running the place. It was only natural for Winnie to assume I expected the same from her."

"Did you?"

Camille shook her head. "I would never. For one thing, she showed no interest in teaching. No aptitude for it, either. To steer her into a role against her will, one that's contrary to her nature, contradicts everything we believe. I wouldn't do it to any other child, and I wouldn't do it to her. I tried to tell her that. What else could she have thought, though? She cast her first Town Hall vote at two. I kept telling her: *You're free.* I said it because I believed it. I do believe it. She must've resented hearing it, over and over, when she'd never left what she perceived as my domain."

Nwodo said, "How old was she when she left?"

"Fifteen. Almost sixteen."

"Where'd she go?"

"I couldn't keep track of her. She went where she pleased, and if I got an update, it was long after the fact. South America, I think. Japan. She wanted to see where her father was born. Niigata Prefecture. They farm beautiful fish, there. I got a postcard, once. *Greetings from Niagara Falls.* That was her, being funny. Otherwise I had to wait for her to decide to show up, which she did, every so often. She'd pop in unannounced, stay for a couple of weeks, then disappear."

"Did you help her out financially?"

"My father left her a small inheritance, but for the most part she managed on her own. She hitchhiked. She's quite resourceful."

Enough to steal credit cards.

"When she visited, a year and a half ago," I said. "Is it possible she took information from the files then?"

Camille blinked. "I suppose she must have."

"What about her friends?" Nwodo said. "Who are they?"

"I couldn't begin to tell you."

"People from school she kept in touch with?"

"She chucked everyone when she left. Besides, that's not how it works around here. There isn't the same social dynamic as in a conventional setting. So-called peer groups," Camille said, waving an airy hand. "Cliques determined by age or gender or what have you. It's fluid. Winnie was accustomed to new faces coming and going all the time. Ever since she was born that was her experience. I imagine it was easy for her to let them go."

Nwodo said, "Ms. Buntley, I have to ask if you know of anyone who might want to harm Winnie."

Camille toed the dirt restively. "You have a list of people she stole from. Why don't you start with them?"

"We're looking into it," Nwodo said. "If you can think of anything that might help us be more directed, though."

No response. Protecting herself, maybe. Blocking out guilt for not knowing her own daughter well enough to provide a lead.

When it comes to grief, normal is a moving target.

Wind thrashed the canopy, wringing out a false rain shower, frigid droplets pricking the back of my neck and lacing down my spine.

Camille Buntley said, "Please tell me she didn't suffer."

I said, "No."

A lie, or not, depending on how you wanted to hear it.

No, *she didn't.*

No, *I can't tell you that.*

She smiled unevenly, wrapped her arms around her waist, parsing the spaces between the trees. Seeing something, someone, that we could not.

A young girl with dirty feet, unruly and incorrigible, naked beneath her gown.

CHAPTER 19

On our way back from the woods Camille left us by the moldering tin-roof shed where the school stored its records. She told us she'd be in her office and walked away.

As promised, the door was unlocked.

A thousand or so manila folders filled three rust-eaten file cabinets. Nwodo and I squeezed in alongside stockpiles of nonperishables: canned tuna in shrink-wrapped stacks, cartons of UHT milk, dried kidney beans in sealed five-gallon buckets. In the event of a nuclear holocaust, the children of Watermark would inherit the earth.

The files dated back to the fifties, obeying a very rough alphabetical order. Compared with a typical school record, the contents were thin. There were no report cards; no grades of any kind. No disciplinary histories. No letters of recommendation or citations for achievement. A standardized form, typewritten on onion paper, noted DOB, parents' home address, Social Security number. A second form detailed medical history and allergies; for recent enrollees, this was more often than not accompanied by a doctor's note exempting the bearer from vaccination. About three-quarters of the folders contained a photograph of the child stapled to the inside left corner. The rest did not.

Whatever the school's strengths as a steward of the future, it did not appear overly concerned with preserving its past.

It took us an hour to dig up info on the women whose identities Winnie Ozawa had stolen, a perfect sixteen for sixteen. She'd put some thought into choosing her marks. All were at present between forty-five and fifty-five—numerically, the largest slice of the general population, and among its most creditworthy. All had spent fewer than three years at Watermark, lowering the risk that they would still be in touch with one another.

I laid out the pages atop the tuna cans and took pictures. It felt right to advise the women of the potential damage to their credit. When it came to their value as suspects, however, I felt less convinced. Neither Leah Horvuth nor Cathie Myers had any clue what was happening, and a stolen credit card seemed like insufficient motive for murder.

Nwodo agreed. "I doubt she knew any of them personally."

Early fifties was Camille's age.

Winnie taking a shot at her mother, unconsciously?

"Maybe," Nwodo said. "What kind of parent stands by while their kid runs off at fifteen and does nothing?"

"She didn't say she did nothing."

"Didn't say she did *some*thing, either. We're talking about a minor flying to Japan. At minimum Camille's getting her a passport. That's some seriously enabling shit."

"Could be her father got it for her."

The photograph in Winnie's file showed her circa thirteen, a scimitar of hair obscuring one eye, smirking like she had a juicy secret.

"That bit about no peer groups?" Nwodo said. "What teenager doesn't have a best friend?"

I set the folder down. "She's twenty-one at time of death. Say Camille's right. Everyone plays with everyone, so plus or minus a few years. That's your potential social circle. What we should be doing is going through the files and writing down the name of anyone under twenty-five."

Nwodo smiled. "I thought they were joking about you."

"Who was?"

She just shook her head.

"Hold up," I said. "Who was joking."

"I read the article," she said.

By "the article" she meant a feature story in the *East Bay Times*, published last year, about an old murder I'd helped solve. The writer had repeatedly solicited me for comment, which I declined to provide: I was under orders not to talk to the press. Strictly speaking, the case wasn't mine; it was considered closed before I forced it back open. That we'd helped exonerate an innocent man was irrelevant. To Sergeant Vitti, I'd disregarded regs and engaged in grandstanding.

I said to Nwodo, "Totally different thing."

"All right."

"For real. It was a unique set of circumstances."

"What's happening with the guy, anyway? Whatsit? Triple-something."

"Julian Triplett," I said. "Application for pardon went in. His lawyers are hoping the governor will want it off his desk fast because of the media. You didn't answer my question. Who was joking?"

"I might've done some research on you."

"Did you now."

"Talked to a friend at Berkeley PD."

"Aha."

"It's my case you're on," she said. "I have to know who I'm

dealing with. All I've heard, you're this guy who comes in and messes around with other people's work."

Once she said that, a number of things clicked into place. She hadn't recognized my name from my basketball days. She recognized it from the rumor mill. I understood her initial reluctance to collaborate, as well as the reversal: she wanted to keep me close, in case I decided to get creative.

I started laughing.

Nwodo broke into a wide grin. "You wanted honesty."

"I guess it didn't help when I asked to tag along at the hospital," I said.

"That was a rude-ass move."

"I apologize. Who was it at Berkeley, though? It was Schickman, right?"

"His partner. Guy I know who used to be at OPD."

"What's his name? Do I know him?"

"Billy Watts."

"I don't even know this guy and he's slandering me?"

"Truth be told he got rather poetic on the subject. 'What's the deal with this guy? I need to watch out or what?' Watts, he goes"— she squeezed her hands in death grips—"'He's like a giant fucking *barnacle*.'"

"That is . . . Wow."

"I think he meant it as a compliment."

"Oh, absolutely," I said.

"Hey, I'm sitting here with you, am I not?"

"What changed your mind?"

She began collecting folders, butting them into line. "Who said I changed my mind?"

CAMILLE'S OFFICE WAS deserted. Nwodo took out a card to write her a note.

"Excuse me."

The young teacher with the rimless glasses hovered in the doorway.

"We're leaving," I said. "We wanted to say goodbye to Ms. Buntley."

"She went into town," the teacher said. "She needed to pick up a few things."

Nwodo said, "Any idea how long she'll be?"

He combed at his chin. The beard was a dense tobacco brown, rising to mid-cheek and stopping in a neat line. Upper cheeks smooth. Like someone had stuck a gag beard on a baby. "It's thirty minutes, each way. Usually she's quick, but." He paused. "Is something going on? She looked upset."

"We can't discuss that," Nwodo said.

"Sure. Of course. Didn't mean to pry."

Nwodo placed the card in the center of the desk. "When you speak to her, please let her know we were here and that we left."

"I will."

"Thank you, Mister . . ."

"Zach. Bierce."

"Thank you, Mr. Bierce."

I said, "Any relation to Ambrose?"

He smiled. Heard that before and liked it. "Cousin."

"No kidding."

"Distant. Like, nine times removed."

"Do you teach him to your students?"

He shrugged. "I teach what they want to learn."

"How's that working out?" Nwodo asked.

Bierce took her question in stride. "Ahh, it's not so bad. They're good kids. They mean well. If you can get them to sit still for fifteen minutes, that's a win."

"Pretty different from other schools," I said.

"I don't have a point of comparison," he said. Another shrug. "It's my first time teaching. I only started last year."

Nwodo said, "You'll give Camille the message."

"You got it."

We exited. Bierce shut the office door behind.

BEFORE GETTING INTO the BMW we scraped the mud from our shoes. Nwodo threw the car into reverse. With a glance at the backup camera, she made as if to gun it. Then, reconsidering, she twisted around, going at a snail's pace, mindful of the presence of children at play.

As we jounced along the muddy track, I stared into the trees, searching for the girl in the nightgown. I thought I caught a glimpse of her, a shimmering wisp of white, but I might have been mistaken.

WE STOPPED AT a San Rafael diner for hamburgers and coffee. Our table afforded an expansive view of the harbor, bristling masts and moody waters like ruffled silk. Gulls, arrogant and rancorous, strutted along the pier, brawling over potato chip fragments before taking to the sky, specks shed by the sky itself.

Nwodo said, "The thing with Jankowski."

I looked at her.

"You asked what changed my mind," she said. "That's what did it. You didn't go banging on the table for credit."

"Too much paperwork."

She snorted benignly. "Whatever. It's not like I got folks lining up to help me. I'll take what I can get."

Understaffed, underfunded, underappreciated: the cop's lament. Behind it, though, I sensed a deeper loneliness. I knew what it was like to live with victims—to have them take up residence in your head, nameless, insistent; to carry on a conversation no one else can hear. Not your spouse or your friends. Not your colleagues, who are themselves immersed in their own private conversations. I knew how much it meant to be able to off-load that weight, even a little.

"My day off," I said. "It's either this or clean the bathroom."

She smiled. "I tracked them down, by the way. The film crew from the rally."

The young cameraman; the older director limping behind. I'd almost forgotten about them. "No way. And? What's the deal?"

"Three guesses."

"Do I stand a chance?"

"None," Nwodo said. "Okay. Night of the party, you remember there was a guy got shot in the leg?"

"Schumacher."

Nwodo whistled. "Go for bonus points?"

". . . Oswald. That was *him*?"

"Him and his cameraman," she said. "He's making a documentary."

"About . . . ?" I stared. "Oh come on. Not about the shooting."

She fashioned air quotes. "'It's my story, too.'"

"He got *grazed*. He wasn't even in the hospital overnight."

"'A story that needs to be told.'"

"That is hella tacky."

"You don't know the half," she said. "He tried to get me to do a sit-down."

"On camera?"

"I mean." She laid a dainty hand on her chest. "It's *my* story, too."

"A story that *needs* to be told."

"Not if I want to keep my job," she said. A beat. "Maybe I should take him up."

The waiter came by to refill our coffees. I added milk, stirred. "Your pal, Watts. He transferred from Oakland to Berkeley?"

"They started him over at the bottom," she said. "Nine-year vet, pulling graveyard patrol. Reset his pension, too."

"Damn."

"Mm-hm."

"Why'd he do it, then?"

"He got sick of the bullshit," she said.

"And you're not?"

"Sure I am," she said. "Who isn't? What's my alternative? Abandon it to the wolves? It's my city. I grew up there."

"That's fair."

"Well, no," she said, "the one thing it most definitely is not is *fair*. Since when's that matter?"

"Never."

"Nope. I chose it."

I told her she had more in common with Camille Buntley than she realized.

Her response was to make grabby motions; a sucking sound through her teeth.

Barnacle.

"Careful," I said, wagging my spoon at the harbor. "That shit'll sink a boat."

"My boat," she said.

I said, "Your boat."

CHAPTER 20

Thursday, January 10

6:35 a.m.

I could see the relief spread through Sergeant Turnbow's face when I told her we'd identified Jane Doe.

"And to think," she said, "he did it on crutches."

I took a wonky bow. No sooner had I straightened up, though, than she was reaching for her mouse.

"What about your other decedent? 'Gomez,' " she read. "Where are you on NOK?"

"Couple decent leads."

She nodded gravely, continuing to click and blink and click.

"Sarge? You good?"

"Yeah. Yeah yeah." She paused. "They buried Benjamin Felton yesterday."

"Right." I'd never known her to get emotional, even when it came to the death of a child. "I think I knew that."

"You heard what happened."

"I don't think so."

"Some guy showed up with a camera crew," she said.

She mashed down on the mouse to close the window. "You believe that? They're carrying the coffin—you know what a kid's coffin is like, it's like a toy, like a, a, a *joke*—and this son of a bitch is chasing after the mother, trying to get her to make a statement."

"Schumacher," I said.

"What?"

"That's his name. Oswald Schumacher. He's the guy got grazed in the leg."

"What's that got to do with anything?"

"He's making a documentary," I said.

"About her?"

"About the whole thing."

She squinted at me, baffled. "What?"

"I don't know."

"Why is that a good idea?"

I shook my head. "I don't know what to tell you."

She swung back to her screen. She looked fit to burst. "Just— find me Gomez, please."

I limped to my desk.

JASMINE GOMEZ'S YEARBOOK page supplied the names of nine classmates, one of whom, I determined, had gone on to play midfield for the UC Irvine women's soccer team. Rosters going back to 2001 listed the players' graduating high schools. By extension, Kevin Gomez had graduated from Hamilton High School, in West Los Angeles, class of 2013.

I called up, reaching a frazzled-sounding vice principal. That she didn't remember Kevin was to be expected: enrollment stood at over three thousand.

"I'm trying to contact her parents," I said.

"Her?"

"His," I said. "Sorry. It could be he had an older brother who went there, too. I'm unclear on the first name."

"Gomez, you said?"

"That's right."

"Uh-huh. Well, I can try to look," she said, "but—"

Background clatter ballooned into a loud argument, two cracked male voices trumpeting for dominance, the vice principal shouting *Knock it off.* The receiver banged against a hard surface and the line went dead.

I tried her again, without success.

My next move was to contact LAPD. If I asked nicely enough, they might send an officer by the school. I ran a gauntlet of voicemail, then spoke to four people, each of whom passed me along, until I ended up back at voicemail.

I hung up.

Scrolling through my contacts, I found a number with a 310 area code.

Alex Delaware said, "Hello?"

We'd spoken twice, met once, but his voice was distinctive: alert and at the same time mellow.

"Dr. Delaware, hi. This is Deputy Clay Edison from Alameda County Coroner's, up north. Don't know if you remember me."

"I do," he said. "Nice to hear from you. Actually, I've been meaning to get in touch. I read about what you did with the Julian Triplett case and wanted to congratulate you."

No reason for him, in L.A., to be following our local news, unless he'd made a point of keeping an eye out.

He said, "I couldn't say so then—not my place—but I always felt he'd gotten a raw deal. Well done."

"Appreciate it. Your help meant a lot."

"Sure," he said. "What's up?"

"You have friends at LAPD, right?"

"A few."

I explained my need for boots on the ground.

"Basically," he said, "you're trying to cut through red tape."

"Basically."

"Man after my own heart," he said. "Let me see what I can do."

THAT AFTERNOON I got a call from a patrol officer named Eric Monchen, out of West L.A. Division. He wanted me to understand that his lieutenant, a man named Sturgis, had instructed him to call. Clearly put-upon. But yeah, he'd swing by the high school and see what he could find.

I thanked him and called Delaware to do the same.

"Glad it worked out," he said.

"You must have some powerful friends," I said. "I've never seen cops move so fast."

"It's good for them to run a little, every now and again."

"You don't happen to know anyone down at the Coroner's, do you?"

"Not well enough to produce similar results."

"Worth a shot. There's one other thing I wanted to ask. By any chance have you heard of a place called the Watermark School?"

He said, "It's up by you."

"That's right. In Marin. You know it."

"A little," he said.

"Have you been there?"

"Never. I remember reading about it in a graduate seminar. Case study for the free school movement. Fad of the moment. Nowadays it's Tiger Moms. I didn't realize Watermark was still around."

"I was just there on a notification," I said. "Interesting place."

"How so?"

I described some of what I'd seen: the Town Hall meeting, the kids running wild. "My decedent, her mother's the principal."

"That's too bad." He paused. "Is there something specific you wanted to know?"

I was thinking about the girl in the nightgown, crouched in the mud.

I couldn't get her out of my head.

I said, "I'm not sure."

When he spoke next I heard mischief. "Just good, old-fashioned curiosity."

"It's a bad habit."

"I wouldn't know about that." He laughed. "Take care, Clay."

I FIGURED PATROL Officer Monchen had been shining me on, but lo and behold he called the next day. A trifle friendlier, now that my request had proven not a complete fool's errand.

Kevin F. Gomez, same DOB as our vic, class of 2013.

Parents Philip and Valentina; brother Dylan, class of 2011.

Phone number and an address on South Halm Avenue.

Monchen didn't volunteer to go over there in person. I didn't ask. Not his wheelhouse. Instead I called the Los Angeles County Department of Medical Examiner–Coroner to request they make notification to Valentina and Philip Gomez.

Hung up, pleased with myself. My week to move the needle.

Saturday, January 12

1:41 p.m.

Or not.

The caller identified herself as Sue Carney, L.A. Coroner investigator. In a rapid patter, she told me that she and her partner had paid a courtesy visit to the Gomez family.

"The father answers the door," she said. "I'm like, 'Mr. Philip

Gomez?' 'Yeah.' 'I'm afraid I have some bad news,' et cetera. The whole time he's staring at me like I'm crazy. He goes, 'I don't have a daughter.' "

I could see where this was headed. "Shit."

"I'm checking the address, see if we went to the wrong place. Mendes, she calls back to the office, like, 'Do we have the wrong Gomez?' Cause this is pretty embarrassing for us."

"I bet. Listen—"

"She calls, they tell her, 'No, that's the address he gave us.' *He,* being *you.*"

Carney read the number on South Halm. "That's what they told me. Is that right?"

"It—yeah, but—"

"Good to know *we* didn't screw up," she said, "cause meanwhile the father, he's telling us no such person. So now I'm thinking he's having some sort of denial reaction. Happens, right? 'Why do you keep telling me that, I don't have a daughter, I don't know what you're talking about.' Mendes, nice and calm, asks is your wife home. Hopefully we talk to her and she can help him, you know, *ease* into it. For some reason that pisses him off even worse. He's going apeshit. 'Why won't you leave me alone, blah blah blah, get your ass out of here.' This is not a small dude, okay? This dude is big. Two thirty, two forty. I'm five-one, okay? Mendes—you see her, she's a stick. Neither of us is carrying. I keep a Taser in the car. Six years I've been doing this I've never had to use it. And here's this guy foaming at the mouth like he's gonna step to us. All of a sudden he runs back into the house. I don't know if he's going to get a knife, a bat, a shotgun, whatever. Me and Mendes, we're like, what do we do? We start backing up to our vehicle, and the dude comes tearing out the door with—I don't think I, did I mention he's naked?"

"You did not," I said.

"He's in his underwear. Technically not naked but I saw plenty."

I said, "Can I interrupt you for one second? What did they tell you about the decedent?"

"What do you mean, what did they tell me?"

"Were you aware that the decedent was born male?"

Beat.

"The fuck," she said.

"They didn't tell you."

"No."

I pinched the bridge of my nose. "I'm sorry about this."

"The. *Fuck*. You think it might be, I dunno, *important,* maybe, to *mention* that?"

"I did mention it," I said. "I told whoever took the call."

"Nobody told me shit."

"I told them. I swear."

Sue Carney said, "Whatever. That don't help, cause I got this maniac in his tighty-whiteys screaming his head off. He shoves a picture at me. It's a picture of a young guy. 'That's my son. I have a son. He's not dead.' And I'm like, 'Sir, I am very sorry, but I am going to have to clarify this situation with my department.'"

"What did he look like?" I asked.

"What? Like a red walrus with ass crack. I told you."

"The son," I said. "In the picture. Can you describe him?"

"No, I can't, because I wasn't paying attention." A beat. "He was in a uniform."

"Marine uniform?"

"I don't know," she said angrily. "I'm sorry, all right? I wasn't taking notes. He won't let us leave. He's blocking our car, whaling on the hood. 'Who do you think you are, come here, tell me that, run off, you come back here, chickenshit motherfuckers, get the fuck out of here.' Mendes and me are like, make up your frickin mind. 'I want to speak to your supervisor.' Mendes goes, 'Absolutely, sir.' She gave him the number and we got out of there quick."

"That's where you left it? He's gonna call you?"

Carney had a sailor's bawdy laugh.

"Hell no," she said. "That's what you think? *Hell* no. She didn't give him *our* number. She gave him yours."

CHAPTER 21

I braced myself for a call from a pissed-off Philip Gomez.

It never came, and the next several weeks slid by in relative peace and quiet.

The orthopedist prodded my leg and declared it to be healing nicely.

A van from a Marin mortuary arrived to pick up Winnie Ozawa's body.

The jail emailed me the results of Meredith Klaar's drug panel. It was clean.

The Sunday after Martin Luther King, Jr., Day, five weeks and one day since the events on Almond Street, the transcriptionist returned Winnie Ozawa's autopsy protocol.

Cause of death was confirmed as asphyxia due to manual strangulation.

Her blood work showed traces of methamphetamine and alcohol.

Two DNA profiles had been recovered from the scrapings beneath her nails.

The first profile belonged to Winnie herself.

The second profile was that of an unknown male.

I picked up my phone to call Nwodo. Stopped myself. She didn't need me to tell her about the results. She would've gotten them.

Five weeks and one day. In some ways it felt like far more time had passed; in some ways, far less. A few tasks remained. Starting with contacting the defrauded women. The Watermark name made it easier to keep them on the line. Now Karla-with-a-K Abruzzo was grateful. Jessica Chen, too. As for those who chose to continue to hang up on me, let them reap the consequences the next time they applied for a car loan.

I ran Winnie Ozawa's Social Security number, looking for a residence, a marriage license, a driver's license, arrests.

Nothing.

I wondered if Nwodo'd had any better luck.

Maybe she'd managed to locate Winnie's friends.

I picked up the phone.

My boat.

I put it down. My dialing hand felt awful twitchy, though.

It didn't help that I had fewer distractions than usual. People kept dying, but I was still on light duty, forbidden from going out on removals. What fell to me instead were notifications.

Shoops and I paid a visit to a woman out on Alameda whose sister had overdosed on opioids. The woman beamed triumphantly. She said, "I told you so."

Bagoyo and I paid a visit to a man in Hayward. His mother had been found in her apartment, dead of a heart attack. We omitted that the apartment was overrun with rabbits, gerbils, and other living things, uncaged. Left without food, the animals had devoured the contents of the pantry before starting in on one another and their host. EMTs broke down the door on a charnel house. The body was positioned upright in bed, missing six fingers, nine toes, and both eyes. She had been dead for a week. Per downstairs neighbors, the stench wasn't noticeably worse than usual.

Zaragoza and I paid a visit to a couple in Berkeley. They lived in a quaint Brown Shingle. He was a computer programmer. She was a microbiologist. The previous spring, their twenty-four-year-old son had left for a solo camping trip in Arches National Park. He hadn't been heard from since. His vehicle, a green 1989 Volvo station wagon, was discovered at a remote trailhead, and a search mounted without success. Now a group of hikers had spotted his skeletonized remains, a mile off the trail. He was piled up on the far side of a rock formation. A nearby backpack contained tabs of LSD. The presumption was that he'd gotten high, climbed up, and fallen, shattering his left femur. The pathologist's report put the probable cause of death as dehydration, rather than trauma from the impact. Identification had been made from dental records.

His mother showed us to his childhood bedroom, still with its hip-hop posters and outer-space duvet. She and her husband had been talking about redecorating. Update it; make it suitable for guests. They hadn't gotten around to it yet, she said, softly stroking the rings of Saturn; not yet, but perhaps the time had come.

The degree to which all this depressed the shit out of me caught me off-guard. Notification was a duty I performed on a weekly basis, but I'd never felt the weight of it quite so hard as I did then.

Amy said, "You're a physical creature."

It was Monday night, and I had my leg up on the couch, watching the Warriors dismantle the Celtics. The coffee table had been moved within arm's reach, a slice of Zachary's deep-dish congealing on a plate. The gel pack on my knee had warmed to room temperature.

I said, "I don't feel very physical."

"You're not, right now." She was sitting at the card table that served as her work nook, answering emails. "That's my point."

She took the gel pack to the kitchen.

"You sit still for too long," she called, "you start to brood."

She returned with a pack fresh out of the freezer, plus three ibuprofen and water.

"Thanks," I said.

She went back to her laptop. "I'm the same way."

"Think about our poor kids."

"I'd rather not, yet."

On screen, Draymond Green was getting T'd up.

Between swallows, I said, "You do want to have kids, though."

"Yes, I want kids."

"Have we talked about this? We should probably talk about this."

"I'm waiting for my ring."

"You said you wanted to pick it out together."

"I do."

"Whenever you're ready," I said. "Or I can surprise you."

She paused her typing. "Please don't."

"What."

"I'm asking you to wait for me."

"You don't trust me?"

"I trust you."

"But?"

"But," she said, "you are a terrible present buyer."

I sat up. "What's that mean?"

"It means that you are good at many things. Buying presents is not one of them."

"Name one bad present I've bought you."

"Tch."

"I'm asking you to give me an example," I said.

"I'm not playing this game."

"See?" I said. "You can't."

Silence.

I said, "How am I supposed to improve without feedback?"

She sighed, clapped her thighs. "My birthday."

"The—? That was an expensive scarf."

"I'm sure it was."

"It had skulls."

"Yes, it did."

"Skulls," I said, "are a thing."

"Are they, though?"

"I thought they'd remind you of me," I said. "You didn't like it?"

She batted her eyes mawkishly. "I love *you*."

"Just to be a hundred percent clear," I said, "when you say you want kids, you do want them with me, right?"

Amy laughed.

The downstairs buzzer sounded.

"I'm not expecting anyone," I said.

"Me neither." She headed to the front-hall intercom. "Hello?"

Yo, Amy. It's Luke. Is Clay around? Can I come up?

"Are you around?" she called to me. "Can he come up?"

"What's he want?"

"Can he come up or not?"

"Yeah. Fine."

She buzzed him in, leaving the door unlocked.

Size thirteen feet came bounding up the steps.

"Hello?" Luke poked his head in. "Hey, dude. You look comfy."

He was dressed absurdly. Nylon shorts over black tights, a compression shirt that revealed his knobby contours. Bleach-stained hoodie, bearing the pirate mascot of San Leandro High. It could have been his originally, or it could have been mine.

I assumed he'd come from playing ball. But Amy said, "Are those weight-lifting shoes?"

Luke held them out proudly: grim wedgelike soles and Velcro instep straps. "Just finished gettin my swole on."

"Where?" I asked.

"The CrossFit box over on Harrison. Hit a snatch PR."

"Since when do you do CrossFit?"

"Like two three months," he said. "You ever tried it? It's awesome. My work capacity has gone up like five thousand percent. Both you guys should check it out. First time's free. Anyway I was in the neighborhood and I thought I'd swing by and say hi."

"Hi," I said.

"You want to go hang out?"

". . . now?"

"If you're not busy. I'm—a carb up. Can't remember the last time I had a milkshake."

I looked down at myself: cold pack, pajama bottoms. "Uh. I'm kinda—"

"Yeah," he said. "It's cool, we can talk later."

He was bouncing from foot to foot.

"Is everything okay?" Amy asked.

"Oh yeah. Totally. I just wanted to have a word with Clay."

Amy said, "I can step out for a bit."

Me: "No." Luke: "You mind?"

"It's no problem," she said, getting up. "I'll take a walk. We need eggs."

"Thanks," Luke said.

I pleaded with her silently not to go. In the thirty seconds it took her to grab her coat and keys, Luke's attention had shifted to the TV.

I caught the replay: Steph Curry, hitting from mid-court as the quarter ran down.

Luke said, "Dude's a freak." He lowered himself toward the sofa, his gaze still glued to the screen. I had to slide back so he wouldn't crush my foot.

I shut the TV off and set the remote on the carpet. "What's going on."

"Not much."

"In the neighborhood."

"Yeah."

"There isn't a CrossFit in San Leandro?"

"I'm trying out a couple different places," he said. "See which I like the best."

"First time's free," I said.

He grinned, not ashamed to be caught. "Yo, their policy, their choice."

"How long before you have to start paying?"

"I think there's one in SF I haven't hit yet."

"Holy hell you're cheap."

"Support a living wage, man."

I laughed. "So what do you want?"

He looked mildly stung. "I don't want anything." He straightened up, smoothing his shirtfront as though preparing to pop the question. "I want you to be my best man."

Idiot, I thought. Meaning me. Because I saw him wide-eyed and hopeful, trussed up in spandex, the hair on his temples plastered with dried sweat, and the back of my throat felt thick. Stupid, sentimental idiot.

He said, "It's, you know. Theoretical, at the present moment. Till we set a date. Andrea said I might as well ask you now. Life happens. I walk out of here, get hit by a bus . . . I mean, I don't need to tell you that."

I said, "Thank you. Sure."

"Yeah?"

"Yeah. Of course."

"Hey," he said. "Thank *you*."

He put out his hand, and I took it, and for a few seconds we held on to each other.

He let go. "How's the knee?"

"Not bad. Brace comes off next week. Then I start PT."

"How soon can I get a rematch?"

"That could be a while."

"Cool, cool. Hey, listen, can I ask you about something else?"

Without waiting for an answer, he started talking. At first I failed to follow him. I was still choked up. I couldn't shift gears fast enough. But then the gist began to come through.

An opportunity had come his way. An amazing opportunity. The laws had changed, the culture was changing. It didn't take a genius to see, people were going to get rich. No question about that. The question was: who. Remember Scott, from high school? Not Scott Kern. The other Scott, Silber. Good guy. *Smart* guy. He had a business degree from Stanford. When it came to this space, man, he was way ahead of the curve.

"Time out," I said. "You want—am I hearing you right? You want to open a dispensary?"

"No no no. You gotta think bigger than that. We're talking the whole supply chain: strain development, grow, brand, retail. Full vertical integration."

"Luke—"

"Let's, for a sec, let's examine this in terms of the market. They did a survey."

"Who did."

"Scott's people. That's what I'm telling you. This is not his first trip to the store, bro. How much are you willing to spend per week for organic, locally grown, top-quality cannabis? You know the average number they got? Sixty. Dollars. A week. East Bay alone, multiply that times a hundred thousand. That's how much is sitting on the table any given moment. *Someone's* gonna take it. It's either Big Tobacco comes in and bulldozes everyone—and that's what happens, guaranteed, unless the little guy gets there first."

"I take it you're the little guy in this scenario."

"Grassroots. People like Scott, or me, or you—"

"Me."

"Yeah you. Why shouldn't you get what's coming to you?"

"Have you forgotten," I said, "that I'm a cop?"

"Read the news. Same as cigarettes."

"Not federally."

"Five years, tops."

"Luke," I said. "You have a drug problem."

"It's not—" He broke off, frustrated. "You need to lose the nineteen fifty-five mentality. This is about helping people in need. It's mission-driven. Scott has three full-time PhDs on staff. The stuff they're looking at, you have no idea. Anxiety, depression, pain, *cancer*. Anyway I'm not out in the fields doing quality-control testing. It's passive income."

I said nothing.

"I didn't have to go to you," he said. "There's lots of people I could've gone to. I'm coming to you as a favor."

"Thanks, but I'll pass."

"Come on, dude. Don't be like that. Look. This industry, it's true, you do get some shady characters."

"No shit."

"The investors Scott's talking to, it's a whole different class of people. These are major names. Top-shelf Silicon Valley. It's important to them everything is on the up-and-up. My history, he's out on a limb for me, okay? Ordinarily he won't take less than a hundred K, but in this case he's willing to go twenty-five, because of the prior relationship."

"You're free to do whatever you want. I'm not interested."

"I'm not asking for money," he said. "I'm saying *I*, me, *I* go twenty-five. Of that, two and a half percent to you. All you gotta do is sign."

I stared at him. "You want me to be your front man."

"Course, you want in yourself, we can talk about that."

"I don't even—Christ alive, Luke. Where'd you get twenty-five grand?"

"Andrea."

"Where'd *she* get it?"

"Rainy-day fund. She's been saving up since she was like nineteen."

"And you think she's gonna hand it over to you? Are you insane?"

"What can I say? Girl's got vision."

"Have *her* sign."

His gaze floated away and back. "I mean, I could. If you stop and think about it, though, it's not the best idea."

"The whole thing is a fucking horrible idea."

"It's a gray area, legally. Lot of shit remains to be figured out. Say the tide shifts, enforcement-wise? Sooner or later we're married. Now we're one entity. This is our future we're talking about. You don't leave it to chance."

"One second ago it's 'five years tops.' Now the tide's shifting."

"You gotta take risks if you want to get anywhere," he said.

"You *just said*—" I shut my eyes, bore down. "You know what, I'm super tired. Can we not discuss this any further, right now, please? Not right now."

"Yeah," he said. "Okay."

I felt him get up off the couch.

"Call me when you've had a chance to think it over," he said.

I nodded, my eyes still shut. I opened them hoping he'd be gone.

He was standing over me, studying me with concern. "You need more ice?"

"I just want to stretch out."

"Cool. We'll talk. I'll circle back to you."

"Fine."

"Discuss it with Amy. I feel like this is the kind of thing she'd go for."

"Mm."

"Whatever you decide," he said, "you're still my best man."

"Thanks."

"Cool." He pressed his palms together, *namaste,* and was gone.

I sank into the cushion, too beat to reach for the remote.

Stupid, sentimental, gullible idiot.

A little while later, the front door opened, and Amy came in, swinging a plastic bag adorned with a piss-yellow smiley face.

She said, "What'd I miss?"

CHAPTER 22

"**C**oroner's Bureau."

"Is Clay—Edison there?"

The connection was poor, the words halting through the speaker.

"This is Deputy Edison."

"My name's Dylan Gomez. I'm calling about my brother. Kevin Gomez."

I snatched up the receiver. "Mr. Gomez?"

"Yeah, hi."

"Would you mind telling me your brother's date of birth?"

"April nineteenth."

"Year?"

"I . . ." The line crackled as he did the math. "I was born in ninety-two. So ninety-five. Am I talking to the right person?"

"I'm the one handling the case, yes. My condolences. How can I help you?"

"Tell you the truth I don't know," he said. "I got this email from my dad that has me pretty worried. I guess you guys went over there and—something happened?"

I gave him an edited version of what had occurred to the pair of LA coroners on their notification call to Philip Gomez.

Dylan Gomez exhaled. "Shit."

He spoke again, but it was lost to static.

"Sorry, I missed that," I said. "One more time?"

"It's this fuckin—pardon my French—this line I'm on, it sucks."

"You want to call me back?"

"No point. It's always like this. I said I don't even know how he died."

Male pronoun: I decided to follow his lead. "He was struck by a car."

"Shit. Did he—was it quick?"

"Very."

"That's good, I guess."

He had the analytical cadence of one accustomed to death, who has seen enough deaths, of enough variety, to assemble his own private taxonomy.

He sounded, in fact, a lot like a coroner.

I said, "I was hoping to speak to your father about making funeral arrangements. I'm having trouble getting in touch."

"Yeah, no shit. He's in a bad place, you know? It messed him up pretty bad, what they told him."

"I apologize for the way he found out."

"Whatever," Dylan said. "It's not like he didn't already know what Kevin was like. He wants to throw a tantrum, that's on him. So what do I need to do?"

"Who else besides him might step up? Your mother?"

"I haven't seen her since I was like five. She left my dad and went back to El Salvador. She could be dead, all I know."

"Do you have other siblings?"

"Just us."

"Okay. Then I'm going to suggest that you go ahead and contact a mortuary. I can provide a list of local ones. Unless you wanted to hold the funeral in Los Angeles?"

"You don't understand," he said. "I'm not—I can't be there, to do this, myself."

"Where are you?"

"I can't tell you that," he said.

I remembered the young man in a khaki uniform; heard the sizzle and zap of the phone line, and I pictured a cartoon arrow spanning the globe, like in an old black-and-white newsreel. Hurtling into space, ricocheting off satellites, funneling through fiberoptic cable.

Landing on the map in a big, blank, hostile spot.

I said, "Is it morning where you are?"

Three beats. "You could say that."

"Gotcha. And you're not getting back to California in the near future."

"That's not up to me," Dylan Gomez said. "But, no. I wouldn't count on it."

"We'll hang on as long as we can," I said.

"And then?"

"Well, at some point, when we run out of space, it's our policy to proceed with a cremation."

Dylan Gomez said, "No. No. I don't want that. I mean, the thought of him, all burnt up . . . There's gotta be another way."

It's rare you can't find a family member willing to cover costs. Aunt, grandparent, a warmhearted cousin. I put these possibilities to him but he cut me off: "I'll pay for it. I'll find the money. I don't give a shit."

"Then . . . ?"

"For one thing, I'm not in a position to start making a hundred phone calls. I'm up to my eyeballs in all kinds of shit you don't want to know. It's not like I can hop on a bus. I mean, fuck. What's that look like? They're throwing him in a hole in the ground and no one's around to witness it? You don't think that's kind of fucked up? Pardon my French."

"Here's a thought," I said. "I've spoken to several of Kevin's friends. I'd bet they're eager to help. I'd have to ask, of course."

There was no reply.

"I'm not sure if you feel that solves the problem for you," I said. "But at least you'll know that he won't be alone."

Again, silence. I wondered if I'd lost him. "Hello?"

"Yeah," he said. "What kind of friends are we talking about?"

I said, "They cared about him a great deal."

"About him?" he said.

I said, "About her."

My line beeped with call waiting. I glanced at the display.

Nwodo.

It took a great deal of restraint not to hammer down the hook-flash.

Dylan Gomez said, "I'd like to talk to them first."

I didn't want to imagine how that conversation might go. If he used the wrong pronoun? Greer Unger, with her anti-cop posters—what kind of earful would she have for an active-duty Marine? Didi Flynn seemed a better bet, but barely. She didn't give the overwhelming impression of someone who had her act together. Could I involve one and not the other without provoking a territorial throwdown?

I said, "I'll see what I can do."

He gave me his email address, with the caveat that internet access was spotty, at best.

I thanked him and switched to the other line.

"Tomorrow morning," Nwodo said. "You busy?"

Monday, February 11

9:29 a.m.

For a second time, the silver BMW coupe pulled up outside my building. The hour was a little more humane, the weather a little better. And I was walking without a crutch, a fact Nwodo took note of as I buzzed the seat back and folded myself in.

"You're new and improved."

My turn to buy coffee. We stopped en route to 580 north.

She said, "Thanks for coming."

"Either this or laundry."

"Man, you are housebroken as shit," she said. "This fiancée of yours pitch in?"

"Cooks. What can I say? She's a busy lady."

"The good doctor."

"Yup."

"Whatever you do," Nwodo said, "don't mess that up."

"Roger."

Northbound again. Instead of continuing toward the bridge, though, she veered onto the 80 fork, through Richmond. Cold sun flashed in the red-and-blue Costco sign, stirring within me an intense need to purchase forty-eight of something.

I said, "You feel like telling me what we're doing?"

"Right now, you know as much as I do."

I knew only what she'd told me over the phone.

A week prior, the DA's office had contacted her.

Isaiah Branch wanted to talk.

He'd asked for her by name.

The meeting was to take place in Antioch, at the home of Isaiah's parents, Curtis and Tina Branch. I told Nwodo she was nice to travel, rather than have him come to the station.

"I want him in an environment where he feels comfortable," she said.

"Then why am I here?"

"Not *that* comfortable."

"Why you? As opposed to Bischoff or Von Ruden."

She shrugged.

"Homeboy's crushing on you," I said.

"Wouldn't be the first."

THE BRANCHES LIVED in a southeastern quadrant of Antioch that consisted wholly of housing developments, a warren of short-run streets ending in culs-de-sac. Bird's-eye, the neighborhood resembled a thousand sunbathing spoons, or a platoon of very tired sperm.

Here, the price of a mildewy Oakland studio bought a four-bedroom Spanish Colonial, vintage 2003, complete with AC, attached garage, and a postage-stamp yard. The schools were solid and the neighbors worked for Kaiser, too. Arid, beige, and peaceful, it felt about as far removed as you could get from the Lower Bottoms on a Friday night.

In short, the burbs.

We came to a home that looked like every other home, except for the number of cars congregated outside it.

Lexus and Prius in the driveway.

Acura and Mercedes at the curb.

The Acura was the oldest of the bunch, with one window decal for Deer Valley High School and another for SFSU.

"What do his folks do?" I asked.

"Dad's a hospital admin. Mom works for the city. Something to do with disability access." Nwodo flicked at the Mercedes. "I'm guessing that's his lawyer."

"So that makes four on two."

"I got ball," she said, ducking out.

I remembered Isaiah's mother, Tina, from our brief encounter at Highland Hospital, when she and her husband came bursting into the room to cut short the interview. The woman who answered the door was a calmer version of the same, but aloof and not much happier to see us. When she told us to please come in it was a command rather than an invitation; she gave us her back and walked ahead into the living room.

The house was pleasant and fresh, with an open floor plan and a broad window overlooking gentle hills. The others rose to greet us.

I'd been wrong about our odds.

Five on two.

Isaiah. Tina, in a yellow-and-lavender twinset; Isaiah's father, Curtis, muscular across the chest through his russet polo. The lawyer, a black man in a slim glen plaid suit and gold-rimmed eyeglasses, who introduced himself as Montgomery Prince.

Center, a tiny woman, gray hair ironed crispy, ankle-length wool dress, orthotics.

Curtis said, "My mother, Harriet Branch."

"Hattie," the woman said. She put a soft hand in mine. "Nice to meet you, sir."

"You too, ma'am."

Montgomery Prince cleared his throat. "Shall we get started?"

Isaiah sat on the sofa, hemmed in on either side by his parents. Hattie took the largest armchair, a proper monarch. The lawyer took the ottoman, and Nwodo and I sat on the pair of dining room chairs that had been press-ganged for the occasion. Stacked atop the coffee table were print-on-demand photo albums, spines dated, one volume for each of the last nine years. The topmost cover showed the nuclear Branch family in better times, smiling, vineyards in the background. There was a daughter, too, younger. At school, presumably.

Mine was the only white face in the room. Hattie smiled at me. I smiled back.

Prince cleared his throat again. "I'd like to go on the record that I have advised my client against speaking with you. Since he insists, I insisted on being present."

To me, Isaiah didn't look capable of insisting on much of anything. His posture was at once alarmed and defeated, his shoulders caved in so close they threatened to touch. He wore a long-sleeved T-shirt, a bulge visible at the upper left arm: the gunshot wound, still bandaged. I supposed he'd had some time to ponder his future.

"As I told the district attorney," Prince said, "my client has information of potential value to your investigation. I would like to emphasize that this information has nothing whatsoever to do with the alleged incident. The information my client wishes to share pertains to a separate incident, which my client only became aware of after you, Detective, mentioned it to him. His willingness to come forth is therefore nothing less than an act of good faith. He is a young man performing a brave civic duty, and I expect you to treat him and it as such."

I found this speech puzzling. Isaiah Branch had yet to be charged. Any halfway decent lawyer would realize that he couldn't prevent Isaiah from saying something incriminating. Nor could he prevent us from taking that to the cops working the shooting.

"You're doing the right thing," Nwodo said to Isaiah.

"Yes, he is," Hattie said.

"Mom," Curtis said.

"If I may," Prince said. "I would like to emphasize as well that if at any point I sense a failure on your part to keep that distinction in the forefront of your mind, I will instruct my client to end the conversation immediately."

I grasped now the lawyer's aim: to scare the shit out of Isaiah, thereby getting him to change his mind about talking to us.

It was a lost cause, though. The prime mover made herself known.

Hattie said, "Tell them what you told me, honey."

"Mom," Curtis said, "please."

"It's all right," Isaiah said. He blew out a breath. "Okay. Earlier that night, I was over at the, the house."

"Sorry," Nwodo said. "Which night are we talking about? The night of the shooting?"

"Yeah."

"He was visiting me," Hattie said.

"Mother," Tina Branch said, "let him talk."

"I'm trying to help them understand," Hattie said.

"You live on Almond Street," Nwodo said to her.

"Forty years."

"They were blasting music," Isaiah said. "I went over to ask them to turn it down."

"The neighbor across the street," Nwodo said.

"Yeah."

"You remember what time this was?"

"Seven thirty," Isaiah said. "Seven forty-five."

Montgomery Prince appeared poised to jump in. Isaiah was admitting to having prior contact with the party people.

"You ask them nicely to turn down the music," Nwodo said. A little editorializing on her part: *We're not out to get you.* "Okay. What then?"

Isaiah said, "I saw a guy."

"A guy."

"A homeless guy."

"How do you know he was homeless?" I asked.

"How do *you* know when someone's homeless?"

"Don't sass," Hattie said.

Curtis Branch sighed.

"Can we, please, move it along," Montgomery Prince said.

"I've seen him myself," Hattie said.

Nwodo turned to her. "You did?"

"Not on that particular night. But a number of these fellows hang around the neighborhood. Before the lady artist moved in they used the house to do their drugs."

"'Artist,'" Isaiah muttered.

"It's terrible, what happens to these poor folks, when they get hooked. My husband, God rest him—"

"If you don't mind, Ms. Branch," the lawyer said, "let's stick to what's directly pertinent."

Curtis shot the lawyer an irritated look—*Don't insult my mom*—but said nothing.

"I ran into him when I was leaving," Isaiah said. "I was on my way out, and I got lost. It's kind of a mess back there."

He paused to glance at Nwodo, who gave him an encouraging nod. "I saw it."

"Yeah," he said. "So, they have this—in the back, there's this area, with a shed."

"That's where you saw him? By the shed?"

"Yeah."

"What was he doing?"

Isaiah said, "Digging."

The nape of my neck prickled.

Nwodo said, "Digging what?"

"I don't know. That's what it looked like," Isaiah said. "I'm walking past and he jumped up out of nowhere. I didn't see him at first. It was dark, and he just ... appeared. Like, from the dirt. We're looking at each other, and ..." He trailed off, caught up in remembered fear. "He had a knife."

"Did he threaten you?" I asked.

"Of course he felt threatened," Tina said. She grabbed Isaiah's hand. "Anyone would."

"All right," Nwodo said. "He has a knife. What does he do?"

"He came up to me," Isaiah said. "Like, this close. He goes, 'Not you.'"

"'Not you.'"

"That's what he said." He freed himself from his mother's grip. "You asked me about that girl. In the hospital. I was thinking about it later and it reminded me. Because of—I mean, I'm not trying to tell you this because he was homeless. All right? I'm not saying that."

"Nobody thinks you think that," Curtis Branch said.

"No, but, see," Isaiah said, "if people need help, we as a society should give them help, right? Not demonize them. It all feeds into the structures of power."

He sounded like a school essay.

Prince said, "Let's wrap this up, please."

"The girl," Nwodo said. "Did you see her?"

Isaiah shook his head.

"Can you describe the homeless man?"

"White, with a beard, messed-up. Messy."

"Would you be willing to work with a sketch artist?"

Isaiah started to nod, but Montgomery Prince said, "I consider that request premature until I've heard back from the district attorney's office regarding his intentions toward my client. For the moment we sincerely hope this has been of help to you, and that you can appreciate the fact that Mr. Branch was willing to come forward."

"We do," Nwodo said, standing. "Thank you, everyone."

Prince rose, followed by Curtis and Tina, and then Isaiah. Hattie remained sitting. Curtis put his hand out to help her up. She ignored him and got up on her own.

We said our goodbyes, and a minute later Nwodo and I were back in the car.

NEITHER OF US spoke until she'd gotten on the freeway. I figured she was lamenting the wasted time. She glanced over her shoulder to merge toward the fast lane.

She said, "I want to have another look at the shed."

We were seven-plus weeks out. That she thought it worth the trouble said she wasn't having success elsewhere. The request for a composite had that same tinge of desperation. Eyewitnesses are notoriously inaccurate; most police sketch artists have rudimentary skills.

"You can come," she said. "Unless you have to wash the windows."

CHAPTER 23

We met on the corner of Almond and 11th, outside the giant Victorian. Oily rain spat down. Nwodo stood beneath a red umbrella, talking on her phone.

I hadn't been back since the shooting. Seeing the mansion now was like visiting a friend who'd succumbed to a sudden, horrific illness. It swooned beneath leaden skies, bedraggled and wan. Crime scene tape hung in sullen yellow shreds, fluttering across flower beds reduced to mud sumps and snaking over a lawn pounded to stubble. The fence gate had been fitted with a beefy padlock and an opaque green tarp added behind the chain-link to thwart gawkers.

None of that compared with the real damage: a rash of graffiti, consuming the façade. There were anarchist *A*'s, and racial epithets, a vile base coat of hate topped by squiggles and tags. The original Painted Lady color scheme, pastel purple and yellow, was all but obliterated. You had to give the vandals top marks for tenacity.

They'd scaled the porch overhang to get at the upper floors. Cardboard filled a broken second-story window.

Nwodo finished her call. "Morning." She joined me in peering up at the house's blighted exterior. "I know, right?"

"When did this happen?"

"I think it's a work in progress," she said.

I said, "Did you know that the Summerhof Mansion was built in eighteen-ninety-something, for a guy whose name I can't remember?"

"Summerhof?"

"He had like a dozen kids."

"Huh. It doesn't look so big anymore."

I eyed the padlocked entry. "Jump the fence?"

"Bold thinking from the man with a bad knee," she said. "No need."

She pointed up the block, where a gold-tone Cadillac Coupe de Ville was puttering toward us. At the wheel sat a woman in her early forties. She parked in the driveway and got out, and I gave myself a pass for failing to recognize her at first.

Like her home, Rhiannon Cooke appeared much the worse for wear. She'd dyed her hair a uniform black. Dressed in baggy sweatpants and a RISD hoodie, she slouched toward us, casting nervous glances behind.

"Appreciate your taking the time, ma'am," Nwodo said.

"Yeah, no problem," Cooke said, sounding like it was a problem.

"Shame about the house," I said.

That was all the prompt she needed.

"Do you have any idea what I've been going through? It's insane. I get death threats. I can't stay in my own home. You can't imagine what this place used to look like. It was a *crack den*. It's this massive white elephant nobody will take responsibility for and then I come along and put my heart and soul into improving it, for the good of the community. My own two hands and now this. It's not enough to throw a tantrum and let everybody know how *mad* you are. You have to *ruin* something. You have to burn it to the ground, on principle. Explain that to me. You want to hate me, fine. But *that*—is a *building*. A beautiful building, and, by the way, historical. You *live* here. You're going to walk past it every day and see it. Why would you do that? It's disgraceful."

Nwodo said, "Tough situation."

"I haven't slept more than four hours in God knows how long. I have to keep moving, every time someone takes me in, they start getting death threats, too. There's a dedicated subreddit called FuckRhiannonCooke. I took down my Twitter, my Facebook page. Twice"—she pointed to her car—"my tires have been slashed."

"Have you reported it?" Nwodo asked.

"Of course I've *reported it*. Half the time no one bothers to come and the other half they write it down and there's literally *zero* follow-up. No offense, but what kind of donkey show are you people running? I have to drive down here and open a gate? You've had since January. What you think you're going to find is beyond me."

We waited for her to run out of steam.

Nwodo said, "If you wouldn't mind."

Rhiannon Cooke raked her stiff black hair. "Whatever."

She undid the padlock, then went and stood beneath the denuded willow, arms crossed, glaring at us from afar.

"Should've jumped the fence," I said to Nwodo.

TWO MONTHS OF weather had worsened the disarray in the yard, paper pulped, vessels overflowing. The rain had petered out, but drops continued to fall from eaves.

No sign of the goat. Maybe Officer Grelling had nabbed him.

The passage to the rear of the property felt briefer than I remembered—compressed, the way a return journey often is. We arrived at the triangular nowhere zone to find the scenery intact, the actors long gone.

Bicycles. Pallets. Crates. Cans.

Shed.

Nwodo opened the doors, causing the hand tools hung inside to rattle on their hooks. From her pocket she removed a tube of Chap-Stick. She placed it on the ground where the doors met, then shut them and set the hasp, leaving the end of the tube sticking out, a proxy for the dead girl's thumb.

She counted off ten paces and faced the shed.

"Isaiah sees this guy at seven thirty, give or take," she said. "Twelve hours till the uniform finds her."

Was it possible Winnie's body had lain in the shed that entire time, while the party swirled on, oblivious? Daylight made the white nub of the ChapStick hard to miss.

I said, "Nighttime. Folks were drunk."

Nwodo conceded with a shrug. An abrupt break in the cloud cover loosed a torrent of perpendicular noonday sun. She stepped past the shed, coming abreast of the trash cans. Shading her eyes, she rotated at the waist, trying to regain lost perspective.

At the heart of Rhiannon Cooke's tirade lurked a kernel of truth: the scene *had* been gone over, extensively.

I said, "You happen to recall if Forensics found a flip-flop? White foam."

Nwodo didn't answer. She was squinting into the space between two of the cans. She seized the burgundy can and drew it away from the house. Her eyes went huge.

"Clay."

I came over to look.

A panel, two and a half feet on a side, was cut into the siding.

The fit was snug. Only the faintest score line at top and sides—invisible in anything less than direct light. The bottom of the panel, like the exterior wall adjacent in either direction, sat an inch above ground level. The gap enabled a person to worm a hand in, grasp the bottom edge, and pull, which is what I did.

The panel popped free with a soft *thunk,* revealing the entrance to a crawl space.

Nwodo clicked on her penlight and crouched down.

Just past the opening, the crawl space widened and deepened considerably. Bare earth sloped down to mazy dimness, defined by soffits and joists and shot through with listing spars of timber and corroded pipe. Not hitting your head would require constant vigilance. But if you could get used to that; if you could tolerate the filth, and the dust, and the droppings; if you could stomach the dreariness and beady-eyed vermin fleeing the light—if all you cared about was getting out of the elements—it would make a fine place to shelter.

Someone had thought so.

On the ground, like a carcass, was a single tube sock. From around a bend, the end of a mattress jutted.

The city garbage cans had plastic wheels on an exposed rear axle, making it easy to tip the can back for rolling. Once inside the crawl space, you could lie on the slope, reach through the opening, and grab the axle, using it to tug the can just about into line.

On the reverse of the cutout panel was a short handle, enterprisingly fashioned from seatbelt nylon and secured with heavy-duty staples. You could use this handle to seal the opening, leaving not a soul the wiser.

One nowhere space, tucked within another.

I said, "Isaiah said he appeared from the dirt."

Nwodo snapped off her penlight. "Let's hear what our cheerful owner has to say."

. . .

RHIANNON COOKE SAID, "I've never seen it before."

Her complexion had acquired a greenish pallor, and she was staring at the mouth of the opening, her head cocked as though recoiling from a foul odor.

She said, "I swear to God. I have no idea how it got there."

"It's always been there," I said. "You just never noticed it."

"You didn't see it when you took the trash out?" Nwodo said.

"I don't . . ." Cooke said, distressed. "My landscaper. He puts the trash out for me."

Nwodo made a disgusted face.

Of course, part of that anger was directed at herself.

How could *she* have overlooked it?

Not her fault. Or mine. Or the techs'.

We don't really see most things, and the panel was made to be ignored.

Nwodo said, "You've been here how long?"

"Two years."

"All that time you never heard anything?"

Rhiannon Cooke bit her lip. "We thought it was rats."

Nwodo threw up her hands and began walking in a tight tense circle.

I asked if there was a way to access the crawl space from inside the house.

"So we don't have to squeeze through," I said. "Ruin my colleague's nice clean shirt."

Rhiannon Cooke remained transfixed, staring at the ground. Reliving nights at the dinner table, kale Caesar salad and Chardonnay, whispery scratches eking up through the floorboards, exchanging a look of mutual admonishment with her boyfriend.

We should really call an exterminator.

"Ms. Cooke," I said.

"I don't think so," she said.

"Is there a basement?"

"Huh?"

"Do you have a basement?"

"It's sealed," she said. "They found mold during the inspection. I had the entrance walled over."

"Convenient for him," I said.

At the mention of *him* she shuddered.

"I don't understand," she said. "How is this possible?"

"It's your house," Nwodo said. "You tell us."

NO EVIDENCE TEAM available till the afternoon. Neither Nwodo nor I wanted to wait that long. Neither of us wanted to be the one to climb in there, either, so we played rock, paper, scissors.

I lost.

I GOT DOWN on my stomach, wriggling backward, feet-first. It was a tight fit, but once I cleared the mouth of the opening I slipped easily down the cold dirt, raising a choking cloud. I straightened up slowly, wary of cracking my head. My pants and jacket-front were smeared brown.

"Good?" Nwodo called.

"So much fun."

Despite the lack of insulation, the space retained an unclean whiff of human being. I crept forward, clawing at cobwebs, high-stepping over the beams, playing the penlight into the crevices. I didn't know how far back the space went. If there was one homeless guy living there, why not two? Or five? Or ten?

Coming around the bend I encountered a heap of items not visible from the outside. There was a men's shirt on a wire hanger, dangling from a wrapped pipe. There was a small pile of paperbacks. There were food wrappers and scraps of toilet paper.

He liked to eat Funyuns.

He liked to read action thrillers.

He was, it appeared, a tinkerer. There were several radios in various states of disembowelment, spare parts sorted by type atop a flattened cardboard box. I got the impression that he had vacated in a hurry.

The mattress was soiled, and thin, like those used on pullout couches.

At one edge, nestled in the stitching, was a syringe.

Needle missing. Residue in the chamber.

To BE ON the safe side, the evidence team also took the shirt, the food wrappers, the books, the electronics parts, and the sock. They left the mattress, but not without blacklighting it first and swabbing for organic material. Taping off the crawl space, they cautioned Rhiannon Cooke not to enter or remove any items that might remain.

"Like I'd do that," she said.

It turned out not to matter. The syringe yielded a hit. Nwodo must've leaned on the lab pretty hard, because a week later I was looking at a mugshot on my computer.

Lawrence Lee Vinson. A.k.a. Larry, a.k.a. Dickfish.

White male, fifty-nine years of age, though his face begged to differ. Basset hound cheeks, long earlobes—he appeared to be melting, vacant blue eyes struggling to stay afloat in the downward cascade of tissue. A tattoo wrapped around the left side of his neck. The intention, I think, was a shark. The artist had botched the job, making the body too wide and the snout too rounded. What resulted was a hilariously unnatural mongrel that evoked nothing so much as an enraged penis with teeth.

Hence the nickname.

Or maybe the moniker had preceded the artwork, and the tattoo had come out precisely as Larry had hoped for.

The eternal question: which came first, the Dickfish or the dickfish?

A Wisconsin native, Vinson had surfaced in California six or seven years back. Our system mostly had him down for minor offenses.

Public intoxication. Resisting arrest. Misdemeanor possession. Misdemeanor assault.

Until fifteen months ago, a conviction for PC 647.6.

Annoying or Molesting a Child.

A third-grade teacher at Malcolm X Elementary School in Berkeley called 911 to report a suspicious man hanging around on the sidewalk during recess. He'd been there several days in a row. When she approached him, he walked away.

Shortly thereafter, the same man was spotted talking with a girl through the fence. Officers were dispatched but he left before their arrival.

Next call came from the principal. The man was back. This time, however, he wasn't talking to the girl. He had his pants around his knees and was masturbating in front of her.

Right there, broad daylight.

Within the hour they'd picked him up near Ashby BART, three hundred yards away.

Larry Vinson had engaged in similar behavior throughout the late eighties and early nineties, back in Milwaukee. His MO was well established. Always underaged girls, always acts of public sexual gratification that stopped short of physical contact. Nevertheless the judge treated the California conviction as a first offense. I would guess the rationale went along the lines of: Vinson didn't enter school grounds, didn't touch the girl. In an area of Berkeley with its fair share of oddballs, the Dickfish was simply one example—and, frankly, not an extreme one. He received minimal jail time and no fine.

As a transient, he was required to register with the authorities every thirty days following his release.

He failed to do so.

No one checked. He dissolved into the streets.

A warrant for his arrest had been languishing ever since.

I called Nwodo. "Congratulations."

"Don't jinx me," she said.

"How hard could it be to find a guy with a giant swimming dick on his neck?"

She allowed a self-pitying laugh. Larry Vinson had managed to evade capture this long. Nothing prevented him from leaving the city, region, state. Nwodo had to hope the powers-that-be now deemed him worrying enough to make him an operational priority.

I meant to wish her luck but she spoke again: "One thing: he's not a total match. It's his DNA in the syringe but the skin under Winnie's nails belongs to someone else."

I felt the air starting to hiss out of me.

She said, "It doesn't mean he's not our guy."

"Sure," I said.

I meant it. The presence of third-party DNA by no means excluded Larry Vinson. I could think of a million explanations.

Winnie was a back-scratcher in bed.

She'd danced at the party, hanging on some guy's neck.

Giving a friend a massage.

Another scenario, horrific: Larry had an accomplice who'd held Winnie Ozawa's throat closed while Vinson did his thing.

"He was there, in that exact spot, on that exact night," Nwodo said. "We have an eyewitness places him by the shed. I sent Isaiah a photo array and he picked him out straightaway. He's a convicted sex offender."

"Sure," I said again.

Even if Nwodo was unable to account for the second DNA profile, it was ultimately the prosecutor's problem, not hers. Larry Vinson was starting with many strikes against him, and convictions had been secured under far shakier circumstances.

"I don't know, though," she said. "All these years, he's a flasher. Now he changes his MO totally? There's no evidence of sexual assault. No semen left behind."

"He could've used a condom," I said.

"You think he's capable of planning that far ahead? Plus Winnie was dressed and arranged. I'm having a tough time squaring it with the mope who jerks off in front of schoolkids."

Her ambivalence was striking. At this point, not too many detectives would miss an opportunity to clear a pain-in-the-ass case off the board.

I strained to imagine how it had happened.

Dickfish Vinson, tweaked and ravenous, peering out from his demon hidey-hole, waiting for a woman he liked the look of.

Bursting to the surface to ambush her.

The stuff of nightmares.

Arguments and counterarguments went pinging around my head, too.

Vinson's history indicated a taste for preteens, rather than grown women.

But: Winnie Ozawa had a baby face, small breasts, slim hips.

But: she *hadn't* been sexually assaulted.

Vinson had never dared to lay a finger on his victims.

But: everybody starts somewhere.

But: he was nearing sixty, an age when bad guys tend to burn out, not accelerate.

Isaiah Branch had seen him wielding a knife.

But: Winnie Ozawa hadn't been stabbed.

But: a knife could coax compliance from a terrified woman.

A new question popped into my head: why would Winnie be near the shed in the first place, with the party happening elsewhere?

I remembered the track marks on her arms, the drugs in her blood.

Perhaps she'd sneaked out back to shoot up.

A rogue thought occurred to me: Winnie Ozawa *wasn't* at the party as a guest. She was, rather, living under the house with Larry. They were meth buddies, lovers, partners banded together for survival. The crime wasn't random, it was the tragic conclusion to a psycho relationship gone sour.

Fighting over their last hit, the way other couples bicker about the remote.

Manual throttling is vicious and relatively rare. You look your victim in the face and watch them die in half-second increments.

Did Larry Vinson have that kind of dedication in him?

I told Nwodo my relationship hypothesis.

She said, "I thought of that. I had them test the rest of the crap in that hellhole to see if they could find a sign of her or anyone else. Plenty of semen *there*. Saliva, too. All his. Again, doesn't rule anything out. For the moment, he's our guy."

It was, I noticed, the second time she'd referred to the killer as "ours"—not hers.

I said, "Speaking with him will help."

"Got to find him first."

"I'll keep an eye out."

"Please do," she said.

I said, "How hard could it be?"

CHAPTER 24

"**S**he was right," I said to Shupfer. "I jinxed her."

Shoops rolled her eyes.

A month had gone by without a sighting of Larry Vinson, despite a countywide Be On the Lookout. But that's theory. Most people put their heads down and do their jobs.

I, on the other hand, had looked for Dickfish with special focus.

Interacting with the homeless is a front-line duty for any Bay Area law enforcement officer, and we at the Coroner's see more than our share of people at their least fortunate. In the tent cities, beneath overpasses, along MLK and West Grand, death is a familiar visitor, manifesting in all its sudden and strange forms: exposure, overdose, cirrhosis, sepsis, violence.

Each time one of these calls came in, I would take a quick refresher peek at Vinson's mugshot before going out. Whenever the body fell to other team members, I would remind them, as they were suiting up, about the guy with the ugly-ass neck tattoo.

I had become a one-man BOLO.

246 / JONATHAN KELLERMAN and JESSE KELLERMAN

That morning's call came from OPD, near start of shift. I was at the coffee station, shaking out a sugar packet, when I overheard Bagoyo starting to take down information, repeating it back to the officer on scene for confirmation.

Sherrice Day. Black female, mid-fifties, DOB undetermined. No fixed address. At present residing at Market and 5th.

I knew that particular encampment. We all did. It had existed, on and off, for years. In response to a litany of neighbor complaints—trash, sewage, belligerent panhandling—the city had more than once attempted to dismantle it. It kept popping back up. Eventually, shifting political winds prompted the council to adopt a new strategy: they voted to provide Porta Pottys and install running water. It was a move not without controversy. Depending on your stance, you could view it as a gesture of compassion, pragmatism, or surrender.

What was inarguable was that the camp had continued to grow. Around fifty people lived there full-time. Rumor had it you could get your mail delivered. Last spring a fire had broken out, ripping through the cardboard and tent nylon, killing two people.

Market and 5th was a mile and a half from the house on Almond Street.

OPD was reporting the death as an apparent homicide.

Sherrice Day had been stabbed in the neck.

He had a knife.

Bagoyo hung up, and she and Zaragoza got ready to depart.

I said, "While you're out there—"

"We know," Bagoyo said, slipping on her vest. "Beware the Cockshark."

"It's Dickfish."

"Oh, well," Zaragoza said. "That changes everything."

. . .

MIDMORNING, SHUPFER AND I drove out to Dublin. White male, early forties, slumped against the wheel of his car in the Target parking lot. He'd been there overnight. Shopping bags in the backseat; a carton of milk, warm. Loose fentanyl tablets on the passenger seat, in the cup holder, in his crotch. It was our seventh opioid-related death of the year. Nothing compared with some parts of the state, and a drop in the bucket overall. But a disturbing trend for Alameda County.

Returning with the body, I ran into Zaragoza in the intake bay.

"You get my text?" he asked.

"What text?"

"Your guy," he said. "Moby-Dick. They got him."

I began pelting him with questions.

He put up his hands. "Hey. Hey. I don't know shit about shit. I just asked them, 'You guys seen a dude with a schlong on his neck,' and uniform's like, 'Oh yeah, that guy, they brought him in last night.' Anything else, talk to them."

I was amazed. Not just at Vinson's arrest, but at my teammates' diligence. I'd assumed they'd been laughing at me behind my back.

I looked to Shupfer, scribbling on the clipboard.

"Go," she said. "I got it."

"You sure?"

"Go before I change my mind."

"Thank you." To Zaragoza: "Thank you."

"Yeah, man. Anytime."

"Seriously," Shupfer said, "leave."

I DROVE TO 7th Street, puzzled. Nwodo's phone kept sending me straight to voicemail and Larry Vinson's name wasn't showing up in any of the county booking logs.

Hauled in but not yet arrested? New problems?

The desk sergeant told me Detective Nwodo was away from the office.

"Who's with her suspect?"

He looked me over, clocking my Coroner's uniform. "Hang on a sec."

I leaned on my elbows while he called up to Investigations.

He replaced the receiver. "Someone'll be out in a minute. Make yourself comfortable."

He meant the row of tubular steel chairs beneath a pocked corkboard. I stayed right where I was, and he went about ignoring me.

Someone turned out to be a woman with a great mane of cinnamon hair—Detective Robin Muñoz, whom I'd met briefly at Highland Hospital. The Jalen Coombs murder was hers, which made Dane Jankowski hers, too. I didn't know what, if anything, Nwodo had told her about me. Her smile was cordial but absent any special regard.

"I remember you," she said. "Delilah's friend."

"Clay Edison. I can't get her on the phone."

"Delilah? She's on a plane. You need something?"

I asked about Larry Vinson.

"Bad Tattoo Man," she said. "They got him in the fishbowl."

"Who does?"

"Von Ruden."

"I was hoping to have a word."

Muñoz tilted her head. "Everything okay?"

"Yeah," I said. "Just—I've been giving Nwodo a hand, here and there, so . . . You know. I know a little bit about it."

Slow nod. She said, "Come on up."

On the stairs, I asked where Nwodo was flying to.

"London. Visit her sister."

"How long's she gone?"

"A week. She left last night." Muñoz checked her watch. "Probably touching down right around now."

"Has anyone let her know about Vinson?"

"Von Ruden did," she said. "I'm assuming."

"So he's briefed on the situation."

Muñoz stopped four steps shy of the third-floor landing. Facing me, she said, "What situation would that be?"

I hesitated. "It's complicated."

"Uh-huh." She was evaluating me with the same skepticism as had the desk sergeant.

He's like a giant fucking barnacle.

"Call Nwodo," I said. "Ask her."

Muñoz resumed her climb. "I'll do that. Maybe I'll let her unpack."

SHE ESCORTED ME to the viewing room, a converted closet with enough space for a desk, a monitor, and two more tubular steel chairs. The walls exhaled burnt coffee and feet.

Muñoz toggled the screen over to INTERROGATION 3.

Larry Vinson, alone and uncuffed, sat at the table, munching on Funyuns and sipping Mountain Dew.

Muñoz told me, "Hang out here."

I sat. Vinson was absorbed in his snack. A second bag stood by for when he finished the first. He'd shed his outer layers, a navy-blue parka draped over the chair-back, a gnarly poop-brown scarf over that, its fringes tickling the carpet. The camera angle was favorable, showing the world-famous tattoo. With each gulp of soda, I saw, or imagined, the shark-phallus pulsing obscenely.

For a wanted man, he appeared mighty chill.

Conventional cop wisdom holds that an innocent person will

rage and protest. It's the guilty who relax, put their heads down, take a nap. Take that as an ironclad rule, and Larry Vinson was in major trouble.

But it's not ironclad. If you've been arrested twenty-plus times, you're going to feel at home in an interrogation room. Guilty, innocent—why get worked up?

Take a load off. Nice and toasty.

Enjoy your Funyuns.

Hell, they were *free*.

Detective Von Ruden appeared in the viewing room doorway. "To what do I owe the honor?"

"I heard you had the Dickfish," I said. "Always wanted to see him in concert."

Von Ruden chuckled. "Oh yeah. Once-in-a-lifetime experience."

"Where's he been hiding out?"

"BART cops spotted him on the steps at Nineteenth Street."

"Good for them."

"Yeah, it takes a village." He smiled. "So what can I do for you?"

On the screen, Larry Vinson shook Funyun crumbs into his mouth.

I said, "How long have you had him?"

Von Ruden yawned. "Couple hours. Most of that's been feeding the poor bastard. We're getting to know each other."

"You haven't arrested him."

"I will if I need to. Nothing else, we have him on failure to register. He ain't leaving."

"He hasn't asked for a lawyer."

"Not yet."

"Nwodo bring you up to speed before she left?"

"Some," he said, starting to get impatient.

"You mind I poke my head in? Talk to old Larry."

"Trust me, you don't want that. Mr. Vinson has not showered in some time. I gotta step outside every ten minutes so I don't suffocate."

"Smells don't touch me."

"Yeah, I guess they wouldn't, huh."

"Has Larry given you anything yet?"

"We're still flirting."

"Have you asked him directly about the murder?"

"Like I said. Flirting."

"I'm wondering if maybe he thinks he's up on the old warrant."

"So let him think that," Von Ruden said. "Look, friend. I'm busy. All right? Whyn't you relax and enjoy the show."

He walked off.

Reappeared on screen, entering the interview room.

Hey buddy. How's your lunch?

Larry grunted.

You want anything else?

Larry shook his head.

For a brief while that was how it went: Von Ruden asking harmless questions, Larry Vinson answering in monosyllables. Gradually, the detective began circling in. Where was Larry living? Where had he been living the last few months?

I couldn't tell if Von Ruden was being intentionally vague, or if he was in fact unfamiliar with the details of the Winnie Ozawa murder.

Week of Christmas Von Ruden said. *You heard about that thing that went down?*

Vinson started in on his second bag of Funyuns.

Some people got shot Von Ruden said. *You didn't hear about that? It was big news. Fancy house party. Buncha people got killed. Everyone was talkin.*

Larry chewed, chewed.

You know the place I'm talkin about, though. Big house, corner of Eleventh and Almond.

A hiccup in the cadence of Larry's chewing; a tiny raising of the antennae.

Yeah, you know the one I mean Von Ruden said. *You stayed there a couple times, right?*

Larry swallowed, took a swig of soda.

So let's talk about why you're here Von Ruden said. *You know why you're here? You want to take a guess? It's about the girl.* Paging through the file. *The girl . . .*

Larry licked salt from his fingers.

. . . in the toolshed.

Larry stopped.

Yeah Von Ruden said. *Someone fucked her up. Real nasty.*

Larry blinked.

You want to tell me about that, Larry?

Larry Vinson had been arrested twenty-plus times. He knew the drill.

He crossed his forearms on the tabletop and put his head down. With his face buried in his sleeves, the word came out muffled. The room microphone wasn't in terrific shape, either, and his voice emerged a clotted ursine growl. All the same, I heard him perfectly.

Larry Vinson said *Lawyer.*

Some cops get up and leave at that point. More than a legal nicety, it's a tactic, calculated to instill second thoughts and panic.

Hey, I'm doing you a favor, letting you talk.

Don't make a damn bit of difference to me. I already got you sewn up.

Von Ruden chose instead to stick around, asking Vinson what did he need that for, we're just having a conversation, you and me, just two guys talking. Offended that Larry would taint their blossoming friendship with accusations of duplicity.

Lawyer.

Larry my man.

Lawyer.

All right. If that's what you think you really want.

Lawyer.

You want something else to eat? While you wait.

Lawyer.

You want to eat a lawyer? Cause I heard they taste like shit.

Lawyer.

Eventually Von Ruden slapped the table. *Suit yourself.*

He got up and left. Minutes later I heard his plodding tread in the hall.

"You see that?" he said, leaning into the viewing room. He had a shit-eating grin on his face. "I say *shed* he sits up like I stuck a cattle prod up his ass."

"I saw it," I said.

Von Ruden said, "There you go."

I nodded. I think he was expecting me to thank him. "Thanks."

"All right then," he said, and departed.

I was still sitting there, staring at Larry's crumpled form, when Muñoz came around the corner, cellphone pressed to her breast.

With a bemused expression, she handed me the phone. "It's Delilah."

I heard a froth of noise. "Where are you?"

"Heathrow," Nwodo said. "Just heard. I'm trying to figure out a flight back today."

On screen, Larry Vinson had gone to sleep.

I said, "Don't rush."

CHAPTER 25

She didn't listen to me, of course. She got on the next available flight, which put her into SFO the following afternoon.

By then Larry had established that he wasn't talking to anyone about anything. That included his public defender, a guy named Lipper who looked like a high school freshman.

Von Ruden arrested Larry on the outstanding warrant as Lipper watched.

Larry held his wrists out for the cuffs, like a groom being fitted for a tux.

NWODO TOOK A cab straight from the airport to the jail. I met her there. Our "interview" with Larry, in the presence of a sleepy-looking Lipper, lasted till midnight. Not once did he speak, not even to thank us for the Funyuns.

Except to enter a plea of not guilty, Larry did not open his mouth in court. After Lipper had prodded him.

The judge denied bond, citing the flight risk.

Larry didn't react other than to stand up and shuffle out in his orange jumpsuit stamped PROP OF ALAMEDA COUNTY.

Nwodo, undaunted, consulted with Lipper, and the two of them went to the cells so she could try to loosen Larry up and Lipper could file his paper.

Larry kept his head down from start to finish.

NINE DAYS LATER, she said to me, "It's a done deal."

We were at a restaurant in downtown Oakland, blocks from the courthouse, having an early lunch of poke bowls and bubble tea. Ours was the sole occupied table, though the line for takeout stretched to the sidewalk, men and women in business attire stabbing their phones with loathing, collecting their orders, and backing out into the buttery spring sun.

She delivered the news with an air of detachment. The DA planned to charge Lawrence Lee Vinson with the murder of Winnie Ozawa. Broad consensus held this to be the best possible outcome. The case was three months old and getting staler by the day. Neither Nwodo nor I had been able to locate an address for Winnie or anyone connected to her, leaving no viable alternative suspects. Why go to the trouble of manufacturing one, when Vinson fit the bill?

Extraneous DNA notwithstanding, the case against him was considered solid. He was a sex offender, in the right place, at the right time. When they'd picked him up, he'd been carrying a screwdriver whose brand matched the other tools hanging in the shed. Of greatest importance to the prosecutor, he would look terrible to a jury. Logic pointed to a plea. If for some reason the case went to trial, Dennis Lipper would have to pray for a courtroom with the jury box located on the right side, away from the neck tattoo.

Sit still, Larry.

Whatever you do, don't turn your head.

Meanwhile, life kept coming, which meant that death kept coming, which meant that Nwodo's docket was overflowing. Her superiors had indicated, not too subtly, that she should quit while she was ahead.

"Everyone's telling me good job," she said.

"Good job."

We clinked plastic cups. It was hard to argue that the world wasn't a better place with Dickfish Vinson off the street, and what doubts Nwodo and I shared were slippery.

She'd rebooked her flight for Thursday, the red-eye. Her sister had managed to secure last-minute dinner reservations at a trendy gastropub.

"It's my vacation," she said, "and I'm taking it."

She wanted to move on. Who was I to deny her that?

"You earned it," I said.

"Been fun," she said. "You ever get bored where you are, call me up."

We shook hands, and she walked out, stuffing her bowl in the trash as she went.

Saturday, March 30

3:04 p.m.

Carmen Woolsey touched me gently on the shoulder. "The car's here."

I thanked her and got up from my desk.

Any coroner's deputy is authorized to release a body. Typically it falls to whoever happens to be in the vicinity of the morgue when the hearse shows up. That day, I'd asked to be informed when Bayview came for Jasmine Gomez.

I'm not sure why. To put a period on the case, I suppose. It's not as though I expected an invitation to the memorial service. I felt ready to say goodbye, not merely to Jasmine and Winnie, but to a defined moment in time, an asterisk in the text of my life and the lives I'd come to know: Almond Street and its aftermath.

Down in the intake bay, I elbowed a flat metal panel. Double doors swung open, and the hearse driver glanced up from his phone and waved. Older gentleman named Sid. A regular. We spent a minute catching up before I went down the hall to cold storage.

I stepped through a curtain of freezing air.

On the table, Jasmine appeared much the same as when I'd first encountered her: a swathed, frail shape. Physically, she seemed scarcely to exist. But halfway around the world a young Marine was thinking about her and doing his best to imagine—over a distance of miles, across a gap of understanding—what she would've wanted. An arrow tracing the globe, a scratchy connection bounced into the heavens and back again, one of the countless invisible threads that bind our souls.

I double-checked the toe tag. Rolled the gurney out to the intake bay.

Forms were signed, the body loaded.

Sid said, "Good seeing you," and got behind the wheel. The hearse crawled toward the driveway, signaled, and turned amid a cough of exhaust.

REENTERING THE SQUAD room, I grabbed the stack from my mailbox and sat at my desk.

My cellphone showed a missed call from Luke; a text.

hey bro call pls

I disregarded it, answered work-related email, finished typing the narrative for the Dublin Target overdose. I spent half an hour dealing with a medical resident at Highland who was refusing to sign a death certificate for his patient. The decedent was eighty-seven and had succumbed to complications from pneumonia, passing in the middle of the night without any apparent irregularities.

Her body was none of my business. All the same the resident insisted that I come fetch it. It happens, every so often; you get one who locks up like that.

While I was talking him down off the ledge, my cellphone rang: Luke again. I silenced it, continuing to reassure the resident that he would be fine, reminding him politely that it was his legal duty to sign the certificate.

In the end he complied. They always do.

I began sorting my snail mail.

Professional development conference. Latest in DNA facial reconstruction.

Tactical gear supply catalog.

Internal memos; mandatory diversity training; an appeal for volunteers to teach neighborhood disaster preparedness, to work the Silicon Valley Soap Box Derby.

Legal-sized envelope, plain white and hefty. The return address had me puzzling why Alex Delaware was mailing me stuff. But no: Delaware, as in the state.

I started to work my thumb under the flap.

My cellphone.

Luke.

At first you're annoyed. Then you worry. It's not as though my parents are old, but I've written mental eulogies for everyone I care about. Occupational hazard.

I picked up. "Who died?"

He guffawed. "Hello to you, too."

"I'm at work, so unless it's an emergency, I'll call you back later."

"Just—real quick, I wanted to ask if you're free sometime next couple of weeks."

"Free for what."

"Andrea picked her colors, she wants us to coordinate."

"Colors . . . For the wedding?"

"Yeah, man. You and me, we're getting new suits. I was thinking we could go and get it done, hang out afterward, if you're up for it."

"Is there a reason this has to happen now?"

"Dang," he said. "Didn't I tell you? We set a date."

"You didn't tell me that, no."

"Memorial Day weekend. Mark it down."

"That's—what is that? Eight weeks from now?"

"What can I say? When it's right, it's right. Right? No need to screw around. We put the deposit down and everything. Make sure you can get the day off. It's carnelian and pearl, by the way. The colors. Andrea's gonna email Amy about it. She wants her in the wedding party. So what do you say? I can do Tuesday morning. I talked to Mom, she said she'd pay half."

"I don't want her to do that."

"Sure, no worries. The offer's there."

"I have PT on Tuesday."

"Oh shit, yeah. How's that going, by the way?"

"Not bad."

"CrossFit, dude. I'm telling you . . . Well, cool, you find a time works for you and hit me up. Don't sleep on it, though."

This was the first conversation we'd had since he pitched me his business plan, and I thought it was weird that he hadn't mentioned it. I should've cut bait.

I couldn't help myself. "Everything else good?"

"Yeah, bro. Alrighty tighty."

"What about your thing?"

"Thing."

I didn't want to say *weed* or *dispensary* in earshot of my colleagues. Instead I ended up talking like a character in a bad spy novel. "Your deal. What we discussed."

"That? Don't worry." Luke laughed. "You're off the hook."

"I wasn't ever on the hook."

"Well, yeah, no. Don't worry about it, though. I got it all taken care of."

"You're not still going ahead with it."

"I mean. Is there a reason I shouldn't?"

"Many."

"Look, man. I appreciate that you care about me. But it's my life. I don't get chances every day. I got to do what I can, when I can. All I'm asking is you respect the effort."

He sounded sober—reasonable, even.

"I thought you didn't want Andrea's name on the paperwork," I said.

"Nah, it's cool."

"No, as in, she's signing, or no as in you are."

"Don't worry about it, I got this. Look, I'll let you go, I know you're busy."

"Hang on a minute."

"Let me know about Tuesday, okay?"

"Luke—"

He hung up.

I stared at my reflection in the phone's screen.

"So?" Dani Botero asked. "Who died?"

I opened up my contact list, scrolled. "No one yet."

I hit CALL.

My mother said, "Hi, honey."

I'M NOT A yeller. Even after she told me she'd agreed to put her name on the contract, I didn't raise my voice. Even though she'd attempted to deny it at first.

"He needs my help," she said.

"He needs someone's help, that's for damn sure."

"Clay. He's doing his best to pull himself up. Do you have any idea what he's up against? The stigma? You should see how people treat him. He goes in for a job interview and they act like he's a leper. He's lucky to be getting minimum wage. I know it's easy for you, in your position, to sit there judging him—"

"I am not—Mom. Please. I'm trying to protect you. Both of you."

"From what? It's *legal*."

Round and round we went. I didn't yell. But when I ended the call, every face in the vicinity was angled toward me.

"Nothing to see here," I said, glaring.

They went back to work.

I snatched up the white envelope from the State of Delaware and tore it open, giving myself a paper cut. I sucked on my thumb while skimming the cover letter.

It was from the Capital One legal department.

Dear Mr. Edison: This is in response to your request of December 28 . . .

Enclosed were records for one of Winnie Ozawa's fake credit cards. Eight to twelve weeks, and they'd used every last one of them.

I turned pages until I came to her mailing address.

I drew my thumb from my mouth; the taste of blood lingered. "Fuck me."

Dani Botero said, "*Now* who died?"

I stuffed some items in my bag, grabbed my vest, and hurried out.

MY GPS ALREADY had the address from a previous search.

I took 580 to the Maze, passing Ikea, where weekend deal hounds filled the parking lot; passing the wholesome minivans lined up for Bay Street, afternoon movie, dinner at California Pizza

Kitchen; exiting at Powell and making my way through the revised Emeryville streetscape to arrive at a bland, pleasant residential midrise.

I parked in the space reserved for visitors.

It was almost one a.m. in London.

What would Nwodo want me to do?

Call, wake her up? I'd already ruined her vacation once.

I sent her a text, waited twenty minutes. Got out of my car.

In the lobby, I flashed my badge at the doorman and kept walking.

"Sir?" he said.

I went to the elevator bank.

The doorman said, "Sir, come back here, please."

I got into the elevator.

"*Sir. I—*"

The doors closed.

On the fourth floor I walked a hallway painted a flaccid ecru and hung with unlimited-edition lithographs. Muted abstract carpeting, green and bark, evoked the forest floor. From within the ceiling, deep within the walls, came the sound of fast-rushing air, as though I were the lone passenger on an airplane, destination unknown.

Inside unit 4011, a TV murmured.

I knocked.

The dialogue snapped off.

Behind me, the elevator dinged, and the doorman stumbled out. He spotted me and started loping down the hall.

"Sir. You can't be up here."

The door to unit 4011 opened.

Meredith Klaar peered out at me, glazed, her mouth a puckered interrogative. Thin to begin with, she'd lost weight and now verged on frail. The blue in her hair had dulled to the color of old bruises.

Sooty smears beneath her eyes. She wore flannel pajama bottoms, woolen house slippers with holes in the toes, a sweatshirt dotted with crumbs.

I could see into the apartment, and I remembered my previous visit, wastebasket full of crumpled tissues, spent boxes everywhere and unopened boxes stacked like a bulwark on the kitchen counter.

All of it had been cleared away.

She'd cried herself out.

"Sir," the doorman said, uncertainly.

"It's okay," Meredith said to him.

She smiled at me. "You came back."

"I have a couple of new questions for you."

She stood back to admit me.

"Easier if you came down to the station," I said.

The natural question: why?

Meredith nodded. "Is it cold out?"

"Not so bad."

"I get cold easily," she said.

"Go grab a jacket," I said.

THREE

Beforemath

CHAPTER 26

The drive to the Sheriff's offices on Lakeside took fifteen minutes. In the rearview, Meredith Klaar slumped low, nibbling her thumb, gazing serenely out the window.

She knew what was happening; had expected it.

Guilty people put their heads down in interview rooms because they're tired. Lying is exhausting. Running is exhausting. Waiting for the doorbell, the phone; petrified of tripping up, straining not to bust out in public confession.

When the spirit is broken, the body follows.

In the sluggish station elevator she smiled bashfully at her feet. She'd swapped out the slippers for eggplant-colored Converse Chucks. She seemed childlike. Like Winnie Ozawa.

"Thank you," she said. "For listening."

At that point she had yet to say a word. But I nodded.

The elevator croaked open. I held the door. "After you."

I got us an interview room, got her a bottle of water. Once we were seated, I showed her the fake credit cards. I showed her the letter from Capital One, listing Winnie Ozawa's mailing address, same as that of Meredith Klaar's studio unit.

When I displayed the photo of Winnie's gray face, she hid in her sleeves.

"Please don't make me look at it."

"'Her,'" I said. "Not 'it.'"

She huddled in her make-believe shelter.

"Meredith," I said.

She sat up. Wiped her nose on her wrist. Her arms were like sticks. She uncapped the water bottle but did not drink. "I'm ready."

THEY'D MET AT school.

"Watermark," I said.

Her reaction: amusement. *Is there another?*

Meredith had arrived at age twelve, after bouncing around several other schools. In the beginning she had a hard landing. She was confused, resentful, undisciplined. She skipped class. She skipped meals. She steered clear of the other kids. They didn't shun her, but neither did they go out of their way to make her feel welcome. She might not have lasted, had she not fallen in with Winnie Ozawa.

"She was my first real friend," Meredith said. "There or anywhere."

Theirs was a relationship forged in common disdain. For authority; for their earnest peers who'd drunk the Kool-Aid. Everyone at Watermark liked to think they were so rebellious and unique, when really they'd bought into a system, no different from that of their parents or their church or the piano teacher.

"They *non*-conformed identically," Meredith said. "'Look how free we are, la-dee-dah.' Nature, arts and crafts, the kind of cheesy garbage that just made you want to barf."

Winnie was a loner, too, and though younger than Meredith by a couple of years, she came off as a sophisticate. She introduced Meredith to weed, which Meredith didn't particularly enjoy, but which she smoked anyway, because she couldn't afford to jeopardize Winnie's esteem. Late at night they'd sneak into the woods to pass a stubby joint back and forth, mocking the other kids, the La-Dee-Dahs, high on life.

What started out as transgressive and cool soon felt silly. No one *cared* if they got high. No one gave a shit if they were in the woods late at night or ran naked or ate leaves or skinned squirrels or cut class.

That was the crux of the problem. What was the point of breaking a rule that didn't exist? "I was the difficult one," she said. "I was used to having an adversary."

She *needed* an adversary.

But you can't push against something that gives no resistance. Swiftly she went from feeling silly to feeling pathetic; from pathetic to furious.

One morning, she stormed over to the main office. Ready to shriek at Camille, demand that Camille call her parents and tell them to come get her right away.

No, Camille said, I'm not going to do that.

But she *had* to.

You don't have to do anything you don't want to do, Camille replied. Nor do I.

"That totally threw me. I didn't know what to say. I pitched a fit. Down on the floor, kicking, flailing. A full-on banshee shitstorm."

It seemed to be a pleasurable memory for her.

"What did Camille do?" I asked.

"Nothing."

I raised my eyebrows.

"She let me carry on for a minute," Meredith said. "Then she went back to her crossword. Fine. I'll yell louder. But it was like she couldn't see or hear me. And then I had this out-of-body experience. I could see *myself,* rolling around on the ground like a two-year-old. By the end I was curled up in Camille's arms, sobbing."

Everything changed after that. Others began to show her kindness. Or it was possible that they had been offering kindness all along, and she'd refused to believe them. She allowed herself to open up. She tried out their stupid activities, found they weren't as ridiculous as she thought. She worked in the garden, hours at a stretch. It wore her out so much that she started declining Winnie's nighttime invitations. She worked the boy who ran the woodshop, and through him her circle began to widen.

She introduced her first resolution at Town Hall. When it passed, the feeling she got was like none she'd ever experienced.

"That was real freedom," she said.

"What was the resolution?"

"Budget." Hint of a smile. "Money for fertilizer."

By May, she dreaded the prospect of summer vacation.

Who would take care of her tomatoes while she was gone?

She returned for her second year a full convert. La-dee-dah. High on life.

As for Winnie, she'd moved on to another newcomer.

With time Meredith came to recognize the pattern: Winnie operating as a black-market welcoming committee, displaying an uncanny knack for identifying those who would fail to fit in—the misfits among the misfits.

I asked if she thought Camille put Winnie up to the task.

Meredith bit her lip. "I don't think so. Camille practices what she preaches. She stayed out of our business."

Even after Meredith and Winnie had gone their separate paths, they retained a mutual fondness, unspoken, not unlike the embers of a first love. By no means did Meredith expect that. Nothing goes cold faster than revoked intimacy, and in the hermetically sealed world that was Watermark you had no way to avoid one particular person.

It might have turned ugly. Yet they continued to smile at each other on the path; to share an occasional meal, share an eye roll across the meeting hall.

"I was keeping her in my back pocket, you know? Just in case. Cause things always break down. I guess she was doing the same."

She sighed. "You can't understand how . . . *off* I felt, when she just upped and went. I don't think I'm the only one who reacted that way. Watermark without Winnie Ozawa, it's like an insult. To the natural order."

The more Meredith thought about it, the sorrier she felt for Winnie. It made her sad that Winnie couldn't appreciate what she had.

"She'd never spent any real time out of the valley. *She* was the naïve one, not me. But there was nothing I could do. Her problems were hers to deal with."

I said, "After she left, you two kept in touch."

"No. Even if I'd wanted to, I had no way to contact her. There was nothing until she found me."

"When was that?"

"About a year and a half ago."

That lined up with Camille's account of Winnie's most recent visit to the school.

I said, "What happened?"

"I come home from work and she's sitting in the lobby. She jumped up and threw her arms around me in this giant hug."

"Where'd she been in the meantime?"

"I don't know."

"You didn't ask?"

"I haven't seen her in four years and here she is behaving like it's last week. I wasn't prepared. Having her there felt warm and good, I didn't want to spoil it."

"Why do you think she came to you?"

"I want to think cause we'd been close. But probably she had nowhere else to go."

Studio apartment, one twin bed.

I asked if she and Winnie had ever been romantically involved.

"Nothing happened."

"Would you have wanted something to happen?"

"No. No. You're not ... If you'd had our experiences, you'd understand."

"Help me understand," I said.

She thought awhile before answering. "It was a spiritual connection."

And yet.

Here we were.

I centered the credit card statement. "Whose idea was this? Yours or hers?"

"I had nothing to do with that. I swear. I didn't know what she was up to."

"You let her use your mailing address."

"Absolutely not. Never. She just did it."

"There are sixteen cards," I said. "Sixteen statements showing up in your mailbox every month."

Meredith shook her head violently. "I didn't get any statements. I swear to God. Maybe the doorman thought the names were wrong and tossed them in the trash. I don't know what to tell you. They never got to me. Never."

I didn't believe her, but I didn't want to push too hard, too soon, before we'd gotten to the main event. I sat back, stretched my legs, eased my tone. "How long did Winnie end up staying with you?"

"I don't know. Awhile."

"A week? Two?"

"About a month." She paused. "A little longer ... maybe six weeks, altogether. Seven? I wasn't keeping a calendar."

"Did you help her out otherwise? Give her money?"

"She took from the fridge. I didn't ask her to chip in rent or anything. That's not what it was about."

"You were helping a friend in need."

"Yes. Exactly."

"After that, where'd she go?"

"Wherever she went. 'I'm a traveler.' She liked how she lived. It was her choice."

Spoken like a true Watermark alum.

I said, "When did you see her next?"

Meredith shrugged. "She'd drop in whenever she felt like it. A night or two. She never gave me any notice."

"Using your place as a crash pad."

"More than that." She bit her lip. "I wanted her to feel she belonged."

I remembered Winnie's lonely, empty pockets.

"Let's talk about the night of the party. How'd you two end up there together?"

Meredith stared at the tabletop, skimming her nails against fake wood. Glossy peach polish, now chipped and bitten ragged.

She swayed, touched her hair. Closed her eyes. Her breathing was rapid and shallow.

"Meredith? The party."

"It was an accident," she said.

A lie. You can't throttle someone accidentally.

The first time I'd met her she'd come right out with it.

I killed her.

I'd assumed then that she meant Jasmine.

But look at it another way: she'd been trying to get ahead of me, to absolve herself.

Trying to do the same, now?

I said, "Let's start with, you hear about a party."

She opened her eyes. Moist, weary. "Winnie did. She read about it online."

"Did you know anyone else who was going to be there?"

"No."

"So you decided to show up at some random thing."

"Yes. I mean, it wasn't random, she thought it looked cool. She didn't want to go by herself, so I was like, 'Fine, whatever.' "

"You remember what time you got there?"

"Late. Probably around eleven thirty."

"And at that point, what was the mood between you two?"

"Okay, I guess."

"Were you arguing?"

"Not really," she said. "I mean, yeah. I was annoyed at her. I didn't want to be there. It was crazy loud. I was tired, I wanted to go home. Now I can't, because she has no car, and so I'm stuck, trying not to go deaf."

"She couldn't make her own way?"

"What?"

"Winnie lived on the street. You didn't figure she'd find a way to get back?"

Meredith fidgeted. "I'm going to *leave* her there? That's so cruel. Like, what if she, I don't know. Gets raped. Think how I'd feel."

The irony appeared lost on her.

"You need to realize," she said, "these people are all strangers to me. To both of us. I don't know who they are or what their deal is. What would you do in that situation?"

"I get where you're coming from."

Meredith Klaar crossed her arms with finality. "Right. So."

"So," I said. "You're at the party. You're not getting along, but it's no big deal."

"I'm like, 'This sucks, let's leave.' She wouldn't listen. Suddenly she goes off on me and starts screaming."

"What triggered it?"

"I don't . . . I mean, I don't think it was one specific thing. She was high. Even when she's sober, she's not the most stable person in the world."

"Were you inside the house or outside, when she freaked out?"

"Outside. They weren't letting anyone in except to use the restroom. They had a rope set up. Red velvet. Like at a club? Anyway, I'd already peed, we were just hanging."

"What did you say to each other?"

"Like the exact words?"

"As close as you can remember."

Meredith cinched her arms across her torso. "It was months ago."

"Did she do or say something that made you especially upset?"

"I don't know. I can't even remember."

"Lots of people get into arguments," I said. "What I'm trying to understand is how in this case it ends up with Winnie dead."

"I told you. It was an accident."

You told me *I killed her.* When I had no idea what you were really saying.

I said, "Remind me what time you got there?"

"Eleven thirty."

"You're sure about that."

She hesitated. "It might've been later."

"Okay. That's fine. So explain to me this argument you had."

"Explain it how?"

"It must've gotten pretty heated."

"She was upset. We both were." Nibbling her thumb. "She pushed me."

"Pushed you."

"Hard. That's what I'm saying. I didn't mean to—I was reacting. She pushed me and I pushed her back and it just . . . happened."

"Okay," I said. "Can you walk me through it?"

"She attacked me. She started hitting me. I—I don't know. I yelled at her to stop. Have you ever tried reasoning with someone on meth? It's not like they're super logical."

"This is happening in the middle of the yard, everyone watching you."

"*No one* was watching us. There was nobody else around. Those guys came to the house to start shit, everyone left to see what was going on."

"Where in the yard is this taking place?"

"I don't . . . I'm having a hard time—it's like everything is disconnected." A beat. "I'm sorry."

"You're doing great, Meredith."

She looked at me. "What was the question?"

"Where you were when Winnie attacked you."

"Toward the, the, the . . . back."

"The back of the yard."

"Uh-huh."

"That's helpful," I said. "Thanks. Could you describe the surroundings any more specifically?"

"I told you what I remember."

"I know, and I appreciate that. But it's little details that really help us."

"Help you what?"

"Understand."

"I wish I understood," she said. "It was dark, that's all I remember."

She wiped her spitty thumb on her pant leg. "Okay. Here's something: when she hit me. All these thoughts, and memories . . . Like, how dare you. You're out of my life, and now . . ." Beat. "I didn't know what I was doing. I was out of control. She got out of control and I caught it from her."

"So what did you do?"

"Hit her."

"With your hand? With an object?"

"A—I think it was a shovel."

"Where'd you get a shovel?"

"There was stuff everywhere, I grabbed the first thing I saw."

"Where on her body did you hit her with the shovel?"

She indicated her flank. The site of Winnie's bruising, the two broken ribs.

"And then?" I asked.

"And then, she fell down."

"Was she alive at that point?" I asked.

"I don't know." Her gaze ran back and forth across the tabletop; she had resumed gnawing on her thumb. "It's like there's a blank." She let out a weird laugh. "Like someone took out a piece of my brain."

I waited for more.

Nothing.

"You hit her with the shovel," I said. "She falls down. What's going through your mind?"

She murmured unintelligibly.

"What's that, Meredith?"

No reply.

"Putting myself in your shoes, I think I'd want to know how

she's doing." Again I waited. "Maybe I'd get down on the ground, shake her. 'Winnie, wake up.' Check to see if she's breathing. If she has a pulse."

"I didn't. Nothing like that." Her nostrils flared. "I was scared. I wasn't thinking."

"Once you realized she was dead, what did you do with the body?"

"I . . . I can't remember."

"Please try."

"I am." She scrunched up her face. "It's not like this is easy for me."

"Sure," I said. "What's the next thing you do remember?"

Her answer, without delay: "The car. I'm driving, they're banging on the roof for me to stop. I got out, and everyone's . . . They were pointing. Underneath the . . ."

She shuddered and fell silent.

"Just to be clear," I said. "You remember hitting Winnie, and then you're in the car and folks are banging on the roof."

"Yes."

"Nothing in between?"

"Uh-uh."

My phone rang: Nwodo.

"Tell you what," I said to Meredith. "We've been going awhile. I think it's time for a break. It might help you remember."

Meredith Klaar nodded listlessly.

"You want something to eat?"

Her response was to lay her head down on the table.

CHAPTER 27

I phoned Nwodo from the viewing room. Four thirty a.m. in London, she'd woken with jet lag to find my texts and emails.

"Tell me it's okay to bug you," I said.

"Sure. But I'm not getting on a plane till I hear something concrete."

I recounted the substance of Meredith's story. "She's lying. No doubt."

"What she did tell you fits."

"She gave me salad and left out the meat. I show up at her apartment, no warning. She gets in a car with me, no questions asked. Doesn't want a lawyer. Has no trouble going on and on about stuff from years ago. Then I ask her to go back to December and it's full of blanks? Bullshit. The question is why."

"Denial," Nwodo said. "She can't seal the deal."

"Maybe. But she admits attacking Winnie with a shovel. She showed me on her own body where she hit her. It matches what we know about the bruises and the ribs. She remembers the color of the velvet rope. When it comes to putting her hands on Winnie's neck? 'Whoops, that part of my brain's been lifted out of my skull.'"

"They see it on TV," Nwodo said. "'I have no memory, I was in a trance.'"

"It doesn't make any sense. The time frame's wrong. ShotSpotter recorded the first gunfire at eleven fifty-five. Eyewitnesses saw Jasmine get run over within a few minutes of that. Meredith said she and Winnie showed up at the party at eleven thirty. They fight, blah blah, next thing you know Winnie's under a hundred fifty pounds of dirt. Meredith's doing all that by herself, in less than thirty minutes? I don't think so. When I pressed her on their arrival time, she said it might've been *later*. Not earlier. She told me she and Winnie don't know anyone else at this party. 'Everyone's a stranger.' She said that more than once. Like she wanted to make sure I got it."

"There was someone else," Nwodo said.

"Male DNA under Winnie's fingernails," I said. "We know it's not Larry Vinson's. Whoever it was, she's trying to cover for him, and painting herself into a corner. That's why she can't say how Winnie died: she really doesn't know. She's present when the argument starts. Then it turns physical. Winnie gets hit with the shovel, goes down. Meredith panics and runs. All she's thinking about is escaping. She's not watching the road. Back in January I interviewed her about the car accident and asked if she was scared of getting shot. You know what she told me? 'I wish I had been.'"

"Two people dead," Nwodo said.

"Can you imagine? She looked a fucking wreck, and at the time I'm asking myself, *Can I walk out of here, or is she going to throw herself out the window?* She's going, 'I killed her, I did it, let's get this over with.'"

"Mr. X," Nwodo said. "Why's Meredith willing to take a murder rap for him?"

"Why do people do anything?"

"Sex and money."

"Not love?"

"Isn't that what I said?"

"Goddamn but you're bleak," I said. "When are you back?"

"Supposed to be Friday. If I could beam myself over there, I would."

"You mind if I go in and take another swing?"

There was a pause. "You think you can crack her."

"Right now she's vulnerable. Wait too long and she could go into her shell. Or pull a Larry on us."

"Mm." Another pause. "Do your thing, Barnacle Man."

I CHECKED THE monitor. Meredith had moved to the floor and was balled up, fetal. I stayed put, letting the minutes drag out, waiting for her to get restless. I felt keyed up, my adrenaline flowing. Not a good disposition to take into an interrogation. You win by staying calm.

I stood, shucking in place to shed excess energy. The cushion of the chair was compressed from too much cop ass. All viewing rooms are the same.

"Look what the mother-loving cat dragged in."

Grinning at me, one hand clutching the doorframe, the other tucked inside his bulging waistband, was Sergeant Joey Vitti, my ex-boss.

"Someone said you were in the building," he said. "I didn't believe em. Clay Edison? *The* Clay Edison?"

"Appearing one night only."

We shook warily. It was Vitti who'd suspended me, emphasizing all the while that it was for my own good. He wasn't a bad guy at heart. He just viewed everything through one lens: *How does this affect me?* Any deviation from protocol had the potential to disrupt his unstoppable, sloth-like progress up the ladder. Your basic bureaucrat.

It felt awkward now to be shooting the breeze, catching him up on the other members of our team. True what they said about Turnbow, tough but fair. Lindsey Bagoyo was working out fine. Zaragoza, how many kids did he have by now, eleven? Shupfer's son Danny: could be better, health-wise, but you wouldn't hear her complaining.

And Big Brad Moffett, his former protégé?

"I heard he caught that shooting back Christmas," Vitti said.

"We all did. Bad scene."

"Gotta say, I don't miss it, not one second." He ran his tongue over his lower lip; I saw his gaze snag on the screen, where Meredith Klaar lay like a stone. "So what brings you to our neck of the woods."

"Incidental shit."

"Uh-huh," he said.

"Favor for a pal. She's tied up out of town." When that failed to satisfy him, I added: "I've met her witness before, she's comfortable with me."

"The Great Communicator."

I smiled tensely.

"Well," Vitti said, "don't stay up too late, you got school in the morning."

"Thanks. Take care, Sarge."

"Yeah, you too." He didn't leave. "One thing I feel I should mention—and I say this cause I care, you know that, right?"

"Yes, sir, I do."

"You know I do. It's been a good year for me, you know? Time to reflect."

"Glad to hear it."

"You might consider doing the same, whether you can be happy there, long term."

I said, "At the Coroner's, you mean."

"Not that I'm suggesting you do one thing versus the other. But we all make choices in life. Right? You and me, we're not that different. Not everybody's cut out for it."

"Yes, sir."

He drummed the doorframe. "Back to our regularly scheduled program."

On the monitor, Meredith Klaar had stirred at last, reaching for her water bottle to drain it. I went down the hall to the vending machine to buy her another.

WHOEVER DEFINED INSANITY as doing the same thing over and over while expecting different results never conducted a police interview.

You ask the same question a thousand times because most people can't stand to give the same answer a thousand times. Human beings crave variety. Eventually, they slip, out of carelessness or boredom.

All interview rooms are the same.

All police stations are, at root, the same: incubators for psychological breakdown.

The risk is that the subject starts inventing things, to please you or to get you off their back.

So far, that did not appear to be an issue for Meredith Klaar.

It was an accident, I was upset, I don't remember.

Her mantra.

When pushed for specifics she embellished some extraneous element of the story. She could tell me about the music. She could tell me about Winnie's outfit. But the critical period surrounding the murder remained a black box.

After a whole bunch of that, I took a risk of my own.

"Who else was with you that night, Meredith?"

Wire-tight: *"No one."*

284 / JONATHAN KELLERMAN and JESSE KELLERMAN

"Come on, now. You and he didn't take the time to get your story straight?"

Silence.

I loomed in, making use of my height. "Is that what you want? To go down for someone else? Why would you do that?"

She was chewing on her thumb so hard I thought she might bite it off.

I switched to the credit cards. Veered back to Winnie's death.

It was an accident.

I was upset.

I don't remember.

"Why don't you *believe* me," she said.

"I don't know," I said. "I guess you just don't seem like the type."

"You don't know anything about me."

"Well, so tell me."

"I *am* telling you."

I said, "Let's go back a second."

"No. No. I don't want to go back. I don't know what it is you want me to say. I'm telling you I don't *remember*. Who cares? She's dead because of me."

"Without a clear sense of what you did and did not do—"

"I *killed her*. What's unclear about that? This is—I don't know what it is. It's crazy. I'm making this easy for you. How often do you get someone coming in saying 'I did it'?"

"Generally they can provide corroborating information."

"I *am*."

"About everything except the main part."

"*I don't remember.*"

Silence.

It was after one in the morning.

Time for another risky bet.

"Here's what we're going to do," I said. "I'm going to drive you home. You sleep on it, and we can try again tomorrow."

I rose. Meredith didn't.

"I'm not leaving," she said.

I felt so punchy, I nearly laughed. "Okay."

"I'm not," she said. "I will not leave."

"I've heard what you have to say. There's no reason—"

"Arrest me."

This was one of the stranger conversations I'd ever had. "You want me to put you in handcuffs and take you to a cell."

"Why else am I here?"

I began gathering up my documents and photographs. "Sure, I'll arrest you."

"Then do it."

"When I'm ready."

She stared at me with utter contempt. "I have to, like, buy you dinner first?"

I rapped the table. "Come on. Time to go home."

She gripped the chair, as if to anchor herself.

I left her there and went to ask for help. The pickings were meager. Graveyard shift, squad room lights doused, a single deputy chicken-pecking while his radio babbled prophecy.

I knocked on the shift commander's door. He put down his fidget spinner. I explained the situation to him. He made me explain twice more. Still confused, he walked with me over to the viewing room.

On the monitor, Meredith sat upright, jogging her leg, her hair tucked behind her ears. She looked like she was waiting for the results of a medical test.

"She's begging you to arrest her and you're telling her no?"

"Pretty much."

He nodded contemplatively. "You're Vitti's guy."

I wasn't sure how to respond to that.

"You managed to bring her in," he said, walking away. "I'm sure you're smart enough to figure out how to get her to leave."

I said, "Yes, sir, I'll do that."

ALL INTERVIEW ROOMS are the same.

There are white or gray walls, thin polyester carpeting, shaded dark to hide stains. Sticky scuffed table. Folding chairs, or tubular chairs, purchased in bulk by County Procurement. You might imagine that the table and chairs are bolted down. They are at the jail. Everything in jail is bolted down, because everything is a weapon. No such care extends to your average station room. Detectives like to move things around, change the layout to their psychological advantage.

What TV gets wrong is the lighting. No matter how good a show is, no matter how edgy the dialogue or gritty the backdrop, the interview scenes invariably take place under two isolating spots, one each for cop and subject, the background gradating into shadow. I understand why they do it—more dramatic—but it gets under my skin. Never have I seen an interview room that was anything less than blindingly bright.

I went down the hall to the room where Meredith Klaar was keeping her petulant vigil, pausing before I entered to change the wall slider from IN USE to VACANT.

I unlocked the door and stepped inside. "Time to go."

Under that bright and unremitting light, I saw it coming: the glossy flash of bruise-blue hair, chipped nails and bared teeth.

A silver tracery as she swung a chair at my head.

I ducked.

This was a reflex, and a lousy one at that. She was aiming for the head of an average man, who's five-foot-nine. Dropping six inches brought me right into the line of fire.

The leg caught me on the temple, staggering me sideways. Meredith lost her grip, and the chair flew into the wall, barely missing the thermostat panel, which concealed one of the CCTV camera lenses.

She fell, jackknifing over the table, then sprang back, assuming a Karate Kid–style fighting position. She looked ludicrous. But ludicrous can still scratch and bite.

I rounded on her, palms up.

De-escalate. Stop this before it got any further out of hand.

"Listen," I said.

She leapt at me. I grabbed her wrists, swung her around, slammed her into the wall.

"Calm down. Meredith."

She thrashed, pumping her legs, trying to knee me in the nuts.

"Backup," I yelled. Her wrists were so slender that I was able to grip both in one hand, freeing up my other arm to pin her across the throat. "Room five."

She spit in my face.

"Backup. Now."

Footsteps.

The chicken-pecking deputy barreled through the open doorway. "Aw shit."

He jumped in to grab her legs, and we wrestled her down to the ground.

"My mistake," I said, cuffing her. "I guess you are the type."

The side of her face was crushed against the smelly carpeting, giving her fish lips. But through that, I could see her smiling.

She'd gotten her way.

CHAPTER 28

As soon as a new form of communication arises, people will find a way to use it to embarrass themselves. Call it Zuckerberg's Law.

I suppose the same held true with the arrival of the camera, the telegraph, the telephone. But I have to believe that the computer age will have us suffering all out of proportion, far beyond any statute of limitation.

You can burn paper. You can hang up a phone. A compromising Facebook post, hasty tweet, or indiscreet selfie? They'll haunt you forever, because nothing digital ever dies.

The best you can do is smother it and pray.

Hence the booming business known euphemistically as online reputation management. Flood the web with redundant sites. Cross-link them. Post bogus reviews. Send bogus lawyer letters and removal requests. Tweak the algorithm, pushing unfavorable content farther and farther down the list, and filling the top spots with applause.

Google has conditioned us to accept that whatever comes up first is what we actually need: instant gratification as a proxy for

truth. Who bothers browsing beyond the tenth page of search results? Let alone the fortieth.

I hadn't.

When you searched for "Watermark School," the first hit returned was the school's homepage. The second was the Wikipedia
entry on C. E. Buntley. The third was the warm-'n'-fuzzy article
celebrating Watermark's golden anniversary, in 2001. There was
the student creative writing journal, and the multitude of ratings
sites that awarded the school five stars.

Then a hundred miles of internet gobbledygook.

I remembered the invoices piled on Camille Buntley's desk.

We-B-Klean.

Their site featured the same vacuum-cleaner/race-car logo.

Their corporate mission statement:

Protecting Your Good Name in Cyberspace

They were based out of Latvia. Basic management packages
began at three thousand dollars per month, but could be tailored to
fit the client's needs.

They, too, had received nothing but five-star reviews.

IF YOU LOOKED, as I had, for "Watermark School," you got the
impression that everything was fine and dandy.

Likewise when you typed in Camille Buntley's name or her father's or any of the top ten most predictable search terms—including
"Winnie Ozawa."

We-B-Klean was concerned with traffic coming through the
front door.

For all their raves, they'd forgotten about side doors. Or they
deemed those doors not worth worrying about. Or they hadn't
been paid enough to close them.

Side doors such as "Meredith Klaar," for example.

It came up as the seventeenth hit, after her numerous social media profiles.

Struggling to find a place

For many children unhappy in conventional settings, the Watermark School has served as a haven. But can it survive in a changing world?

February 21, 2009

Meredith Klaar has never enjoyed school.

"I hated it," Klaar, 13, says, of her previous school, located in her hometown of Somerville, Massachussetts. "Everything was so programmed. The people were programmed, too. It's not like that here."

The "here" Klaar refers to is the Watermark School, a private educational institution for ages six through seventeen, located in a remote valley at the northwestern edge of Marin County . . .

Like the article celebrating the fiftieth anniversary, this one appeared in the *Marin Independent Journal*. But the tone of the coverage had soured in the intervening eight years.

The Buntley approach, always controversial, had begun to appear obsolete in a high-speed, highly competitive culture. Hands-off had given way to helicopter parenting, free play to Mandarin lessons and coding club. Watermark's failure to adapt, the piece suggested, had had material consequences: in recent years the student body had shrunk by more than 50 percent, giving rise to a chronic shortage of funds.

Camille Buntley's response was, in effect, to shrug. Since its inception, she said, Watermark had faced naysayers, busybodies who would force upon others a single model of education. Parents who wanted robot children were not the parents they aimed to reach. She pointed out that the school's track record for college placement remained excellent—on par with other top private schools. Several recent graduates had gone on to the Ivy League.

Far more meaningful to her, however, was knowing that those students who had not gone on to college had done so of their own volition. She challenged the assumption that a bachelor's degree was the be-all and end-all of a young person's life.

Certainly not when it comes to personal happiness she said.

Nor were financial straits anything new. Her father had plowed his life savings into buying the land. He'd operated on a shoestring budget and spent much of his tenure fighting off creditors.

The beauty of Watermark Camille said *is that its success does not depend on fancy equipment or expensive facilities. It springs, rather, from the fertility of the child's own mind.*

A few bills did not trouble her. They had yet to complete their annual fundraising drive. Last year they'd had enough left over to buy a new kiln. Without fail, their families and alumni came through.

To understand their devotion, she said, all you had to do was speak to the children. Ask how they felt.

For her part, Meredith Klaar wouldn't have it any other way.

"This is more than a school to me," she says. "It's my home."

On balance, the piece was unflattering, but not damning. The portrait it sketched was one of gradual decline, rather than a downward spiral. It would hardly seem to merit the expense and hassle of an internet scrubber. To the contrary: I detected a gleeful note in Camille's stubbornness. Suffering fools had become the Watermark way, overcoming persecution a mark of pride.

Yet the link to the article appeared nowhere in the first four hundred Google results, at least not in response to conventional search strings. Suggesting that she—or someone—had paid to have it suppressed.

I began trawling the paper's online archive.

In short order I'd reached the marrow: a dozen other headlines, detailing a protracted conflict between Watermark and local authorities. Notably, none of the links returned with a standard search.

September 2008: *School fined $5,000 for improper electrical line*

March 2009: *County investigates allegations of hazardous materials*

Some of these skirmishes were substantial.

May 2009: *Measles outbreak sends two to hospital*

Others felt like much ado about nothing.

February 2010: *Student veggie stand dinged for missing vendor license*

You could chart the rising friction on a graph, a line peaking in October 2010.

HHS wants school shut down

Citing numerous safety and public health code violations, Marin Health and Human Services yesterday submitted to the County Board of Supervisors a letter requesting the temporary closure of the Watermark School . . .

Reasons for the closure included rodents in the kitchen and structural problems with the Quonset hut. I saw those as pretexts— final straws. Camille had spoken out against the establishment one too many times, for too long failed to pay her fines. The matter had also been referred to the California Association of Independent Schools, which planned to open its own investigation.

> This is not the first time Watermark has come under the microscope. In 2005, Children and Family Services responded to complaints of child endangerment, after a seven-year-old student was found wandering the highway, several miles from the campus . . .

That charge had been overturned on appeal.

Still. It was a bad look.

By the opening of academic year 2011, the situation had improved, enough so that Watermark had regained its accreditation on a probationary basis. A settlement was reached for the outstanding fines, and the county agreed to back off.

For a while, things went quiet.

Then:

Coroner rules boy's death an accident
December 21, 2012

> A single-car crash that took the life of a sixteen-year-old student at the Watermark School last month has been ruled an accident, the Marin County coroner said in a statement Wednesday.

The boy's name was Charlie Sepp. He was described as quiet and well liked, known around campus in his capacity as manager of the woodshop. An inset photo showed a young man with a lopsided smile and floppy white-blond hair, settled amid a tangle of disembodied limbs.

According to the article, Watermark kept an old Ford F-150 that licensed students were permitted to use, provided their parents had signed a waiver. It wasn't uncommon for Charlie to drive into town to purchase lumber or other supplies from the hardware store.

The week before Thanksgiving, 2012, he helped himself to the keys.

The next day, the driver of a FedEx van called 911 to report a vehicle off the road, its front end buried in the trunk of a redwood. Without a seatbelt, Charlie Sepp had gone through the windshield.

When you searched for his name, the link came up as the two thousand two hundred thirty-ninth hit.

Saturday, April 6

5:55 p.m.

Nwodo landed on a Friday afternoon and went home to sleep. The following evening we convened at my apartment, where I'd commandeered the kitchen table to lay out my dossier: laptop, notes from my interview with Meredith, inch-thick stack of printouts.

She said, "I leave you alone for one week."

I made a sucking sound: *Barnacle.*

We reviewed the newspaper articles.

"You can see why Camille's afraid," I said. "They've just pulled through a rough patch. They're getting back on their feet and a kid dies."

"It could bring everything crashing back down."

"So she buries it. Soup to nuts."

"You have to admit, it worked," Nwodo said. "They're still around."

"True. There's nothing illegal about what she's doing. She's protecting her school."

"And herself."

"Feels skeezy, though."

"One hundred percent."

I said, "What I do find unusual is the radio silence from Charlie Sepp's parents. I'm them, I'm suing the shit out of Watermark. I checked. Nothing in the news, no court filings."

"Even if they signed a waiver," she said, "how often do those hold up?"

"There are a million lawyers out there who'd be happy to take a run in civil court. Worst-case scenario, sue and settle."

She said, "They're rationalizing. Charlie knew how to drive. Accidents happen."

"Okay. Now ask yourself how they react if it wasn't an accident."

Nwodo looked at me.

I said, "I had Coroner's in Marin send me a copy of the report. He drove straight off the road. No skid marks. Far from conclusive, but you have to wonder. A lot of single-car crashes are suicides. I've heard numbers as high as thirty percent. We get faced with it all the time, and we rarely know for sure. You don't have access to the main variable, which is the decedent's state of mind."

"What was Charlie's state of mind?"

"Parents and friends describe him as a normal teenager, but people will do anything to avoid a suicide tag. 'Could I have prevented it? What did I do to make his life so unbearable? Is there some genetic time bomb, ticking away inside *me*?' Without strong evidence, I go with accident. Reading between the lines, that's what Marin did."

"So what's the issue?"

I drew her attention to a paragraph on the ninth page of the Coroner's narrative.

I (Willis #543) interviewed Camille Buntley, principal of the school where decedent Sepp was enrolled. I inquired regarding ownership of the vehicle (CA lic. 9Z78354) driven by decedent Sepp. She advised that the vehicle belonged to the school and was available for general use.

"Now look here."

I paged ahead to a section of the narrative added later, by a different coroner.

I (Morawiecki #199) contacted the California Department of Motor Vehicles to obtain a copy of the vehicle registration for the truck CA lic. 9Z78354. This was furnished to me (item 22). The registered owner of the vehicle is Donald Bierce of San Francisco, CA. I telephoned Bierce. Bierce advised that he was the registered owner of the vehicle and stated that the truck was used primarily by his son Zachary Bierce, a classmate of decedent Sepp's at the Watermark School.

Nwodo said, "That guy. The teacher with the beard."

I nodded. "It's his truck Charlie's driving. Camille lied. And when we were up at the school, Bierce lied to us about being a newbie. I made a remark that it must be different teaching here than at other schools. You remember what he said?"

"He didn't have a point of comparison."

"Right. Which is true."

"Because it's the only school he's ever been at."

"Yeah. Exactly. Then he realizes what he's said and tries to backtrack. He tells us it's his first time *teaching,* he's only been there a year. A guy who goes from student to faculty? He's not going to mention that? These people have institutional pride. *As a matter of fact, I'm a graduate, myself.* Unless you don't want us to know you were around back then."

"They're close in age," Nwodo said. "Bierce and Winnie."

"And Charlie Sepp. And Meredith Klaar. They're classmates."

"If Watermark had real classes," she said. "I understand Bierce distancing himself from Charlie. His car was used, his pal's dead. What's the connection to Winnie now?"

I clicked my laptop to a new page and showed it to her.

She said, "This reads like bad student poetry."

"That's cause it is. It's the Watermark creative writing journal. Third from the bottom."

She scrolled down. "'The valley is my mother,'" she read. "'My father, the stones.'"

"Keep going."

"'My sisters and brothers are animal bones.'"

"See the author?"

Nwodo said, "'Chief Wyn.'"

"Our victim kept a blog," I said.

It detailed—in photos, in words—Winnie Ozawa's travels, thoughts, experiences. There were quiet periods and periods of frenzied writing; bursts of lucidity and incoherent, drug-addled screeds. She used her pen name, never her real name. The entries began shortly after her departure from Watermark, and they ended the previous November.

Lately I've been thinking a lot about my friend Charlie who died six years ago this week. Normally I'm not the type of person who gives a shit about anniversaries but hey it's been on my mind.

A lot of people when someone dies they say that he or she didn't deserve it but when it comes to Charlie it's true. He was a really good person. I don't say that lightly, I've met a lot of people and I know how bad people can be. Charlie was good inside. Not everybody understood that because he was very private, he didn't like everyone to know what he was thinking.

Teenagers die from cancer or another disease, people feel sad but they aren't afraid. They get excited and organize a bike ride to raise money. Suicide is different. No one talks, it's like the word is a curse. In my opinion that's a shame because one of the best things you can do to help someone who wants to hurt themselves is to speak to them directly. I regret that I wasn't able to do that for Charlie. I tried. I'm not making excuses for myself though.

People still don't know the truth about what happened. Even his parents don't. That bothers me, they deserve to know. It's taken me some time to admit this to myself. I was scared back then. Now that I'm older I can understand why it's important for them to know the truth even if it's painful. Not just his parents but everybody, maybe that way some good comes out of it. For example if someone out there is having the same feelings, they should realize they don't have to feel alone like Charlie did. We have to bring it into the open otherwise there's no way to learn and the same shitty mistakes can happen again.

Whose fault is that?

November 18, 2018 @ 3:49 a.m. by Chief Wyn   0 Comments

CHAPTER 29

Monday, April 8

It was my turn to drive.

Nwodo had coffee waiting. I didn't need any; anticipation had sharpened my senses. She didn't touch hers, either.

Over the San Rafael Bridge, the sky arched smooth and delicate, like the rim of a china cup, the edges of the Bay tucked in tightly along the coast.

We made good time. It helped that we'd been there before, knew what to look for.

The Watermark School

2.2 miles

Nwodo said, "Go slow."

A DRY SPRING had baked the track, leaving hard, jarring ruts. The car lumbered, its weight slopping from side to side. Wildflowers tunneled up through the dirt, spots of purple and yellow, forget-me-nots, redwood sorrel, western bleeding heart. The blooms lurked in the mottled shadows along the side of the road, like escapees hoping to hitch a ride.

Nwodo leaned forward, one palm braced against the dash, peering through the bars of tan light that spliced the canopy.

Watching for small bodies at play.

As we came through the tree line and the prow of the campus pushed into view, I was surprised to encounter a riot of noise and movement. For some reason I'd been expecting the stillness that had greeted us on our previous visit. But it was a beautiful day. The kids were out in full force to take advantage of it, kicking up a haze, mingling cries of delight and distress.

Only in freedom will the child come to integrate both halves of the personality, the Shadow and the Light.

In the air hung a tang of smoke; a charcoal thread drifted from the chimney in Camille's office. Nwodo and I headed in the opposite direction, toward the classrooms.

We found Zach Bierce sitting one-on-one with a boy of ten, who was reading aloud from *The Lorax* with difficulty, stammering the rhymes. Seeing us, the boy immediately stopped and shut the cover, glaring at the ground.

"Mr. Bierce," I said.

Bierce frowned. He had on the same purple down vest, the same beige Dickies. His beard had grown out, its sharp edges ragged, as though he hadn't moved from that spot in many months.

He laid a hand on the boy's shoulder. "We'll pick it up tomorrow, okay, Cyrus?"

The boy bolted the room.

Bierce waited until Cyrus had disappeared from view, then removed his glasses and began cleaning them on the corner of his shirt. "I don't appreciate you barging in. He has it hard enough as is without feeling judged by strangers."

"Nobody's judging him," Nwodo said.

"You're strangers," Bierce said.

From a distance came the ringing of the forge, dull wallops from the woodshop, a drunkard's rhythm.

"Is there a good place to talk?" I asked.

"About what?"

Nwodo said, "Someplace more private."

Bierce worked his lips and replaced his glasses. With a grunt he raised himself up. He'd been sitting in a child-sized chair, and his joints cracked and popped as he reassumed adult stature.

THE SIX MEMBERS of the Watermark faculty occupied a squat house set behind the dining hall. You couldn't accuse them of extravagance. Zach Bierce shared a bedroom with two other teachers. No closet. No television. Good housekeeping; everything tidy by necessity. Even so, an odor lingered, the brooding funk of captive male.

There was one twin-sized bed along the wall and, perpendicular to it, two more stacked in a bunk, curling snapshots thumbtacked to the rails. Unfinished cube bookcase, white pine and bare screws. Chest of drawers in the same boxy style. A multicolor rag rug, trampled flat, covered scant floor space.

Before entering, Bierce slipped off his shoes and asked us to do likewise.

He plopped down on the open bed. There was nowhere for us to sit unless we wanted to fold ourselves into the bottom bunk. I positioned myself in front of the dresser, resting an elbow along the upper bedrail. Nwodo switched on her phone's voice recorder and set it atop the bookcase.

Zach Bierce said, "Is this going to take long? I have an afternoon meeting."

Nwodo began by telling him we had Meredith Klaar in custody. She lied and said Meredith had confessed to everything.

I said Winnie Ozawa had male DNA under her fingernails, and that, in claiming to have started at the school only last year, we knew he was attempting to mislead us.

We knew it was his truck Charlie Sepp had been driving when he died.

We'd read Winnie's blog, where she wrote that Charlie's death was not an accident, but suicide, and that she intended to make that information public.

We stopped, leaving the splintery walls to suck up the echo of our voices.

Bierce cleaned his glasses again, checking the lenses for smudges. He was young, and handsome in a cozy, rumpled way, his brown eyes ringed with gold. Watermark's very own resident poet-philosopher, rubbing his belly and dispensing life lessons.

Girls giggling and whispering in his wake.

Evoking, in a certain kind of woman, feelings of protectiveness.

He put his glasses back on and gazed at us. "Where should we start?"

"The party," Nwodo said.

"It might be better to start at the beginning?"

A teacher. Posing a question. Expecting a certain answer.

When he didn't get it, he tried again.

I said, "Tell us about Charlie."

Bierce could've walked away.

Instead, he lectured.

THEY WERE FRIENDS. Him, Charlie, Meredith, a few others around their age. They regarded themselves as the wise elders of Watermark. Not many kids made it all the way through to seventeen. The attrition rate during the early teens was high. Most couldn't hack it. Freedom was easy at eight. An eight-year-old had little self-awareness.

Then the shock of puberty ripped your moorings loose, forcing you to reckon with your own individuality.

Easier to quit, retreat to conventional society, slip on a straitjacket. Find a nice, normal, *expected* form of rebellion to carry you through to adulthood. Then: shackle yourself to a job. Procreate. Watch TV. Climb, meek and numb, into your waiting grave.

Watermark prepared you for a life extraordinary. It required a special kind of courage. Those that did manage to hang on until graduation were a special breed.

They shared a powerful bond.

Winnie had occupied the periphery, drifting in and out when it suited her. She was an exception—her own special case.

For her, Watermark was the straitjacket.

Zach was the oldest chronologically. That didn't mean he was in charge. If we thought that then we didn't understand the first thing about Watermark.

It was a democracy. A real democracy, unlike the sham most people referred to when they used that word. Everyone had a say. Roles shifted. Alliances formed and dissolved. Feelings came and went. They were figuring it out. Instability was inherent to the process.

You grew accustomed to autonomy. At first you wallowed in it. Then it became like oxygen. You didn't know any other way to be. To have the outside world poke its snout in, gobbling at the core of your being, came as a rude awakening.

Charlie Sepp was from San Diego. His parents were divorced. His father was a fashion photographer, a complete piece of shit who'd never shown a speck of interest in Charlie. His mother, a former model, had full custody. Over the summer, she'd gotten re-married. Her new husband had kids from a previous marriage who lived back east with their birth mother. Now the man wanted to move to New York City, so he could be present as they grew up. Not only did Charlie's mother consent, she decided to drag Charlie along, as well: uprooting him in the middle of the academic year and tossing him into some preposterous Connecticut prep school.

Everyone agreed that this was an act of pure selfishness. None of her justifications held up. She claimed, for instance, that she wanted Charlie to be a role model to his new step-siblings. But the prep school was hours from Manhattan; at most Charlie would come home one weekend a month. Anyway, if he ended up going to college, he'd be out of their lives soon enough. So that was bullshit. Also bullshit was her claim that she didn't want to leave Charlie behind in California. As if she couldn't afford a cross-country plane ticket. As if she ever came to visit him at Watermark.

No. Her real purpose was to compensate for the stepfather's control over her by asserting her own control over Charlie. Adults did that constantly—impose arbitrary rules to reassure themselves of their own power. They treated children as dumb extensions of parental will, and most of the time, they got away with it, because children were conditioned from birth to think of themselves as needy. Your time was not yours. Your physical safety was not yours. Your bodily functions occurred at the whim of another.

The children of Watermark knew better.

They knew, because they were living, breathing counterexamples. They had been awakened.

Which made Charlie's mother's behavior even more wicked.

Bad enough to keep a child locked in captivity. Far worse was removing the blindfold; letting him gape, dazzled, until he could finally see ... then *returning* him to his cell and pretending like there was no sun and never had been. It was the most craven form of abuse. The sheer condescension: who did she think she was fooling? Once you'd felt freedom you couldn't unfeel it.

Charlie Sepp had a sense of self. He wouldn't stand for it.

His reaction was that of any rational being with dignity threatened with extinction.

You go out on your own terms.

I said, "Did he tell you what he intended to do?"

Bierce nodded. "Of course."

"You didn't try to talk him out of it?"

"We talked about it, sure. We all did. We opened it up to the group for discussion."

Nwodo said, "Who's the group?"

Instead of answering, Bierce said, "Not everyone felt the same way. Some of us thought he was making a mistake. But our feelings weren't Charlie's. Our life situation at that point in time wasn't Charlie's."

I said, "Winnie—"

"Was opposed. Vocally."

"She didn't do anything to stop him, though."

"No."

"Why not?"

Bierce's smile implied the question was meaningless. "She was outvoted."

Nwodo said, "Was Camille part of it?"

Bierce started. "No. No. Absolutely not. Camille knew nothing. She still doesn't. To be quite honest I don't think we trusted her right then. We couldn't be sure whose side she was on. She hadn't tried to persuade Charlie's mother to change her mind."

"She took your side when the cops asked about the truck."

"Which I appreciate. But she did that to protect me, the individual. And—before you start making assumptions, let's be clear: I didn't tell Charlie to use the truck. You think I wanted him to do that? That was my truck he destroyed. He took the keys without asking. If he had asked, I would've told him no way, figure it out on your own."

I said, "What did you expect him to do?"

"We never got into specifics. It was in theory."

"You voted. That's specific."

"We voted not to interfere," Bierce said. "Ultimately the decision was Charlie's."

Nwodo said, "He was sixteen."

"If he'd been six, the result would've been the same. His choice. His right."

Silence.

"Look," Bierce said, "I'm not necessarily saying I'd vote again the same way, today. But what happened, happened. Obviously no decision-making process is perfect. I could sit here and tell you we made a mistake. Who would that benefit?"

"Not Charlie," I said.

I was poking at him, but Bierce seemed to take my words as an endorsement. He nodded. "Precisely. There was no clear and present benefit to Charlie, given his unique life circumstances. He wanted to make a statement about what Watermark meant to him. I didn't dishonor that then, and I won't now. I have a responsibility to my current students."

Nwodo's jaw tightened, briefly, before she regained a noncommittal detective's stance. "Was Charlie's death the reason Winnie ran away?"

"I assume that had something to do with it."

"Did you vote on whether she could go?"

Bierce laughed. "That's ridiculous. Rights of free passage are inviolable. Besides, Winnie didn't ask for our permission. She did what she wanted. She always did."

"Who decided to deal with her, now? What was the vote count there?"

Bierce looked at the far end of the bed. "That's not how it occurred."

"You read her blog. She was going to talk."

"Wrong," Bierce said, as if correcting poor grammar. "I never saw the blog. I had no idea it existed until a second ago when you told me. Meredith called me. Winnie had showed up at her place, high on meth, ranting about how it's wrong that Charlie's parents don't know. After she'd passed out on the couch, Meredith texted me, could I please talk some sense into her."

I said, "Why did Meredith come to you for help?"

"It's always like that. She has a panic attack, and I have to clean it up."

He sounded annoyed, but I could also see him puffing out, warming to his position of authority. "'You need to talk to her, Zach. You *need* to talk to her.'" His imitation of Meredith Klaar—nasal, badgering—was regrettably accurate. "I said, 'Forget about it, she'll sleep it off.' But Meredith wouldn't let it go. And when Winnie woke up, she wouldn't, either. That's *their* dynamic. Meredith refuses to talk about things, which pisses Winnie off, and makes her talk about them more. 'Silence is a form of consent,' et cetera."

He fluffed his beard. "It was nonstop for weeks. That's why I came down: so Meredith would stop pestering me already. If you think about it, she's the one who created the problem. Winnie was sitting on it for years, there was no reason to assume she was being serious. Anyway, why would Charlie's parents believe her? She's a junkie. If Meredith could learn to relax, we wouldn't be having this conversation. Whatever. That's how she is. I accept it."

Nice of you, oh great sage.

"And honestly, the entire situation sucked, because on the whole I admire Winnie. I might disagree with her, but at least she had the courage of her convictions, which is more than I can say for Meredith."

"What would you say about her?" Nwodo asked.

"She's weak. She votes with whoever is going to win. Her interest was never Watermark, it was what might happen to her."

We let him sit there.

He said, "Okay? Anything more?"

Did he really think that we were done? That we would nod and smile and encourage him to resume the more pressing business of teaching?

Nwodo said, "You came down for the party."

"Also Meredith's idea. She thought the atmosphere would be more conducive than confronting Winnie in private and making her feel cornered. But the place was so loud we couldn't talk. You can see how Meredith's mind works, though. Pure avoidance tactic. I was waiting for the right moment to say *Let's leave,* but she went ahead and preempted me. And, of course, Winnie was high and paranoid, so she lost her shit. She said she didn't care, she was going to tell Charlie's parents, going to talk to the press, write an article. Completely unhinged."

He glanced at us, hoping to find sympathy for his predicament. When we refused to give it to him, he went on. "I told her: 'Stop making this about you. It's bigger than one person. Think about the consequences for the school.' I was attempting to do damage control." He paused. "I suppose I could've framed it better."

Nwodo said, "What happened next?"

Bierce shrugged. His moment of introspection—if that's what it was—had passed. "It was Meredith hit her first, with the shovel."

Not him. Never him.

"Then Winnie fell over, and Meredith ran. I can't believe she did that to me. Well—I can. I should've expected it, from her. But, really? You're the reason we're in this mess and you bail? She took her car. I ended up having to call an Uber."

Shaking his head at the indignity.

I asked Bierce why he felt compelled to keep going. Why couldn't he have stopped, called an ambulance? For this he had no ready answer.

Nwodo did: Bierce had intended to kill Winnie all along. "You said it yourself. She's a loose cannon. You're the one that stands to lose the most."

"No," he said.

"Maybe you don't know how you're going to do it, but you know you have to."

"No, that's wrong."

"No, Zach, it's right," Nwodo said. "You're waiting for your chance. Then the fight breaks out and everyone's distracted. Here it is. You go for it."

He removed his glasses and began polishing them.

"Once you got started, though?" she said. "I think you liked it."

"You're free to believe whatever you want," Bierce said.

He was shaking his head again, and smirking.

I scanned the bookcase, lined with field guides and Nietzsche.

Nwodo's eyes had settled elsewhere, on the upper bedrail, along which ran the tacked snapshots. She nodded me toward the leftmost picture.

A band of teenagers, arrayed in front of a fallen log.

Crunched together with that mixture of self-consciousness and avidity that is the defining feature of adolescence.

I recognized a younger Meredith Klaar, wearing a drab pageboy and looking startled by the camera flash. I recognized Charlie Sepp by his shock of platinum hair. Gawky, a mouth that couldn't decide whether to grimace or grin.

The young Zach Bierce, leaner, confident, clean-shaven, and strong-jawed.

Winnie wasn't present. Yet I felt her by her absence.

A life extraordinary. According to Zachary Bierce, that was what Watermark prepared its children for.

Charlie Sepp, dead.

Winnie Ozawa, dead.

Zach Bierce and Meredith Klaar: killers.

I imagined them gathered in the woods, counting hands.

All in favor.

All opposed.

There were two other teenagers in the photo.

A girl with a frizzy mass of curls.

A boy half a head shorter than the rest.

Who's in the group?

Bierce saw what we were seeing and shoved his glasses back on. His features bunched as if against a frantic gust of wind.

I untacked the photo.

Bierce said, "You can't do that."

I used my phone to take a photo of the photo. I showed it to Nwodo for approval, then tacked the original back up.

Nwodo said, "It's time to go, Zach."

Silence.

"You have no idea what you're doing," Bierce said. "What this place means. The students who come here have nowhere. You're ruining something beautiful."

"It was you who did that," Nwodo said.

Bierce sighed. We would never understand.

He indicated the dresser, which I was blocking. "Mind if I get my coat?"

Such a tiny room. Hard to believe three grown men could live there without losing their minds. I scooted sideways so that Bierce and I could exchange places. I wasn't watching him. I was grinning at Nwodo, ready to start celebrating with her.

Behind me a drawer opened with a wooden squeak.

Nwodo leapt up, grabbing for her weapon. *"Gun gun gun gun gun."*

Looking back, I know I screwed up. I'd turned my back on him in the first place.

I pivoted, too slowly. My right knee was still stiff.

Zach Bierce had pivoted, too, to face us dead-on, the rising profile of a blued pistol silhouetted dimly against his torso.

In my memory the ensuing seconds have an element of slapstick to them, Nwodo and I jostling against each other, skidding on the rag rug in our stockinged feet. You can all but hear a manic player piano.

My hand is up. Through a strained bloodless V of thumb and forefinger, I see the luxuriant underbelly of Bierce's jaw, the yielding flesh beside his Adam's apple where he drives in the barrel.

Then a missing frame.

Whip-crack of the shot.

The bullet traced a more or less vertical path, crossing slightly from front to back and slightly from right to left and exiting through the top of Bierce's skull four inches behind the coronal suture. The crown of his head ruptured. A jammy starburst of gray matter and blood dashed the wallboards. Tumbling, malformed, the bullet continued along, embedding itself, along with chips of bone, up near the juncture of wall and ceiling.

Backspatter stippled my palms and sleeves; my face and scalp ran warm and wet.

Nwodo's white blouse would never again be worn.

Bierce collapsed and fell straight down, the base of his skull grazing the front edge of the dresser drawer and tipping his chin toward his chest. He landed in a compact pile with his legs tucked beneath him. His spine bowed and he folded in half, coming to rest with his forehead touching the rug, exposing the rictal obscenity of the exit wound, as though he'd somehow put his face on wrong, and was leering up at us inscrutably.

CHAPTER 30

Hours later, when long shadows merged and darkness stole over the valley, the campus of the Watermark School lay in repose. Behind the dormitory windows welled the occasional sob. The children had been shepherded inside, doors closed and curtains drawn.

Camille Buntley hunched on a tree stump in the carnival light of ambulance flashers.

What will happen?

Over and over during our conversation she returned to that same question. I took it less as a call for information, more of an existential problem.

If Watermark ceased to be, would she?

I showed her the snapshot taken from Zachary Bierce's room and asked her to identify the unknown girl and boy.

She blinked at it stuporously. Began to mumble.

They were two of her best teachers.

She couldn't afford to lose half her staff in a single day; the children couldn't bear it.

"I need their names, please," Nwodo said.

The boy was Myles Spencer. The girl was Shannon Swint.

Camille regarded the photo. "I forgot how Shannon used to look before she shaved her head. She used to complain about how itchy it was."

I remembered the meeting hall, a woman with close-cropped hair, sprawled on her stomach, wiggling her toes like a sunbather.

"Everyone's changed," Camille said.

I disagreed. I wasn't about to argue.

3:09 a.m.

Inching through the trees, I toggled the wipers to clear away a gauze of dust and pollen that had accumulated on the windshield.

Nwodo had stretched out in the passenger seat, shutting her eyes. She didn't have her seatbelt on, and I didn't want to disturb her. When I had to brake suddenly, she pitched forward.

If we'd been going any faster than five miles per hour it might've been serious. As it was, her elbow bashed into the glove box. She'd wake up the next day with an ugly bruise.

She faced me, breathless, seething; turned to face the road ahead.

The blond girl in the nightgown sat cross-legged in the dirt, picking at a scabby knee.

Nwodo got out of the car and advanced. "Hey."

The girl didn't respond. Nwodo grabbed her by the arm. *"Hey."*

The girl shrieked, squirming as Nwodo yanked her to her feet and hauled her close.

"You little *shit*. What the fuck is the *matter* with you?"

I hurried to unbuckle my seatbelt.

"You're going to get *hurt*. You're going to *hurt someone else.*"

The girl was putting up a struggle, thrashing and letting out high-pitched noises. In the white blast of the headlamps her face glistened with tears. Nwodo continued to shake her and yell.

If she did get killed it would be her fault. Was that what she wanted? Maybe it was, if she was that stupid. Whatever she thought she was proving, she was wrong. She wasn't proving anything. She was just another idiot like the rest.

"Delilah." I got between them, prying at Nwodo's fingers.

With a moan the girl tore away from us and plunged into the void between the trees. Darkness snuffed the pallid flicker of her body. I could mark her receding path by the sound of twigs snapping, bare feet slashing through the grass.

Nwodo stumbled over a root, cupping her mouth to scream.

"Stay out of the fucking road."

The cords in her wrists stood taut. The musculature of her neck bulged. I waited for her rage to abate, listening to the fleeing girl's dying footsteps, the ascendant forest nocturne.

FOUR

Aftermath

CHAPTER 31

My brother got married on a grim, gray Saturday afternoon in December, six months after the original planned date of Memorial Day.

Several factors had conspired to cause the delay.

First Andrea got into a fight with her stepmother, who wanted to wear a dress in a color of her own choosing. Somehow this disagreement morphed into a referendum on their entire relationship, including how Andrea treated her father, which by the way was disgusting, even though he would never say anything about it, but somebody had to, because it was disgusting.

One could say that Andrea's response lacked the nonjudgmental equanimity she strove for in her moment-to-moment life: she disinvited the both of them. Then Andrea's younger half sister wrote an email chewing Andrea out about it, and Andrea disinvited her, too.

The stepmother and half sister next went to Andrea's biological mother, who—for some reason—attempted to intercede on behalf of her ex-husband and the woman who had supplanted her. By the end of that phone call, nobody from Andrea's immediate family was coming, and the deposit for the restaurant was withdrawn. In the three weeks it took to reestablish peace, the desired date had been given away to another party.

Next came the Great Gluten-Free Cake Debate, and a second venue change after the vegetarian option proved inadequate. Then there was Andrea's dearly beloved college roommate, confusingly also named Andrea, who was due in September, but who ended up going into labor in July and spending the next several months trapped with the baby in the NICU, unable to leave Denver. For my suggestion that they have her participate over Skype, I was rewarded with a frosty request to mind my own business.

There was the argument over who should officiate. All four of Andrea's parents agreed that it should be a minister. Andrea didn't want a religious ceremony. She wanted a mindful one. Although my parents didn't care one way or the other, they sided with Andrea, because they wanted to be supportive of their future daughter-in-law, a gesture that led to Andrea's stepmother referring to my mother as a "loony tunes bitch" in an email that she accidentally CC'd to Luke.

I was spared most of these gory details. Amy served as the primary conduit for information. Whenever the train had again jumped the rails, my mom would call her up to cry. After performing thirty minutes of free therapy, Amy would hang up and summarize for me: *Back on* or *Back off,* depending.

To which I would encourage Amy to look on the bright side: for the rest of our lives, she would be known as the Good Daughter-in-Law.

To which she would reply either *All part of my master plan* or *Not worth it,* depending on her mood.

In the end it felt nothing short of miraculous that the wedding came off, let alone that calendar year.

The ceremony took place at the Salinas Vipassana Center for Human Insight and Planetary Harmony, a brown adobe box whose main meditation hall offered a panoramic view of lettuce fields. The bridesmaids wore saffron. Luke and I sported matching saffron ties. My mother wept. The officiant was a woman who held a master's in divinity from the Graduate Theological Union at UC Berkeley as well as a Certificate in Soto Zen Buddhist Studies. Amy had found her on Craigslist.

IN OTHER WAYS, it had been a busy summer, followed by a busy fall.

Informed of Zachary Bierce's death, and faced with the audio recording of his confession, in which he freely advertised his contempt for her, Meredith Klaar changed her story.

No longer was she a free and independent actor. Now she was a victim, forced under threat of retribution to go along with Bierce and the others. It was their idea, Meredith declared. Finally— *finally*—she felt ready to tell the truth. She volunteered to lay out the whole foul chain of events, starting with Charlie Sepp and leading up to the present day. She appeared genuinely taken aback when the DA brought her up on murder and conspiracy.

But that's not fair she said.

A partial fingerprint taken from the handle of the shovel was found to be a match to Meredith Klaar's right thumb.

In light of the circumstances, the DA was also reexamining the accident that had killed Jasmine Gomez to see if it might be upgraded to vehicular homicide.

FOR FAILING TO register as a sex offender, Lawrence Lee "Dickfish" Vinson received a ninety-day jail sentence.

Shortly after he began serving, he requested a meeting with his court-appointed attorney, Dennis Lipper. Larry informed the lawyer that for the majority of 2018 he had been residing in a crawl space beneath an old mansion in West Oakland. He didn't mind living there, despite the frequent loud parties; it was dry and relatively warm, and there was a convenient toolshed, from which he would occasionally borrow items for use. He liked to build things, radios and so forth.

On the night of December 21, he was in the crawl space, working on a project, when he heard a disturbance taking place outside. It had to be a knock-down fight because he could hear the noise over the blasting music.

Larry waited a little while, then opened the entrance panel and peered out between the cans. He witnessed a man, bent before the open shed doors. He could not state definitively what the man was doing, but it looked like he was shifting sacks of soil. The man closed the shed door, then placed a flowerpot in front of the doors, as if to pin them shut, before walking away.

Larry didn't get a chance to investigate. Within a few minutes, sirens had begun approaching. Gathering his things together, he left the property via the 11th Street gate.

In exchange for a reduction of his sentence, Larry Vinson offered to testify about what he'd seen.

Lipper was skeptical. He'd see what he could do. He contacted the district attorney's office.

No deal, they replied. They didn't need Larry's testimony; they had DNA, prints, a confession. The word of a man with a bad neck tattoo could cause more problems than it solved.

DANE JANKOWSKI PLED down to two counts of voluntary manslaughter, for the deaths of Benjamin Felton and Jalen Coombs. A lot better than Murder Two and a potential life sentence. With luck he'd be out in three years.

IN MAY—THREE WEEKS after Zachary Bierce's suicide, and eighty-five miles to the southeast—Patrol Officer Annette Cho of the San

Jose Police Department observed a white 1997 Infiniti exiting the parking lot of El Pollo Loco on Story Road. When the vehicle proceeded to make an illegal U-turn, Cho pulled it over. The driver of the vehicle, a twenty-four-year-old male named Sammy Nguyen, complied, slowing at the side of the road. As Cho typed the plate number into her mobile data center, the passenger door of the Infiniti kicked open, and a second young male jumped out and took off running.

Body camera footage captures the ensuing pursuit, Cho huffing and puffing as she radios for assistance. The young man cuts across a 76 station, running up a short embankment dotted with knee-high shrubbery and tossing an object, later recovered and identified as a baggie of marijuana, into the bushes. They weave through a parking lot, coming to an eight-foot cinder-block wall. For a moment it appears as though the young man is going to clear it. His sneakers lose their purchase. He slips. Cho grabs him by the shirt collar.

Under questioning, Sammy Nguyen reveals that the young man has been living with him for the past five months. The young man's mother is Sammy's first cousin; technically, that makes the two men first cousins, once removed. But they grew up playing together, and they've always been tight. For this reason, when the young man came to him—desperate for help, with nowhere else to go—Sammy took him in, no questions asked. That's what family does. The young man's name is Tuan Trang. Back in Oakland, he is wanted for murder.

Hi Deputy Edison this is Dylan.

What's up, I hope everything is ok with you. I wanted to update you on whats been going on since I was able to get in contact with both of the individuals you recommended. You thought I should start with didi so that's what i did but to tell you the truth she didn't seem too interested in talking to me. She said some friends of theirs already held a memorial on their own, she didn't see any point in doing another one.

Greer unger on the other hand was more open to the idea. I wanted to be up front with her about the fact that I thought we should put both names on the gravestone. That way maybe I could get my dad to feel okay with coming to visit the grave. I spoke to him a couple of times and I think he's feeling pretty bad about how it ended between him and Kevin. I thought having both names could help him accept it in a way. I wanted to be upfront with Greer though. Based on what you told me I was expecting her to turn me down flat but she said she would think about it. So for a little while I was hopeful but then she got in touch and wrote that she would be willing to come herself but she didn't think we could invite any of my brother's friends because it might upset them. I got where she was coming from but it pretty much defeats the purpose and in that case maybe we should just forget about it. She agreed that was the right thing to do. I told her the name of the cemetery so she can come visit if she ever gets down to la.

I guess we're not going to do anything, its just me and i'm not even there. I'm bummed about it but it is what it is, you can't make everybody happy. Nobody's happy but that's life, ha ha. Hopefully I get back at some point and i can go pay my respects in person. Who knows though, its hard to say whats going to happen.

I think about my brother a lot and its tough because we didn't speak that much after i joined up. Both of us had our own issues to deal with, thats why I joined up to begin with. Everyone has to take care of their own shit but it bothers me because I'm his big brother and it was my responsibility to be there for him, but I left him behind because i was looking out for number one and getting out of a fucked up home situation. Whatever i had it was worse for him. It's hard to sleep, I lie in bed and i can feel my heart racing, when i wake up it's still racing like it's been doing that all night long. This place makes you nuts.

I'm sorry to ramble but theres nobody around who knew him and so i don't know who else to talk to about it. Anyway I appreciate your help, it was cool of you.

I wasn't the only one getting mail. A note came, addressed to the entire team, thanking us and singling out Deputy Lisa Shupfer for her kindness. It was signed *Bonita Felton*. Sergeant Turnbow let it stay up on the bulletin board for a few days. Then Shoops took it down and we all went back to work.

RHIANNON COOKE DECIDED not to sell her house. She wrote on her newly resurrected Facebook page that she'd come to this conclusion following a lot of soul-searching. Part of her had wondered if her time in West Oakland had come to an end.

I felt the flux of the universe calling me in new dimensions.

But that was before neighbors started approaching her, pleading with her to stay. They loved what she'd done to beautify the block. For her to pack up and run sent the message that this wasn't a safe place to live—a misperception they'd been fighting for years. What would happen if the house fell back into the hands of drug dealers and addicts?

She refused to let a few bad apples halt the march of progress.

She wasn't a quitter, either.

She owed it to the community to give it another try.

There was a lot of work to be done. With a little help, though, they could not only restore the house to its recent glory, but make it better—banish the winter's bad karma.

To that end, she was throwing a Summer Solstice Painting Extravaganza. Everyone was invited to pitch in. Sort of like a modern-day barn-raising. Admission was ten dollars and went toward the cost of supplies. Alternatively, bring brushes, rollers, trays, or cans of Benjamin Moore Aura Exterior in the quantities and colors listed below.

They'd start at seven and go until the job was complete. Wear clothes you don't mind getting dirty. DJ Fooye spinning. Cash bar.

TEN WEEKS LATER I swung by Almond Street to have a look.

Sloppy blotches of cream-colored paint, ribbons and runnels and drips, covered less than half the siding. Barbs of graffiti poked out, and missing altogether was the fine trim work that had made the scheme so grand in the first place.

A FOR SALE sign was staked on the lawn.

I got out of my car. An attached plastic bin contained a sheaf of tear sheets.

MASSIVE Victorian in vibrant, diverse neighborhood . . .

Front and center was an exterior photo, taken prior to the vandalism. A questionable strategy. If I were a prospective buyer who showed up expecting a pristine Painted Lady and got her diseased twin? Forget it. What else are they lying about?

Evidently Sean Godwin, Licensed Realtor, took a different approach. Bait the hook with big dreams.

Close to BART . . . Stunning original details . . . Fabulous natural light . . . 360 degree views . . .

Priced to sell at $2.85 million.

I put the tear sheet back in the bin.

"Not interested?"

On the opposite sidewalk, Hattie Branch stood beside a wheeled shopping cart stuffed with grocery bags.

I smiled. "Out of my price range."

She nodded and began dragging the cart up her front steps.

I jogged across the street. "Can I get that for you, ma'am?"

"I'm fine, thank you, sir." The cart wasn't much smaller than she was. It thunked against the stairs. The tread edges bore divots from previous beatings.

At the door, she paused with her key out, glancing over her shoulder at me: why was I still there?

I was out of uniform; I didn't think she'd recognize me. But then she smiled.

"You're that young policeman," she said.

"Clay Edison. How are you, Mrs. Branch? How've you been?"

"Oh, not dead yet. Yourself?"

"Good, thanks."

She seemed content to rest awhile and catch her breath. Warm day, but she was wearing a woolen sweater and long skirt. Her shoes looked like shiny loaves of brown bread.

"Are you in the market for a new home?" she asked.

"Not at the moment, no. I heard she had plans to fix the place up again."

"Well," Hattie said, motioning: *See for yourself.*

I nodded.

She clucked her tongue. "It's a shame, what they did."

Did she mean the vandals? Rhiannon Cooke & Co.? Tuan Trang and Dane Jankowski?

"You must be cooking for an army," I said.

Hattie smiled again. "My grandson's coming for dinner. Which reminds me: I never did express my gratitude. To you, or the lady detective."

The leniency shown Isaiah Branch hadn't come about because of Nwodo or me. Once his tip turned out to be useless, she had seen no reason to intercede on his behalf. As far as I know, she never mentioned to Detective Bischoff that we'd spoken to his suspect. She told me—deadpan—that she didn't want to get a reputation for meddling.

If Hattie Branch owed thanks to anyone, it was Tuan Trang. In his statements to police, he remained consistent that Isaiah did not know about the gun when the three of them went over to talk to Rhiannon Cooke. No way. He'd known Isaiah since they were six. Boy was *soft*. If Tuan *had* told him about the gun in advance, he probably would've pissed his pants. They didn't go over there to threaten, but to talk. The gun only came out because the other guy pulled his first. The racist motherfuckers were going to lynch them.

No doubt there was a self-serving aspect to Trang's version of events. But elements of the story were confirmed by two eyewitnesses—party attendees, dug up by the Branch family lawyer, Montgomery Prince. Both described Isaiah's demeanor throughout the initial conversation as civil; Rhiannon Cooke as voluble and drunk.

That testimony, combined with the YouTube footage showing Isaiah surrounded by a chanting mob, led to waning prosecutorial interest. They had Trang. They had Jankowski.

One Shark, one Jet.

Tie game.

I started to tell Hattie there was nothing to thank us for, but stopped myself. She wanted to believe her good deed had borne fruit. I saw no reason to rob her of that.

I looked over at the Victorian. "Think she'll get her asking price?"

"Oh, I don't pay any attention to that sort of thing." Hattie put her key in the lock. "You'll excuse me, now, please. My ice cream's melting."

"Enjoy dinner."

"I will. Take care, Officer."

"You too, Mrs. Branch."

She turned back to grasp the shopping cart. A sly pause. "Three hundred twenty-five dollars a square foot?" she said. She hauled the cart over the threshold. "I suppose someone'll come along."

. . .

OSWALD SCHUMACHER'S 39-MINUTE film, *Anatomy of a Shooting*, was accepted into the Napa Valley Film Festival, where it took second place in the category of Best Documentary Short. Opening with shots of the trashed Summerhof Mansion, Schumacher, in voice-over, discusses the challenge of treating a subject to which he maintains such an intimate connection.

This is a story written in my very flesh . . .

In the spirit of goodwill, a portion of the prize money would be used to establish a foundation, the Benjamin Felton Project, whose mission was to encourage and empower aspiring young filmmakers from low-income backgrounds.

THE WATERMARK SCHOOL remained shuttered through fall semester. An open letter from Camille Buntley, posted to the website, stressed that the closure was temporary and would last only as long as it took to complete necessary and long-deferred renovations.

Most costly was the Quonset hut, which had to be torn down and rebuilt. It was her belief that Watermark would not be Watermark without its traditional venue for Town Hall. She had polled the students. A strong majority agreed. Rather than proceed by half measures, therefore, she preferred to suspend operations until they could once more take up the cause of educating children who embodied the core values of independence, curiosity, and responsibility.

Saturday, December 14

10:47 p.m.

A moist pressure on my shoulder, a sluice of words. I looked up from my chicken breast to find Andrea's stepmother, Regina, leering at me through yards of golden tulle.

"Congratulations to *you*," she slurred.

"Thanks," I said.

"Can I see it. Lemme see. Give it here."

Amy dutifully extended her hand. Regina took hold—not gently—and ogled the engagement ring. "Verrrrry pretty."

"Thank you so much," Amy said, extricating herself.

"When's the date."

"We haven't decided," Amy said.

"Sometime next summer," I said.

"Well I'd better be invited or you can bet there'll be trouble."

With as much apathy as I could muster, I raised my wineglass to her.

Regina tittered. "You're cute." To Amy: "He's a cutie."

"I think so," Amy said.

"It's cute how you and your brother do everything together. Even getting married in the same astral plane."

Before I could answer, the DJ's voice came booming through the PA.

"Ladies and gentlemen, keep on enjoying your dinner. It's time now for the best man to say a few words. Put your hands together for Clay Edison, brother of the groom. Clay, get on up here."

I took my glass and started across the parquet. Regina, applauding wildly, seized the opportunity to occupy my chair.

Stepping to the microphone, I looked out at a grinning menagerie.

The remnant of Luke's high school circle. Some of them had been my friends, too. Our extended family, in from points near and far; my uncle Gunnar and aunt Becka, who'd driven their camper down from rural Washington State, one of the rare occasions they consented to leave the confines of their farm.

To the left, a very white smile: Scott Silber, CEO of Bay Area Therapeutics, LLC.

Plenty of strange faces, too. My brother always did have a gift for making friends. I wondered how many of them had served time.

Andrea's side: square women packed into gowns, stringy men-folk twitching for a cigarette.

Paul and Theresa Sandek.

My father, agreeably dazed.

My mother, torturing her napkin.

I said, "When Luke and I were kids—"

From the back: *Can't hear you.*

"When we were little," I said, louder, "people used to mistake the two of us for twins. At least, that's what my mom tells me. Ask me, I never saw it. For one thing, I'm obviously a lot better-looking than he is. But enough about that, I don't want him crying on his special day."

Too late someone called.

I said, "First, I'd like to take this moment to publicly acknowledge that my brother's jump shot is better than mine."

Luke laughed and shook his head.

"It's true," I said. "It used to frustrate the crap out of me. Hours and hours we're playing against each other, putting in the same amount of work, and he's getting better results. Why? I told myself that there was nothing I could do. I'd never shoot like him. Because he was talented.

"So I focused on other aspects of my game. I became a different kind of player, a different kind of person, in response to Luke. In a literal way he shaped who I am today, and I'm grateful for that.

"But—and this is the thing I missed, and what a lot of people tend to miss about Luke, because he can be a laid-back guy. They take his talent for granted. I'm as guilty as anyone here. More so. I know what it took to make that talent flourish. I just have a hard time admitting it to myself.

"Once, I must've been about six or seven, I woke up in the middle of the night to go to the bathroom, and Luke's bed is empty. There's this weird stomping sound coming from the living room. *Dup. Dup. Dup.* So of course, I go to check it out.

"Let me see if I can describe it to you. Here's Luke. He's standing there in his underwear, holding"—catcalls—"a basketball. He's got the TV on, and the VCR, and he's watching a video that we got as a free bonus when we subscribed to *Sports Illustrated*. It's a bunch of music videos, each featuring a different NBA player. Michael Jordan, 'Take My Breath Away.' Charles Barkley, Dr. J, Magic. Luke has on the Larry Bird video."

"'Small Town,'" Luke yelled.

"That's right," I said. "John Cougar Mellencamp. Except Luke's not actually watching the tape. It's paused, on a frame of Bird, at the top of his shot, right before he releases. There's a full-length mirror propped against the couch so Luke can watch himself. And he's starting with the ball at his waist, and jumping up, trying to copy Larry Bird and get his arms into the same position.

"He's just doing that, again, and again, and again.

"I must've stood there for five minutes before I went back to bed.

"He never noticed me.

"I have no idea how many nights he spent doing that, while I slept. Even if it was the once, it's more than I ever did.

"My brother is a hustler. I mean that in the best sense. I respect him for it. I respect that, no matter where he is in life, he's striving to improve. And I think that what you did here today, getting married, is the next step in that process.

"Now I want to tell you a story about when I met Andrea, on the night we learned she and Luke were engaged. It took place right after they announced they had some big news. You'd expect Andrea, when we ask what it is, to say, *We're getting married*. That's not what she said. The first thing you said, Andrea, was, 'Luke's playing ball again.'

"I didn't grasp the significance of those words then. Remember, I've just met this person, and suddenly she's marrying my brother. It flew right past me. But as I've gotten to know you, Andrea, I've come to appreciate what you were doing, and why it was important."

Andrea was nodding, and smiling, tears streaming down her face.

At last, someone gets me.

"It's easy to feel sympathy for someone when they're flat out on the floor. A lot harder is sharing their joy without fear of losing yourself in the process. Andrea, I remember the pride on your face when you told us about Luke. His happiness was your happiness. That takes love, and it takes courage. It's what makes the two of you good together."

I raised my glass. "It's a lesson we could all stand to learn. It's what I'm striving for, and I thank you both for showing me a path. To my brother the hustler, and the woman who is his equal. Your happiness is ours. I wish you a lifetime supply of it, getting better every day. Cheers."

2:01 a.m.

Amy kicked her shoes toward the bedroom closet. "I'm gonna burn this dress."

She turned around, lifting her hair so I could unzip her. "Your speech was sweet."

"Thanks. It wasn't easy. I didn't want to get up there and lie."

"I'm sure it meant a lot to them." She hopped out of the dress and padded semi-nude to the bathroom. I watched her go, savoring her form, then peeled off my suit and rolled onto the bed.

As a rule, I go to sleep early and wake up early. Two in the morning is not my finest hour. I was drifting downward, grateful for having the day off, feeling around for my phone so I could silence the four thirty a.m. alarm.

"Clay? Can you come in here, please?"

"Everything okay?"

"It's fine. Come here."

She was perched on the edge of the tub. She had neglected to flush the toilet. I reached past her to do it but she stopped me by holding out a white plastic stick.

"Look at this, please," she said.

Bristles at one end. A window displayed a pair of pink lines.

"That's two, right?" she said.

On the counter by the sink sat an open pink-and-white First Response box. *Results in 3 minutes.* The set of instructions accordioned out on the counter.

I found the diagram, held it up for comparison.

"Looks like two to me," I said.

"I'm not imagining it."

"The second one is faint, but it's definitely there." I showed her in the instructions: "'Any two lines means positive, even if one is lighter than the other.'"

I put the paper down. "This is why you weren't drinking?"

"I took half a sip. I had to. Your mom was giving me funny looks. You don't think that's a problem, do you?"

"I'm sure it's fine. How long have you known?"

"Three minutes," she said.

"How long have you suspected?"

"A week. My boobs are bigger. I'm kind of insulted you haven't noticed."

"Sorry. I'm noticing now. They look awesome."

"Thanks."

"Like, amazing."

"Thanks, honey. I appreciate that."

We looked at each other.

"So," Amy said. "What do we do now?"

"We could dance," I said.

"Good idea," she said.

So we did.

ACKNOWLEDGMENTS

Dep. Erik Bordi, Capt. Melanie Ditzenberger, Sheriff Gregory Ahern, Melissa Lewkowicz, Jesse Grant, Brian McMahon.

Special thanks to Sgt. Patricia Wilson.

Also by Jonathan and Jesse Kellerman:

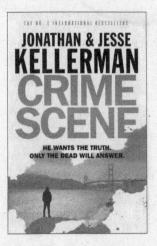

Eccentric, reclusive Walter Rennert lies cold at the bottom of his stairs. At first glance the scene looks straightforward: a once-respected psychology professor done in by booze and a bad heart. But his daughter Tatiana insists that he has been murdered, and she persuades Clay to take a closer look at the grim facts of Rennert's life.

When Clay learns that Rennert's colleague died in a nearly identical manner, he becomes even more determined to discover the truth behind the man's death. The twisting trail Clay follows will lead him into the darkest corners of the human soul.

It's his job to listen to the tales told by the dead. But this time, he's part of a story that makes his blood run cold.

HEADLINE

Also by Jonathan and Jesse Kellerman:

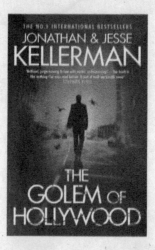

A burned-out L.A. detective . . . a woman of mystery who
is far more than she seems . . . a grotesque, ancient monster bent
on a mission of retribution. When these three collide, a new
standard of suspense is born.

The legend of the Golem of Prague has endured through
the ages, a creature fashioned by a sixteenth-century rabbi to
protect his congregation, now lying dormant in the garret of
a synagogue. But the Golem is dormant no longer.

And for Detective Jacob Lev the mystery of how he spent last
night pales in comparison the one he's about to be called
upon to solve.

HEADLINE

Also by Jonathan and Jesse Kellerman:

It's been over a year since LAPD detective Jacob Lev learned the remarkable truth about his family, and he's not coping well. He's back to drinking, he's not talking to his father, the LAPD Special Projects department continues to shadow him, and the memory of a woman named Mai haunts him day and night.

And while Jacob has tried to build a bridge to his mother, she remains a stranger to him, imprisoned inside her own tattered mind. Then he comes across the file for a gruesome, unsolved murder that brings the two halves of his life into startling collision.

Finding the killer will take him halfway around the world, to Paris. It's a dangerous search for truth that plunges him into the past. And for Jacob Lev, there is no place more frightening . . .

HEADLINE

THRILLINGLY GOOD BOOKS
FROM CRIMINALLY
GOOD WRITERS

CRIME FILES BRINGS YOU THE LATEST RELEASES FROM
TOP CRIME AND THRILLER AUTHORS.

SIGN UP ONLINE FOR OUR MONTHLY NEWSLETTER AND BE THE FIRST
TO KNOW ABOUT OUR COMPETITIONS, NEW BOOKS AND MORE.

VISIT OUR WEBSITE: WWW.CRIMEFILES.CO.UK
LIKE US ON FACEBOOK: FACEBOOK.COM/CRIMEFILES
FOLLOW US ON TWITTER: @CRIMEFILESBOOKS